More Critical Praise for Joe Meno

for *Marvel and a Wonder*

- Winner of the Society of Midland Authors
Award for the Region's Best Books of 2015
- Named a *Booklist* Editors' Choice for 2015
- Long-listed for the American Library Association's
2016 Andrew Carnegie Medal for Excellence in Fiction

"Evoking William Faulkner and Cormac McCarthy, Meno's suspenseful, mordantly incisive, many-layered tale can also be read as an equine *Moby-Dick*. As he tracks the bewildering seismic shifts under way in America, Meno celebrates everyday marvels, including the hard-proven love between grandfather and grandson."   —*Booklist*, starred review

"Meno makes the most banal prose—grunts and salutations, small talk over meals—compelling and necessary . . . [He] has a knack for giving small happenings emotional weight . . . Meno knows how to make you love his characters, want what they want. But don't think he's going to let things turn out well for them. Marvels and wonders aren't worth the trouble. Fortunately, this book is."
—*New York Times Book Review*

"[A] rugged page-turner . . . There's a bit of the country noir of Daniel Woodrell's *Winter's Bone* in the stark atmosphere Mr. Meno evokes ('A faded town, fading, harried with dusty light, midafternoon'), and a bit of the Clint Eastwood movie *Gran Torino* in the story of the vigilante grandfather. But the writing is propulsive enough to make you forget its influences. And at moments the book's consuming darkness is lifted by potent, if inscrutable visions of the talismanic horse—a flash of lightning curving along the horizon."   —*Wall Street Journal*

"Talented Meno has penned a wise and touching novel of love, loyalty, courage; an extraordinary book not to be missed."
—*Library Journal*, starred review

"*Marvel and a Wonder* . . . is a unique take on the generation gap between a Korean war vet and his sixteen-year-old grandson, exploring themes like faith, sacrifice and family . . . With a bit of crime, tragedy and even love."   —*MTV News*

for *The Great Perhaps*

"Meno is thinking hard about why the world is the way it is and about where hope for change might reasonably lie . . . For most of the last decade, a lot of prominent fiction writers interested in establishing their realist bona fides, the relevance of their work to the way we live now, seemed to feel they had no choice but to incorporate 9/11. But Meno dares to consign it, and our response to it, to a larger historical and spiritual context, and even to suggest that there is nothing new under the sun. A few years ago that might have seemed heretical, but traditionally such farsightedness is part of a novelist's job."
—*New York Times Book Review*

"Laugh-out-loud funny but frequently sad, Joe Meno's new novel runs the gamut of emotions and techniques as it depicts a Chicago family in turmoil . . . They achieve no earth-shattering insights, and neither does the author; he simply reminds us with wit and compassion that the human condition is 'both astonishing and quite ordinary.'"
—*Chicago Tribune*

"Tender, funny, spooky, and gripping, Meno's novel encompasses a subtle yet devastating critique of war; sensitively traces the ripple effect of a dark legacy of nebulousness, guilt, and fear; and evokes both heartache and wonder." —*Booklist*, starred review

"This postmodern portrait of an eccentric family delivers equal parts humor and heartbreak, raising questions about love, identity, and faith." —*San Francisco Chronicle*

"The text contains more elements of magical realism than Meno's previous work, yet even the human-shaped cloud that Madeline chases for weeks somehow seems real thanks to the note-perfect dialog and narrative. Highly recommended for all public and academic libraries."
—*Library Journal*, starred review

"Meno's writing seems to have hit a new gear . . . The overall effect is one of mature mastery of form and a deepened compassion for his characters." —*Poets & Writers*

for *Demons in the Spring*

- Finalist for the 2009 Story Prize
- A *Kirkus Reviews* Best Book of 2008
- A *Time Out Chicago* Best Book of 2008

"An inspired collection of twenty stories, brilliant in its command of tone and narrative perspective ... Creativity and empathy mark the collection ... Illustrations enhance the already vivid storytelling."
                                    —*Kirkus Reviews*, starred review

"Spanning worlds, generations, cultures, and environments, each of Meno's short stories in this stellar collection explores depression, loneliness, and insanity in the world, while never quite offering a clear solution or glimmer of hope. Misery loves company, and Meno's assortment of off-center, morose characters fit seamlessly together ... Catering to all the odd men out in the world, this short story collection succeeds word to word, sentence to sentence, and cover to cover."
                                    —*Publishers Weekly*, starred review

"These playful, postmodern stories find the Chicago author's artistry reinforced by illustrators who provide perspectives on his prose ... The range of illustrations adds to the volume's appeal, but Meno's writing is strong enough to stand on its own ... There's a profound empathy in Meno's work that makes it more than just a stylistic exercise."
                                    —*Time Out New York*

"The author of *Hairstyles of the Damned* and *The Boy Detective Fails* is back with a handsome new collection, pairing twenty short stories with original artwork from illustrators like Charles Burns and Nick Butcher. Meno is at his best when he mixes raw emotional realism with tender insight."   —*New York Times Book Review*

"Meno knows just how to press a variety of emotional buttons ranging from giddy delight to not-quite-hopeless despair. Highly recommended."   —*Library Journal*

"Mr. Meno's fiction pops with the energy of youth, its purity and heart ... Mr. Meno has a finely tuned grasp of the fumblings—romantic, existential and otherwise, that make up the first twenty-five years of our lives."   —*New York Observer*

for *Hairstyles of the Damned*

"Captures both the sweetness and sting of adolescence with unflinching honesty." —*Entertainment Weekly*

"Joe Meno writes with the energy, honesty, and emotional impact of the best punk rock. From the opening sentence to the very last word, *Hairstyles of the Damned* held me in his grip." —*Chicago Sun-Times*

"The most authentic young voice since J.D. Salinger's Holden Caulfield . . . A darn good book." —*Daily Southtown*

"Sensitive, well-observed, often laugh-out-loud funny . . . You won't regret a moment of the journey." —*Chicago Tribune*

"Meno gives his proverbial coming-of-age tale a punk-rock edge, as seventeen-year-old Chicagoan Brian Oswald tries to land his first girlfriend . . . Meno ably explores Brian's emotional uncertainty and his poignant youthful search for meaning . . . His gabby, heartfelt, and utterly believable take on adolescence strikes a winning chord." —*Publishers Weekly*

"A funny, hard-rocking first-person tale of teenage angst and discovery." —*Booklist*

"Captures the loose, fun, recklessness of midwestern punk." —MTV.com

"Meno's language is rhythmic and honest, expressing things proper English never could. And you've got to hand it to the author, who pulled off a very good trick: The book is punk rock. It's not just punk rock. It's not just about punk rock; it embodies the idea of punk rock; it embodies the idea of punk—it's pissed off at authority, it won't groom itself properly, and it irritates. Yet its rebellious spirit is inspiring and right on the mark." —*SF Weekly*

"Funny and charming and sad and real. The adults are sparingly yet poignantly drawn, especially the fathers, who slip through without saying much but make a profound impression." —*Chicago Journal*

for *The Boy Detective Fails*

"This is postmodern fiction with a head *and* a heart, addressing such depressing issues as suicide, death, loneliness, failure, anomie, and guilt with compassion, humor, and even whimsy . . . Meno's best work yet; highly recommended."　　　　　　　　　—*Library Journal*, starred review

"Comedic, imaginative, empathic, and romantic . . . Atmospheric, archetypal, and surpassingly sweet, Meno's finely calibrated fantasy investigates the precincts of grief, our longing to combat chaos with reason, and the menace and magic concealed within everyday life."
　　　　　　　　　　　　　　　　　　　—*Booklist*, starred review

"Mood is everything here, and Meno tunes it like a master . . . A full-tilt collision of wish-fulfillment and unrequited desires that's thrilling, yet almost unbearably sad."　　　　　—*Kirkus Reviews*, starred review

"[A] delicate blend of whimsy and edginess . . . Meno packs his novel with delightful subtext."　　　　　　　　　—*Entertainment Weekly*

"[A] radiantly creative masterpiece . . . Meno's imaginative genius spins heartache into hope within this fanciful growing-up tale that glows like no other."　　　　　　　　　　　　　　　　—*PopMatters*

"Billy's search for truth, love, and redemption is surprising and absorbing. Swaddled in melancholy and gentle humor, it builds in power as the clues pile up."　　　　　　　—*Publishers Weekly*

"At the bottom of this Pandora's box of . . . mirthful absurdity, there's heartbreak and longing, eerie beauty and hope."
　　　　　　　　　　　　　　　　　　　—*Philadelphia Weekly*

"Visually and verbally delectable."　　　　　　—*Chicago Tribune*

"Marinated in mood, richly crafted and devoid of irony, Meno's newest novel . . . is imbued with both the hopeful and the romantic."
　　　　　　　　　　　　　　　　　　　—*Time Out Chicago*

"Moving, elegant prose."　　　　　　　—*Washington Post Express*

BOOK OF EXTRAORDINARY TRAGEDIES

Other books by Joe Meno

BOOK OF EXTRAORDINARY TRAGEDIES

JOE MENO

BROOKLYN, NEW YORK

Published by Akashic Books
©2022 Joe Meno

Hardcover ISBN: 978-1-63614-060-5
Paperback ISBN: 978-1-63614-061-2
Library of Congress Control Number: 2022931852

Portions of this book were previously published in an earlier form in the *Chicago Tribune* and *Phoebe* magazine.

Akashic Books
Facebook | Instagram | Twitter: AkashicBooks
info@akashicbooks.com
www.akashicbooks.com

But a man's character is his fate, says Heraclitus, and in the end there isn't any way to disguise the nature of the knocks by acoustical work on the door or gloving the knuckles.
—Saul Bellow, *The Adventures of Augie March*

Keep my planets in orbit,
Never forfeit or quit,
Move forward . . .
—RZA, *"Tragedy"*

For K.Z.

MOVEMENT ONE

BEGINNINGS, ENDINGS, AND OTHER MUSICAL FIGURES

Allegro vivace e con brio.

CHAPTER ONE

BEGIN IN F♯ MINOR WITH A SYMPHONY OF GHOST NOTES. Why not a concerto that details every known silence? Or the most noiseless overture in all of history? Let the trumpets go mute and the cymbals be still. Let the lull from the concert hall destroy every awkward moment, every long-standing argument, with cannons raging in unheard fury and the closing note being fireworks exploding soundlessly in the sky, so that everything finally goes quiet. What would Mozart have to say to that?

Orfeo is booming through the house. I am struggling to do a single pull-up before work. My sister calls and says she is not feeling well and then asks if I can drop my niece off at day care. I slowly catch my breath and tell her I'll be there soon.

I put on my red hat and my winter coat with the Polish flag on the back, grab my bicycle, and then pedal toward my sister's apartment on 95th. I pretend I'm a car and ride in the street, much to the annoyance of other vehicles. Someone honks their horn and shouts, *GET OUT OF THE WAY.* As I ride I ignore all the noise, all the distractions, and try to imagine an entirely new, improvised composition.

I lock my bicycle up and climb the stairs to my sister's apartment. I make sure my niece is wearing her gold gym shoes and find my older sister Isobel leaning against the refrigerator in in her high school track jersey and exercise pants, although I have not seen her exercise in a long time, several years possibly. Her ragged blond hair is unbrushed and something in her eyes appears to be off. I ask her: "What's up?"

"I'm just not feeling so good. Feminine problems."

"Like in eighth grade when you wrote a love letter to Patrick Swayze?"

"You're not funny. You're almost never funny." She touches the side of my head. "I'm not so sure about this haircut. You have a big bald spot in the back."

"I tried cutting it myself." I ask: "Are you sure you're okay?"

She nods and we stare at each other for another moment. With my eyes, I ask, *What's really going on?* but she doesn't answer. So I help my niece on with her coat, and then, once we're outside, I put her on the bike.

I go faster than anyone with a three-year-old on the handlebars should. It feels like we are flying. A car from the 1980s pulls out in front of us and my niece, Jazzy, laughs and screams at exactly the same time and it is one of my favorite sounds ever, a profound, musical experience, always in D minor. If you could only see us, darting among the traffic and January slush on Kedzie Avenue, you would know that we are majestic, we are glorious, we will be triumphant!

Somehow we break our long-standing record and get to the day care on 87th on time. As I help Jazz off the front of the bike, she murmurs, "Your hair looks weird," and I nod. I walk her inside and help her hang her coat. With her hat off, her hair is dark and frizzy and her eyes a sparkling green. She doesn't look much like my older sister but they have the exact same personality. I get her set up at a table, coloring with Magic Markers. On the way out, the day care worker in the large pink sweater eyeballs me angrily because she and I have an unfriendly competition going and today we will not have to pay the ten-dollar late fee, which is the best thing to happen in the year 2008 so far.

Back outside, the snow has made everything look new. It is one of the most beautiful mornings in a long time and I put on my CD player and fast-forward to the second movement of a symphony by Verdi and then a utility van swerves in front of me and I collide with a parked car right in front of a funeral home. Oh the irony. For a moment I feel myself go flying through the air. I hit the ground and watch the world spin around me, hearing the music repeating itself again and again. As I'm lying on my back, my thoughts begin to circle and I think of my sister and her pained expression and all that it might mean.

Is there any way to escape your fate? Even *Orfeo* has no suggestions.

Beginning at the age of three, Isobel and I had our own language, first playing music together—my father installing me in front of the piano, while Isobel, at five, was already playing short pieces by Beethoven on the cello. My father would tilt his head toward her, focused on each and every note, the phrasing, how she held the bow. I, on the other hand, was more than happy to exist only as background noise.

When I was five, my mother suffered from a months-long bout of insomnia and took my older sister and me out on midnight excursions to familiar and sometimes magical places, a convenience store or a far-off car wash on Central Avenue, all while my father happily slept at home. Sitting in the back of the station wagon in my pajamas, eating a candy bar, I was both afraid and excited. My mother's eyes were round and bright in a way they usually weren't during the day. I think she was trying to show us something about life, to get us to see what other people never took the time to notice. I remember my sister reaching across the backseat and holding my hand as we watched the foam rollers cover the windows in an other-worldly, milky haze. I stopped being afraid then and accepted whatever befell me, knowing my sister would be there for me.

Three years later, when I was eight, I had the chance to play before the Jugoslavian ambassador—a friend of the family—who promised to get me into an exclusive conservatory on the East Coast. My father was ecstatic but the dignitary never showed. A snowstorm had created an enormous traffic jam downtown. I sat on a stool on the small stage and stared at my family and music teacher, Mr. Gennaro, gathered together in the front row. Even my baby brother Daniel was silent in my mom's arms.

On that cold evening, with the wind coming in off the lake, you could hear the doors and windows banging—the opposite of applause. Someone had carved their initials *EM* on the top of the piano. I imagined all the names that started with E.

As we waited for the next forty-five minutes, I kept my eyes on Isobel, who never looked away. She mouthed knock-knock jokes and folded a bird out of the program my father had gotten printed. What do you call this other than magic or ESP? In the end my father asked me to play, even though the dignitary was not coming. I did as I was told, placing my fingers above the dull white keys, imagining the paper bird swooping over the empty concert hall, as I glanced up at my sister whenever I could. I don't know if I ever played that way again.

I'd do anything in the world for this person is what I'm trying to say.

I go by the no-name convenience store on the way to work. The same hoods are out front with their conventional, south-side Irish American faces. There are four of them, all in drab green uniforms from the nearby cemetery. The cemetery in Evergreen Park is one of the largest in the Western world, stretching on for miles and miles. What does it say about a neighborhood, an entire place, that its biggest claim to fame is that it happens to contain one of the most popular locations to leave your dead? As I open the door to the convenience store, one of the thugs knocks the headphones from my ears.

"Fa," one of them says.

Then another: "Fa, your sister talks about how you're always listening to music. Come on, let's hear you sing something."

I ignore them and go inside, walking over to the freezers. I grab a bottle of chocolate Yoo-hoo. When I come out, someone gets me in a headlock and I immediately remember why I hate this place.

I'm half deaf. I have to tell you. I have partial hearing loss in both ears. It's asymmetrical, which means it's worse in my left.

I began losing my hearing when I was ten. I first started missing certain words, then certain notes, then entire frequencies by the age of twelve. In the end, the look of empathetic disappointment on my music teacher's face was the hardest thing to take. No one knew why or how it happened—if it was from some accident, or from some virus, or was possibly genetic, passed down from generation to generation through my family, alongside mythical stories of Poland and Jugoslavia.

I don't know any sign language, I'm embarrassed to admit. I don't like talking about my hearing loss but it makes it easier when other people know. Most of the time I just pretend to understand what everyone is saying.

I work at a high school, St. Josaphat, where I once was a student. No one knows this fact but I do. I find it hilarious and also humiliating, depending on the day. I put on my uniform and ignore the misspelling of my name. In the hallways, mop in hand, I make myself invisible. That afternoon, there are some girls from an after-school club hanging out by their lockers. Two of them see me and whisper to each other in ninth-grade French. I think maybe they recognize me as someone who used to have potential but then I remember no one outside my family cares about classical music. These girls are only laughing at a twenty-year-old person talking to himself, mopping the same spot over and over. I look up and watch one of the girls glare at me as she takes out a wad of gum and sticks it against a locker door. After they leave, I am obligated to scrape it off. I look down at the hardened lump and think: *Why won't these people let me be excellent?*

Later I find several cardboard boxes full of old math textbooks in the second-floor storage closet. I ask my boss and he shrugs and I carry the box under my arm all the way down

Western Avenue while piloting my bike. I climb up the metal fire escape to my sister's apartment and leave the books beside her back door without asking.

When I was ten and a half and Isobel was twelve, we both got chicken pox at exactly the same time. My mother put us in the basement, set us up with a pile of blankets and sleeping bags to keep Daniel and my father—who had never had chicken pox—from getting sick. For days we read comics and watched television and listened to the radio together, made up our own language consisting of elaborate knock-knock jokes, hand signs, and whistles. We imagined entire cities of our own invention, which somehow led to a game where we tried to come up with the worst thing that could happen, a game which later came to be known as *Who Suffers More?*

I'd say, "Everyone forgetting your birthday," and she'd say: "Every person in the world forgetting your name."

I'd say, "Amelia Earhart," and she'd say, "JFK."

I'd say, "The *Titanic*. Hitting an iceberg. Except there are no survivors."

And then she'd say, "The *Hindenburg*. Crashing into an orphanage. Where all the children are deathly afraid of balloons." There was a ferocious pleasure in her voice, a gleefulness in imagining just how bad things could be. I came to understand, over the years, that in our family, there was always a preference for the tragic, as it was predictable, reliable, and reinforced a powerful kind of Eastern European fatalism. Unlike everything, catastrophe would never let you down.

I come home from work that night and go to check on my mom. She has not moved from her bed for the last several hours. Her dark hair is pasted to her forehead. I put a clean glass of water on the table and turn the volume down on the television, which is playing a movie from the 1990s. She looks over at me and says, "I have a feeling Julia Roberts might be Polish."

I tell her, "Um, I don't think that sounds right."

"The way she's suffered in her life and also some of the bad movies she's made, I think it's a possibility. A lot of famous actors are secretly Polish."

"Name one."

"George Clooney."

"George Clooney isn't Polish. You just can't decide who's Polish and who's not."

She stares at me for a long time and then glances away.

I wave my hand around the air and ask, "By the way, have you been smoking in here?" and she completely ignores me. I study the side of her face, look at this incredible woman who supported us for so many years, a woman with two degrees and a fierce intellect, a former librarian who used to read to us from the *Atlantic Monthly* and other scholarly journals, and cannot understand what she has become.

Later I go into our bedroom and find my younger brother, Daniel, drawing in his notebook at the desk. He is thirteen and all he ever does is trace figures from his favorite comics. But in his sketches the superheroes are always doing depressingly real things, like filling out their taxes or crying in the shower. I lean over his shoulder and ask, "What's this?"

"Captain America. Going to a movie alone."

"Uh-huh. Why is he doing that?"

"He has a hard time understanding other people."

"You did a good job with his expression. It looks he's very conflicted."

Daniel nods proudly, his dark hair falling into his face. I put on a Chopin record from my grandfather and then slip the headphones over my ears. Soon my thoughts begin to follow the music, spinning around the corners of the room. I start to imagine AMAZING COMPOSITION #167: Why not a symphony that describes the shape of the Big Bang or all of history, one that goes on and on forever? Why not a different opening depending on the conductor's mood or the weather or the state of the world? Why not an endless number of beginnings and as many endings as one could imagine?

I almost never tell people the truth of my name. Everyone calls me Aleks, which is short for Wolfgang Amadeus Aleksandar Fa. I am the only person I knew who is Polish and Bosnian on our block or in our neighborhood on the far southside of Chicago. The first and second names came from the child prodigy who began composing symphonies at the age of eight, the third from my grandfather who emigrated from Sarajevo in the middle of the twentieth century, and the last from my father, a Bosnian American who lives several blocks away but who no one talks to anymore. There are three of us, each named after some important cultural or historical figure: my older sister Isobel, after Isobel Loutit—a famous twentieth-century female mathematician—myself, and Daniel, named in honor of the biblical hero who fought the lions. The circumstance of our ridiculous-sounding names and the fact that all of us had been reared by well-meaning pseudo-intellectuals to appreciate books and music made us strangers on our block and in our neighborhood.

All of our hair had been cut using the same pair of clippers, each of us standing over the sink. Our skin was olive, less pink.

We dressed different—like Eastern European immigrants—in out-of-date clothes my mother used to pick up at Goodwill—T-shirts advertising cartoons that were no longer on the air, generic sneakers found in the discount bins at the supermarket. None of us were allowed to use a computer or the Internet outside of school until I was eighteen. No one in the house had access to a cell phone. Our parents had raised us to think of ourselves as extraordinary, as exceptional, had read us poetry in the crib and played classical music each night as we went to sleep. Our bad haircuts and poor clothing choices only exaggerated these differences—zip-up tracksuits, turtlenecks and vests, floods with off-color socks. In the end, none of it mattered. All we did was disappoint everyone, including ourselves.

I call my sister the next day to ask how she's feeling. There is a long pause and then she says, "Like Margaret Thatcher falling down a well."

Later that morning, I ride my ten-speed to the bus stop and get on. I play a requiem by Chopin and turn it up as loud as I can. I am the only one who nods my head along to any kind of music. Everybody else is dead or is already doomed.

I go to community college because that's all I can afford. I take all the poetry and music and film classes I can. I have a humanities class at the moment, which I am not a fan of. The instructor acts like the twenty-first century did not happen. I raise my hand and ask about current films and hip-hop and he completely ignores me.

After class I go to my other part-time job, ride my bike down to 55th Street, show my ID at the entrance of St. John's, a juvenile detention facility, then show it again on the second floor. The boys are already in the classroom cutting each other up, cracking jokes.

Your mother this, your mother that. The thing is, most of these kids haven't seen their mothers in months, some of them years. All of them are in lockup; the youngest is eleven, the oldest is seventeen. Whenever they have a birthday they get evaluated. The older kids move into the adult general population once they turn eighteen. I am paid to do poetry with them two times a week. I got hired as an assistant as part of a city program in high school, then stayed on after I graduated. Maria, the coordinator, basically lets me run the entire hour and a half while she sits in the corner of the room, checking emails on her computer. All of the kids carry their loss like some indefinable, unforgettable object that sits in the room with us. What I do is talk about European poetry and music. But what can I possibly say that will mean anything? Life has already made most of them a whole lot wiser than me.

On the bus ride back home, I watch two teenagers scrawl a mural of a giant boom box on the back window with silver paint markers. One of boys looks over at me and asks, "What kind of music are you listening to?" and I say, "Bach," and they stare at me and say, "Yo, that's hard core." Eventually everyone gets off the bus and I experience one of the rarest kinds of silence—riding public transit alone, which I imagine as geometric, conical, a glowing orange shape.

I have come to appreciate these silences, all their mesmerizing colors and configurations, after being part of a family whose constant emotional expression was like something out of Stravinsky, where someone was always singing, fighting, rehearsing, or storming off, where disjuncture and disagreement were seen as essential intellectual pursuits, and where CNN was on all the time, rounding out our lives with some other historical catastrophe.

I remember how, when I was almost eleven and did not know how to explain that I had begun losing my hearing, there was a pop quiz in social studies. I only heard some of the questions as everything seemed muffled by a constant, insistent ringing. I did the best I could, leaving several questions blank. I remember I had never left a question blank before and was agonized by it. When I came home, there was news of the discovery of a mass grave in Bosnia, in Korićanske stijene. My mother was standing at the kitchen sink with a broken glass in her hand, her eyes on the television screen in the corner of the room. I remember how small and pale she looked, like she was made completely out of paper. On-screen, a reporter was saying that the bodies belonged to Bosnian Croats and Muslims. One of our great-grandfathers on my father's side was born in Korićanske stijene. Eyes locked on the screen, my mother was motionless. For once, she seemed to have confirmation that the world was as mad as she had always believed. I noticed then that one of her hands was bleeding. I said her name but she was silent, and this silence was the most terrifying thing of all, as it seemed to divide everything into the past and present.

Later my older sister came home and called my father, who drove us all to the emergency room. No one said a word. After that, the doctors doubled my mom's lithium and put her on several other kinds of mood stabilizers, Paxil, then Xanax. She has not been the same since. Now she mostly stays in her room and listens to music—jazz, classical, and opera—or sometimes songs from her childhood in the 1970s, like the Carpenters and the Beatles.

About two years ago we found out she was sick and that her kidneys were failing from all the lithium and other anti-depressants she'd been taking, and so now she goes to dialysis twice a week. I ride with her on the bus, there and back. We have the most compelling conversations in those moments, when she is still halfway between the land of the living and the land of the dead and dreaming. Today she turns to me and says, "I don't know about this haircut. You look like a young communist."

"I read an article in *GQ* in the waiting room that says people appreciate it when you pay attention to your personal hygiene."

"*Dobrze wyglądasz,*" she says, touching the short hairs on the back of my head. She has begun talking in Polish, even though she hasn't spoken it since she was a kid.

Later, when we're back at home, I look at her lying in bed and don't know what to think. When she speaks Polish, when she murmurs odd phrases in her sleep, it's another remarkable kind of quiet, sad but also sort of beautiful, like she is a child once again at the beginning of everything.

Fate will find a way, says Virgil. But then Camus says, *There is no fate that cannot be surmounted by scorn.* So which are you going to believe?

The next morning, I struggle to do two chin-ups before work. *Orfeo* is once again reverberating through the house. As I'm catching my breath, my sister calls and says she's in the hospital.

"What? Where?" I say, and she asks if I can come. I imagine the nurses in the background mumbling to each other, can almost hear the silence of the near-empty hospital room. Static from some machine buzzes in my left ear and does not stop. I tell her I'm on my way.

I pull on my hat and winter coat then slip my headphones over my ears and ride as fast as my ten-speed will go.

CHAPTER TWO

I DON'T HEAR ANY PARTICULAR SOUND, NOTHING BUT MY OWN embarrassing heartbeat struggling to keep up as I pedal toward 95th Street. I pull up to the emergency room entrance, hop off my bicycle, and look for a spot to lock it up.

All the hospitals in our neighborhood have the names of saints no one believes in anymore: Little Mary, Flower of Manufacturing, and St. Loretta the Doubtful. The faces of the statues out front have been washed away by pollution and their folded hands are missing most of their fingers. Some of these sculptures are also covered in particularly lewd graffiti. I decide to leave my bike in front of the building, hoping someone will steal it and put it out of its misery. I get a paper name tag at the information desk and look for my sister's room. Every hospital sounds the same, I realize, as I make my way down the hallway: it's the sound of everyone holding their breath at exactly the same time. Finally I find Isobel sitting up in the hospital bed in a semiprivate room, drinking a plastic cup of orange juice, looking confident but pale. Jazzy is sitting in a chair beside her, watching *Sesame Street*.

In her hospital gown, Isobel is hard to ignore. Part of it is her dyed-blond hair, cut short like an eighties pop star. The other part is her eyebrows, which are intimidatingly Eastern European. Also she never stops moving. Sometimes it seem like she isn't listening but then when she turns and looks at you, you understand she's been with you all along and is now probably several steps ahead.

"What happened?" I ask.

My sister whispers into my right ear, "I think it's cancer."

"What? Are you sure?"

"I don't actually know. It hurt so bad this morning I had to bring myself to the emergency room. Jazzy was sleeping but there was nothing else I could do."

I nod and see the IV they have running into her arm, where a bluish-yellow bruise has already formed. "So how long do you think you're going to be here?"

"I don't know. I had an ultrasound but they're still running some other tests."

"No problem. I can wait."

"Okay. I appreciate it." She looks over at me and nods as I pull Jazzy onto my lap. Then we all watch *Sesame Street*, sounding out the words together.

At the age of eight, Isobel had already begun to show the glorious talent for which she would become momentarily famous. Not only was she musically proficient but she was also able to memorize entire chapters from books, complete musical scores, a list of numbers up to seventy-five digits long. My mother called it *hyperperception*. My sister seemed to see, hear, feel everything, all at once. "Try this," I'd say, and give her a section of the Bible or *Moby-Dick*. Sixty seconds later, she could recite the whole thing, word for word. When she did, her eyes would go blank, and it was like she was only a voice, like she wasn't even a person anymore.

At ten years old, she turned her focus toward mathematics, reciting theorems and quotients, solving complex equations without a second thought. Both my parents would grin and clap as she stood at the blackboard in our basement. All they wanted was for one of us to get into an Ivy League school or MIT, anywhere that offered a scholarship.

During that same time, I continued playing piano under my father's watchful eye. My father had been a phenomenal cellist when he was younger, just like my grandfather, but his musical career had ended when he was eighteen and lost his temper during an audition at the Berklee College of Music in Boston, kicking a music stand across a rehearsal room. Once my sister began studying math full-time, he shifted his musical ambitions toward me. Beginning at the age of eight, I sat in front of the piano for two or three hours a day, going to lessons twice a week with Mr. Gennaro, laboring over violently difficult pieces by Bach and Mozart, especially his eighth symphony, which he composed when he was a boy. My father played that record all the time, pointing out the tonal shifts in the different movements until I finally got the idea to scratch its vinyl surface with a paper clip so that it would skip. After that he was less inclined to play it so frequently.

By the age of eleven, I could no longer follow Mr. Gennaro's whispery voice as he spoke beside me. No one understood what was happening.

When I was twelve, I bombed an audition for a children's conservatory in downtown Chicago. My father took me on the train and, on a small stage, I brutalized a piano composition by Britten. I stopped in the middle of the performance because I couldn't hear half of what I was playing. I lowered my head and began to cry, something I almost never did. On the train ride back home, my dad didn't speak. It cost him weeks of working overtime just to get enough money together for the application.

When I got home I hid under the bed until Isobel came and found me. She didn't say anything, just turned on her tiny portable radio and then the two of us listened as the music echoed along the carpeted floor. I didn't recognize most of the songs except for "Life on Mars?" by David Bowie. *Believe*, the radio seemed to tell me. It was the first time I came to understand that some other entirely complicated music existed outside the kind I had come to know.

"Life on Mars?" became our song. One week later, our father moved out while we were at school, finding an apartment eight blocks away, beside the Mobil gas station. It became hard not to connect those two seemingly unrelated events— listening to David Bowie and finding out our father was gone, the beginning of one world and the end of another.

Another hour goes by and we are still waiting in the examination room. A nurse comes in and checks my sister's vital signs. *Sesame Street* ends and the daytime talk shows start. Isobel turns to me in the hospital bed.

"Do you mind dropping Jazzy off at day care? I don't want her hanging out here any longer than she has to."

I can see the name of my niece tattooed on my sister's wrist in an almost indecipherable script. I can also see the tattoo of a panther on her neck that looks like a black blotch. I study her face and see what seems like much more than twenty-two years of life etched in her eyes, see all that she has lost, given up on, see who she now is, all the different versions of herself made plain by the angles and lines of her forehead and cheeks. Anyone else probably wouldn't notice she's hiding something, how afraid she is at the moment, how trapped she feels. Even though she got into MIT, my sister, the genius, works as a bank teller during the day and, on weekends, as a cocktail waitress in a low-class Polish bar. That dissonance is what you feel when she looks your way.

Finally the doctor comes in. He is young with slicked-back hair. His name is Dr. Parrot and when he introduces himself both Isobel and I laugh. Isobel asks, "Is it broken, doctor?"

The doctor asks, "Is *what* broken?" and we laugh again and then he gives us the results of the ultrasound. Isobel has a complex cyst attached to one of her fallopian tubes which needs to be removed.

"Is it cancer?" I ask.

"It's not cancer," he says. "But it's not not-cancer."

Isobel's eyes go wide as she looks over at me. "Did you just say it's *not not-cancer?*"

Nobody is laughing as the doctor leaves the room.

In 2001, I am thirteen. I stand before the rows and rows of re-cord albums and CDs. Anton Miri's recording of a Stravinsky score for violin glows before me. The cover is meant to be fu-turistic with an abstract neon design even though the music is nearly a hundred years old. I grip the record tight in my hand. Always wondered why the covers of these classic records didn't match the sound. Who were they trying to fool?

Isobel is fifteen and tells me stealing music doesn't count. She urges me on with her forceful eyebrows. She wears a jean jacket with a picture of David Bowie on the back. I balk, over-come by nerves. Previously, Isobel had invited me to her room to listen to the record: a rare occasion. She put the earphones over my ears as I sat on the floor and listened to *Hunky Dory*. It was like nothing I'd ever heard before. I remember asking, "Is it a man or a woman?" Later I let my sister put blue eye shadow over my eyes. Days after that, I asked to borrow the record but she told me I had to get a copy of my own.

So here we are, at the record store. I begin to put the CD back in the stack and she grabs my hand. She slips *Best of Bowie* into the front of my pants and I'm forced to hold my 1990s windbreaker over it as I stumble outside. Worse than not get-ting caught is the feeling of not being noticed. But once we pass through the glass doors I hand my sister the CD and she grins her dogtoothed grin. "Other girls you meet will thank me one day," she whispers. I have no idea what this means: who will be these other girls? She places the CD in her backpack, which has been Magic-Markered with the names of bands I have never heard of, and then pedals off. I struggle to keep up.

Back at home, we see that all my sister's clothes have been put on the lawn. My mother has found several pills and some empty beer cans under my sister's bed. Isobel frowns and walks over to a box of hastily gathered clothes, searches for a balled-up sweatshirt and finds a small baggie full of pills inside one of the pockets, and then shoves it down the front of my shirt. Then she rides off. I won't see her for another three days. I still have no idea where she went, even to this day. I don't touch the pills but that David Bowie CD ends up saving my life. I play it again and again over the next few days, looking for answers in "Rock 'N' Roll Suicide" while my mother cries in the other room.

* * *

When I pull up in front of the day care on 87th with Jazzy on the handlebars, I know we are late. The woman in the pink sweater gives me a satisfied look and I hand over ten dollars. "I like your sweater," I say as she gives me a receipt.

I go back home and sit in front of the old upright piano for a half hour with my hands resting on the keys. At first I don't play anything. I just sit there. In those moments I like to imagine all the songs I could play but don't. It's like the few seconds before you go into a museum or just before a fireworks show. Any shape, any color, any sound might suddenly fill the air. I don't mind not being able to hear everything just then. It feels like the most majestic kind of silence of all. Eventually I make my way through a quiet piece by Debussy, missing half the notes.

Later I lock up my bicycle in front of the mediocre Catholic high school and punch in. Some girls in their fancy winter coats laugh at me, speaking French to each other. One of them balls up a piece of notebook paper in her small hand and then looks at me and purposefully drops it on the floor. I sigh and pick it up as I go past and then they laugh once again.

After work, I get on my bike. Scarlatti's harpsichord plays through my headphones, upsetting the gray sky, as a ray of sun breaks through the clouds just for me. At the stoplight, I think of my sister again and switch the CD to *Hunky Dory*.

In 2003, Isobel got accepted to MIT at the age of seventeen. She was there less than a year. In January of 2004, during the early days of her second semester, she was sent home, and my parents were told by the institution that she had suffered some kind of breakdown. Someone incorrectly diagnosed her as having bipolar disorder.

Isobel later said that she had been told she was smart so many times that she had come to believe it, when the truth was the only thing she knew how to do was memorize things. She loved math, loved college, but had no idea how to do what was being asked of her, realized at once that she was in way over her head, was in the wrong place, and then did the only thing she could think of, which was to bomb out in the most dramatic way possible.

For the first week after she came back, everyone held their breath. I was sixteen and had no idea what was going on, I kept looking at her, kept waiting for her to scream, to throw a plate at the wall, but all she did was sit in her room and listen to the Velvet Underground and Talking Heads and then walk around at night in gray sweatpants, lounging on the couch like a heroine in a nineteenth-century British novel. Later she cut off most of her hair and dyed it blond. I thought it looked a lot better, like she was the person she was always meant to be.

One night shortly after she'd returned, she shoved me awake. I looked up and she held her finger to her lips. We went downstairs and she said, "I haven't slept in fourteen days."

"Fourteen days is a long time."

"Maybe it's not been fourteen exactly but it feels like it. It's those damn lights."

"I don't see any lights."

We went out the back door and she pointed to the sky. There was an eerie glow in the east, right alongside the railroad tracks. "Let's go see," she said.

I shrugged. I was already awake. I grabbed my sweatshirt and even though both of us were in jogging pants and pajamas, we rode down 99th Street and over the train tacks.

There was some kind of construction on the tracks but the

workers were all on a break. Isobel walked over to one of the spotlights and held out her hand. The heat from the light was incredible. You could see waves of it, rising in the air.

She looked over at me and said, "It's like the line between two worlds. The visible and the invisible." Something was going on with her eyes. Everything about her face looked momentarily electric. Then she moved her hand closer to the light, and before she could touch it, I pulled her wrist back. She stared at me for a moment, judging me harshly for not being courageous. Then we rode back home without saying another word.

Only later did I find out that she was pregnant.

On Wednesday night, a week after Isobel is in the hospital, I get a call from one of the endless line of Irish bars on Western Avenue, asking me to come get my sister. I wish I could say this is the only time this has ever happened, but it's not. I ride my bicycle over the icy streets, pull up to the entrance, point to my sister sitting at the bar arguing with the bartender, and the bouncer finally lets me in.

I go over and see my sister with her short blond hair and jean jacket leaning against the counter, holding herself up. She is slightly inebriated and is murmuring, "There's a sadness to solving differential equations that's not like anything else in the world and I really miss it."

I tap her on the shoulder and say, "Come on, Isobel. Let's go home."

She turns and looks at me as if she doesn't recognize who I am for a moment and then gives me a shove. "I don't know what you're doing here but I want you to know I think it's an invasion of my privacy."

"Noted," I say and take her purse.

She stands and then grabs the purse from my hands. As we're walking out, two southside girls who look like they used to be in a sorority together bump into my sister. I can't tell if it is on purpose or not, but Isobel stops and says, "Excuse me? Aren't you going to say something? You just bumped into my jacket," and one of the girls with bleached hair turns to face my sister and says, "Your jacket is from 1973. And it looks like you've got bigger problems than that," and in a flash Isobel has her arm around the blond girl's neck and the bouncer comes over and Isobel is shouting a string of magnificent curses, words never associated with each other ever before. Even I have to marvel at her ingenuity as the bouncer forces us both out into the unwelcoming cold.

Inside the cabin of her frozen Corolla, I sit and listen to her ragged breath. I finally ask, "Are you all right? Who's with Jazzy?"

"Brian finally made an appearance. And then we had a big fight. I told him I have to get this operation and he told me I should get a second opinion."

"It seems like Brian has the right idea for once."

"Ha. The thing is, I did get a second opinion," she mutters. "At Cook County. Have you ever been down there? It's bleak. Like not even the doctors seem to think anyone's going to make it. I'm sure they still do bloodletting and use leeches and everything. But it's free, if you don't have insurance. Which I do not."

"So what did they say?"

"They said the exact same thing. I need to get laparoscopic surgery to remove the cyst. They said it should only take a few hours. But I'm still paying off the emergency room bill from a week ago. And if I get it done at Cook County, I have to wait three months unless someone cancels. So I don't know what to do."

I am not certain what to say and so those words hang in the brutally frigid air between us. I shove my bike in the back of her car and drive her over to her apartment and then ride back home in the cold alone. For a moment it feels good, this oppressive, interminable chill. It temporarily quiets all other thoughts.

I come home and find my mother in bed, talking to the television. She is sitting up on a pile of pillows and smoking, even though she is not supposed to smoke anymore. She asks, "Do you think it's possible Tom Cruise is Polish? Because I think he could be."

I tell her no. I frown and take the cigarette from her mouth and crush it under my sock. It burns my heel slightly.

Other people my mother has incorrectly assumed are Polish:

> George Washington
> Abraham Lincoln and Mary Todd Lincoln
> Grace Kelly
> Jennifer Anniston
> Brad Pitt
> Julia Roberts
> George Clooney
> Condoleezza Rice or anyone who becomes famous enough to face a series of very public tragedies

I pull the blanket up to her neck, say good night, and turn off the light.

* * *

Back in our bedroom, Daniel is in his underwear, drawing at the desk, sketching Spider-Man buying antidepressants at a run-down pharmacy. I look at him and say, "They're going to lock you up someday," and he only shrugs.

Later I watch as he takes out his money and counts it. I know he's been saving up for some old *Fantastic Four* comic. Before he goes to bed, I notice where he hides the money, in the back of shoebox under his bed. As soon he is asleep, I reach under and take out fifty dollars. The water bill is due this week and I'm not fooling around waiting on my mother's disability check. Then I lie on my back and try to hear the sounds of the house creaking. I have to concentrate hard. Finally I notice a pipe echoing somewhere in A♯ and focus on that. I think of my sister and how, if in any way, I might help, but I come up with absolutely nothing over the next several hours.

I call my cousin Benny the next day and explain the situation. Benny is my second cousin and emigrated from Poland seven years ago when he was fourteen. He has never lost his enthusiasm for Chicago or America. To him, every crack in the pavement, every broken window, is a marvel, some kind of a discovery. He knocks on the front door, ignoring the doorbell. I can hear music rattling from his van parked at the curb.

"Aleks, hello, my kuzyn. Are you ready?"

He gives me his wide-toothed smile and I see his blond hair has been cut even shorter than mine. I nod and somehow we get the piano down the back stairs and into his white utility van. 1990s hip-hop blares from the radio as he mouths along, with his unavoidable accent. By the time we get the piano into the music store on 95th, we are both out of breath and covered in sweat. The old Italian with silver hair inspects the instrument with one glance, running his finger along the keys.

"Five hundred. And not a penny more."

Is it the "not a penny more" that makes it feel less like a complete violation and more like he is a villain from a eighteenth-century opera? He gives me the last dollar in change for some reason, and I wonder if it is just to make me feel bad, but who can tell?

I go home and stare at the blank spot where the piano used to be—you can see the outline from where the sun has done its work over the years and in its place sits a now-invisible piano, an instrument of absolute silence. I sit down in front of its outline and hold my hands over the empty air, imagining the opening chords of "Life on Mars?"

When I ride by the day care to pick up Jazzy the next afternoon, the lady in the pink sweater politely adjusts her glasses and asks, "Did you ever notice your niece has a hard time following directions?" and I immediately think, *No, I did not, but thank you very much.*

I help my niece with her coat and she and I look over our shoulders as we're getting on the bike, both of us thinking the exact same thing. Finally she says it out loud: "I don't like that place," and I nod and hand her some snow to eat before we ride off.

We head back over to Isobel's apartment where I give my sister the money from the piano. "For your emergency room bill," I say.

She looks at the money, shaking her head, and seems angry at first. Then she says, "You don't have to do this. You really don't have to," and gives me a hug, a completely unexpected phenomenon.

Isobel calls the next day and says her surgery is going to be on Wednesday. Apparently there's been a cancellation at Cook County. I go over to my sister's on Wednesday morning and get Jazz up for day care, help her put on her gold gym shoes. Isobel has to take the train early to get ready for the operation, which is its own particular kind of sadness. "All-day parking down there is too expensive," she says.

I think: *Why don't we live in a world where everyone getting surgery gets a ride in a limousine, or at least free parking? Isn't this supposed to be some kind of civilization?*

Later I call Daniel from a pay phone to remind him that he has to pick up Jazzy from day care. I take the bus downtown to the hospital and sit in the deadened waiting room. Someone is singing to themself, someone else is shouting on a cell phone, someone is looking for someone named Mona. I wonder if Mona has drugs, and if I can borrow any. I go over to the window and see that it's begun to snow, as if the city can read everyone's thoughts. I close my eyes and put my hand against the window and let the noises fall away until there is only the high-pitched, constant drone that is always with me.

And then, like everyone else in the world, I sit down, put on my headphones, and wait.

CHAPTER THREE

Beethoven and the symphonies of Europe do nothing to distract me, so I go by the gift shop to look for an elephant for Jazzy, but all the stuffed animals look slightly depressed, their expressions sewn on at improper angles. There is a pink elephant with a baby attached that costs thirty-two dollars. I think about stealing the baby elephant by itself but don't. Still, I line all the animals up in a provocative way in order to show my disapproval.

After that I walk outside and look at the uninterrupted bleakness of the snow. Everything is covered in a grim layer of frost. I hear a soft murmur, like a ghostly voice in a magnificently high C, and go in search of the sound. I walk a block and find two silver Mylar balloons stuck together on a power line. Something about the way the balloons move in the air is mesmerizing and, if I listen hard enough, I can hear them brushing against each other, creating a remarkable, almost silent friction. I stand there and listen as long as I can until my hands get cold, seeing the tall buildings rising downtown to the east, looking like someone else's city.

I wipe my nose. The public hospital sits at the exact dividing point between the north and south sides. Traffic passes on the highway nearby and you can see how isolated, how distant each part of the city is from the other, and how purposeful this was, keeping the immigrants from Ireland and Poland and Bosnia and the migrating African Americans all on the southside. It becomes easy to imagine why some people have better jobs, have well-funded schools, live longer lives, depending on which zip code they live in.

Benny shows up half an hour later and we sit in the waiting room, playing music for each other. I put on a track from Puccini and he plays the Wu-Tang Clan, mouthing along with the words. I watch him nodding his head and realize he is probably my best friend in the world, whether he knows it or not. When Benny emigrated from Poland in 2001, he brought with him his love of nineties hip-hop, something I had never really listened to. It seemed so far from the music my parents played when I was growing up. Over the course of that long morning, Benny and I listen to two complete symphonies and an entire Wu-Tang album while we wait.

After about three hours, a nurse with powerful gold eye shadow asks my name. I am so surprised by her makeup that I almost forget who I am. She says I can go see my sister but there's only one visitor at a time. I look back at Benny and he nods. I am led to the recovery room, where my sister sleeps balled up. When she finally wakes, she looks over like she doesn't recognize me and says, "Where have you been?" before turning over and going back to sleep. Finally the doctor comes in with his all-competent, self-assured grin and says, "Your sister did wonderfully. We made three incisions, three keyholes if you like, and removed the cyst. There were a few minor complications but nothing to worry about. She should be okay to go home as soon as the anesthesia wears off." Then in a flash of starched white, he's gone.

I take hold of Isobel's hand and squeeze it but she doesn't squeeze back.

"How do you feel?" I ask.

"Like someone removed something important from my uterus."

I look over and I can see she's trying to stop herself from crying. She keeps on blinking. "What is it? Are you okay?"

"The doctor said the cyst was a lot bigger than they thought. He said it might affect having other children. Apparently it would take some serious medical intervention, or Patrick Swayze, or an act of God or something."

I can tell, by the doubtful look on her face, she's doing these different calculations all at once. I sit beside her throughout the rest of the afternoon. The care at Cook County goes as you might expect. The woman sharing the room with Isobel keeps coughing a wet cough and sounds like she might have the bubonic plague and maybe should be isolated. I have to ask the nurse three times if Isobel can get some pain medication, and then, as we're leaving, one of her shoes goes missing and it takes a half hour to find it.

Later that day we take the L train back to the southside. Isobel holds an ice pack to her lap and nobody stares because it is Chicago after all. There is no hiding it. Everyone wears their heartbreak across their face and refuses to apologize for it.

Back at my mother's house, I find Daniel tearing through our bedroom. My dresser has been turned inside out and half of my clothes are thrown all over the floor. My grandfather's classical records have been scattered everywhere. He turns to me with a furious expression.

"I know you took it."

"Took what?"

"Took my money. I was saving up for the first appearance of Doctor Doom."

"Daniel, some people are dealing with some bigger things right now than some stupid comic book. I used it last week so we could have some water."

"I know, but it was my money. You didn't even let me decide."

"Wait. Would you have given it to me if I asked?"

He is quiet for a moment and then shakes his head, "No. Probably not." He itches the side of his nose and adds, "I happen to like the Fantastic Four a lot more than my family."

I look at him and put my hand on his shoulder. "I appreciate your honesty. But you need to find a way to start contributing around here. You need to start pulling your own weight," and he slowly nods, but in complete disagreement.

I go to sleep at my sister's apartment later that night so she can have some time to recover. I put on a Rachmaninoff record and she comes out of her bedroom and immediately puts on an album by Nick Drake instead. Jazzy sits in front of the television, cutting out elephants from colorful pieces of construction paper, trying to get them to match perfectly. When they don't, she crushes them up into infinitesimally small balls of paper, which she places in a line, with an expression of profound frustration. I have seen that same expression on my sister's face all my life. I look over and see Isobel lying on the couch and groaning, holding an ice pack between her legs, with the exact same look.

"How are you feeling?" I ask.

"I'm okay. I keep thinking that the worst part of all this is that I'm still not done paying the emergency room bill from three weeks ago. And what happens if I need another test? Or some other kind of surgery?"

I ask, "Have you talked to Dad at all? Maybe he can help?"

"I saw him last month, in the parking lot of the convenience store. He didn't look like he's in a position to help anybody right now."

"What about your imaginary boyfriend, Brian? Where's he at?"

"He's been at his mom's the last couple of weeks. We're not talking at the moment," she says, clutching the bag of ice between her legs. "He says I'm too intimidating. He says I love people too deeply."

"You got surgery and he didn't even show up."

"I know. I think I scare men away."

"I think it's your eyebrows. They're super scary."

"Ha ha, you're never funny." She groans, turning on her side. "You're going to make me pop my stitches."

"So what about that guy from college?" I ask. "Is he sending money for Jazz like he's supposed to?"

"Ha."

Jazzy stops playing at the mention of her father. Isobel tilts her head toward her, ending the conversation right then and there.

I look at my sister and say, "I don't understand, how can you be so smart and such a bad judge of character?"

"I don't know either. It has to be related somehow, don't

you think? Like I know they're jerks but I really don't care because I already know how it's all going to end. I can see the entire trajectory. I can map it out before they even say anything. But I can't do anything to change it."

I give her arm a small shove. "You need to think better of yourself. You need to start aiming a little higher. You're an amazing person."

"Thanks for the advice, Oprah."

"I have been watching talk shows while Mom gets her dialysis. I want you to benefit from all of my recently acquired wisdom."

"I'll get on turning my life around as soon as I'm not convulsing in pain."

I fall asleep on the floor that evening and wake up in the middle of the night with the Nick Drake record still spinning relentlessly on the turntable. Something about this image seems poetic and appears to be communicating something about our lives, but I don't know what it is.

I ride over to pick up Jazzy from the day care the next day. The woman in the pink sweater pulls me aside and whispers, "I just want you to know your niece bit another child today."

"Are you sure? She's never bitten anyone before."

"You should know we take these things very seriously."

I tell her, "We just need to make it until the end of August when kindergarten begins."

"That's not my problem."

I ask, "Okay, well, is there a fee if she bites someone again?"

"No. But it'll be a second warning. And then after that . . ."

I take out five dollars and hand it to her. "Here. In case there's a next time."

* * *

I go to the convenience store later that day and grab a Yoo-hoo. I see Siobhan, my ex, out front, leaning into the window of a parked El Camino. She curses me like a madwoman. *Siobhan. Siobhan, what happened to you and me?* I think. Seconds later a half-full can of soda sails past my head.

The sound of it, the feeling of it spinning by, is like something from the past, present, and future all at once.

When I get home, I go through some old, racy Polaroids of Siobhan, which I have held on to for some reason. I lie in my bed and feel terrible looking at them and decide to throw them in the trash, but not before looking at them once more.

I come back inside and find Daniel sketching something at the kitchen table. Mr. Fantastic looks like a lifeless blob of flesh.

"What's going on here?"

"Mr. Fantastic is sad and so he's lost his shape. He wants to leave but he can't. Him and the Invisible Woman aren't in love anymore."

I look at a corner of his drawing and point to a shadowy figure hiding behind a potted plant. I ask, "Who's this?"

"That's where Doctor Doom is going to go. He's going to be hiding behind that plant. Invisible Woman is in in love with him. They're meeting in secret."

I say, "Daniel, this is getting pretty weird. I mean, this is starting to seem like a cry for help."

"A cry for help would probably go unheard around here," he says to himself.

"That is completely true," I say and pat him on the shoulder as I exit the room.

* * *

Benny knocks at the back door in the middle of the night asking for help. I get in his van and we drive over to an abandoned-looking warehouse on the eastside of Chicago, close to the Indiana border. *Perlmen's Music Emporium,* a faded sign that has fallen to the ground, says.

I ask, "What are we doing here?"

"I read in the paper this place has recently gone bankrupt because I am always on the lookout for the good kind of disasters. So we can go take a look around and see if there are any opportunities for us to exploit financially."

I follow my cousin out of the van and see the lock on a sliding door near the side of the building has been smashed. Benny waves me inside and we find piles and piles of oboes— literally a pyramid of them. Some of the copper wire has already been pulled from the walls and ceilings and I ask what he is looking for exactly. He walks among several boxes of discarded sheet music and finds a mean-looking tuba. Somehow he knows how to play it perfectly. "Orchestra," he says. "Back in Poland. I was the best in my class." We sit in the half dark as he thumps through every polka he knows.

Later we carry as many musical instruments as we can into the back of his van. I look at him and ask, "Are we just taking these? Isn't this stealing?"

"At the moment no one owns them. The bank does, technically. But the bank is not a person. And so we are relocating them, so that they can be put to use. They're musical instruments. They are meant to be played."

It is hard to argue with this kind of logic and I wonder where he gets this entrepreneurial spirit, this resiliency, from. It must be from some other part of our family.

Later, after we pull up to my house and carefully place the

instruments in my mother's garage, I wonder what I've gotten myself into. Something possibly, definitely illegal. Benny
hands me twenty dollars and then gives me a hug.

"Oh, I almost forgot," he says and takes a CD from inside
his leather jacket. It says, *Dear Kuzyn, I Think You Will Enjoy
This!* When I get back up to our bedroom, I slip on my headphones and put on the CD and find he is exactly right. I listen
once all the way through and then go back to the opening
track by the RZA again and again.

I pick up Jazzy at day care the next day and take her back home.
When we get inside, Isobel is lying on the floor beside the couch
in a pair of too-big sweatpants, listening to David Bowie.

"David Bowie? Uh-oh, are you feeling that bad?" I say.

She nods. I can tell she's been crying.

I turn to Jazz and say, "Why don't you see if *Dora* is on?"

Jazzy nods and plunks herself down in front of the television.

I ask Isobel: "Did you go to work today?"

"I took a personal day. Nobody cares if I'm there anyway.
It's not that kind of place. I could be a robot. Or a cat dressed
up as a teller. No one would even notice."

"What happened?"

"I called Brian because I was in pain and he came over
and I was in the tub and he was being so nice to me. He even
washed my hair. And then he asked about the surgery and I
told him what the doctor said, about how it was going to be
difficult to have more kids. And then he said he didn't know
if he wanted to be with someone who couldn't have children."

"But you already have a kid."

"Yeah, but he said he was really looking forward to having
children of his own."

"I think you could do a lot better than him, Isobel."

"Everything else in the universe is telling me the opposite. Think about it. Even that cyst ended up leaving me," she says smiling.

"You have a really strange sense of humor."

I go get her some ice and we sit behind the couch like it is just another one of the hidden forts from our childhood.

I come home and find my mother typing at the kitchen table using a pale blue typewriter from the 1980s. A stubbed-out cigarette is in an ashtray Daniel once made in the shape of a white and blue tiger. She looks up at me and says, "I'm thinking of writing a play about Tom Cruise."

"Oh no. Please don't."

"In the play, George Clooney is going to be his father and Julia Roberts his mother."

"I think they're all the same age."

"It doesn't matter. In the play they're part of the same family. I'm working on the first scene where Tom Cruise, as a young actor, comes home to ask his parents about joining the Church of Scientology."

I quietly walk away as I hear her hitting a single key every few minutes or so.

Later that evening I find Daniel in bed, surrounded by a moat of comic books. He has a notebook out with the names of different comics with different prices beside them. I see him counting his money and then he walks over to the old computer on the desk and puts some comics for sale on eBay. It looks like he has a plan of some kind. I study his face for a moment and he seems to look happy. Then I notice he is only wearing underwear and so I have to look away quick.

In bed, I put my headphones on and let Puccini do battle with the persistent ringing in my ears.

Just as I'm about to ride to work the next day, Benny comes by to pick up all the appropriated musical instruments. Carefully we place each one in the back of the van, oboes and trombones and flutes all piled high on top of each other. In exchange, he hands me three dozen black balloons, all of which say, *Condolences.*

I look at them and say, "Benny, Jesus, what am I supposed to do with all of these?"

"Just hold on to them for a while."

"Benny, they're balloons. How long do you expect me to hold on to them for?"

"Don't worry," he says, "if you can get rid of them, the money's yours."

I hold the balloons in my hand for a while and then tie them to the handlebars. As I ride away, I can feel the front wheel lifting off the ground.

I go get Jazzy from day care and she hands me three paper elephants she made.

The lady in the pink sweater shakes her head at me. "She did it again," she says. "Your niece bit two other kids."

"No, no way," I say. "Two?" I am horrified and also kind of proud, as this must be some new sad day care record. I glance over at Jazzy who is getting her coat. She has the look of a mournful convict. I look back at the lady in pink.

"So is she kicked out?"

"We can't have her back if she's going to bite other children."

"But it's the middle of February. Where else is she going to go?"

She shrugs in her infinitely pink sweater. I nod and lead

Jazzy outside and get her up on top of the handlebars. Balloons knock in the air around us. Jazzy's eyes go wide.

"Who are these balloons for?" she asks.

"Are you kidding me?" I say cheerfully. "These are for you."

CHAPTER FOUR

AT THE AGE OF TWENTY I HAVE COME TO KNOW THAT EVEN OUR best-laid plans are often overthrown. I have seen this with my older sister and myself again and again. My brother Daniel, on the other hand, is only thirteen. On Tuesday, he asks me to go with him to the comic book store so he can buy a rare comic without getting molested by the knuckleheads from the neighborhood. But when we get there he struggles at the glass counter. *Fantastic Four #5* is gone. All the masked villains and superheroes look down in disbelief.

"But how can this be?" my brother asks again.

The clerk, an overweight, abstract shape in a Thor T-shirt sitting behind the counter, barely turns. "I just explained. I sold it to someone else a week ago."

A blank spot stares back from the high-priced, collectible comics shelf where, apparently, *Fantastic Four #5* used to sit. For the past eight months my brother has been saving up every cent to add the first appearance of Doctor Doom to his collection, has mowed lawns in the neighborhood, has even sold some of his other comics. Even when I borrowed fifty dollars for the water bill and did not repay it, he did not give up. It's all he has talked about for the last eight months and now it's gone.

Daniel stands there and, even though he is thirteen, I can see his thin face tighten and the tears already coming. Then it's too late and even the other nerds in the store with their abnormal lack of social awareness seem to be getting embarrassed.

I tell him, "This is nothing to cry about. Buy something else. Get *Iron Man*."

"Fuck this and fuck *Iron Man*."

I don't know if I've ever heard my brother swear before. I put a hand on his shoulder and he brushes it off, then hurries outside. I slowly follow him.

He turns and points at me angrily. "I would have had enough two weeks ago if you didn't take that money," he says and starts unlocking his bike.

"I'm sorry," I say. "I had no choice. Also, can you loan me ten dollars?"

He shakes his head furiously.

"Come on. You were the one who asked me to come up here with you because you were worried about getting jumped."

He cuts his eyes at me and hands me a five.

"Wow, you're a real philanthropist," I say as I get on my bike. "Anyway, I've got to get to work. See you later." I put on my headphones and Daniel, who is still unlocking his own bicycle, disappears behind me.

At the dilapidated high school, one of the girls' bathrooms is full of water. The sink has been clogged with a pile of sanitary napkins (used or unused, I don't know). Someone has also left all of the faucets running. When I come out from cleaning up the mess, I think I hear laughter echoing from somewhere down the hallway.

I break the five dollars into quarters and get the saddest vending machine lunch of all time.

I come home and check on my mom that afternoon and find her asleep, speaking in Polish. On the bedside table, celebrity magazines are scattered around. At the foot of the bed is the blue typewriter. There is a piece of paper in it with a few words typed across the center of the page:

TOM CRUISE
Mom, Dad, we need to talk.

GEORGE CLOONEY
Of course, son, what is it?

Good Lord in heaven. Why is this woman, this intellectual powerhouse, this person who raised us as she went through graduate school, why is this individual writing a play about Tom fucking Cruise?

Before the walls came tumbling down, everything was a fairy story.

Before: my mom at the kitchen table reading to us from the *Economist, Mother Jones,* the *New Yorker.*

Before: her hair, long and black, sometimes braided. Eyes with flecks of green and gold.

Before: sound of her singing as she hung the laundry on a line in the upstairs bathroom. Her painting some abstract watercolor, surrounded by light in the front room. Her leaving books on our beds. Her rushing off to her job at the public library.

Before: her telling us strange stories about all our relatives back in Poland, some real, some possibly not.

Before: each day she would write out quotes from Shakespeare, Jung, Karl Marx, on the chalkboard in the kitchen.

Now: Unmoving in bed. Her hair uncombed, feet bare. Weeks without showering. Corner of her mouth covered in cold sores. Now: the same quote from Sophocles has been on the blackboard for the past eight years, which no one has the courage to wipe off: *Dreadful is the mysterious power of fate; there is no deliverance from it by wealth or by war, by walled city or dark, sea-beaten ships.*

I carry Jazzy up the apartment steps on my back after begging forgiveness at the day care the following morning and then being told to leave. When we get to the top of the third floor, I'm out of breath. We turn down the hall and I see someone who is dressed like a drug dealer from an after-school special in the 1980s, standing in a beige overcoat by Isobel's door, handing her something, what anyone in the world would recognize as cocaine. I pause and stare and realize this person actually looks more like the crime dog McGruff from the antidrug ads. Could there be a more obvious and illegal transaction in the history of humankind? I seriously doubt it. Jazzy and I wait at the top of the steps until this person walks past. Isobel looks over at us, surprised, and I can see the panic and humiliation in her face as Jazzy runs up and hugs her.

"Hi, Mommy."

I stare at my sister but Isobel's trying to avoid my gaze. She murmurs, "I took the day off of work," so quietly I can barely hear her because of my deafness, which infuriates me even more.

I hand Isobel her daughter's backpack and watch my niece go inside and then whisper, "Tell me that's not what I think it is."

"It's nothing."

"Where's your boyfriend? Where's Brian?"

"I don't know. Nowhere. We're still fighting."

I ask, "Isobel, what is going on with you?"

"I don't know," she says. "I have to go," and then she quickly closes the apartment door. I stand in the doorway and hear the Senegalese neighbors across the hall speaking in French. The silence is irreconcilable then, like a silver circle, turning and revolving, pulling in all the other shapes from the surrounding space.

Who among us hasn't been hurt? Who hasn't been forced to give up on the one thing they thought mattered or had their heart broken in some other way? I often wonder, what if the past is never past? What if the problems you had as a child come around again and again, like an object in an ever-widening orbit, or like a fugue where the same terrible melody plays over and over? What if everything you were afraid of, all the tragedies, catastrophes you had been unable to confront kept coming around again until you learned how to face them?

I do both of us a favor then and decide not to ask her about it later. Seeing that look on her face seems like punishment enough.

That same week Isobel gets Jazzy enrolled in pre-kindergarten at a Catholic elementary school where my aunt was once a kindergarten teacher. As always in this neighborhood, strings have been pulled. For the rest of the school year, Isobel, a devout atheist, will have to pretend to be Catholic, which for us, raised as intellectuals, and Isobel in particular, with her fierce, independent streak, is particularly hilarious. It just goes to show you what love can do, how it can break you into one million completely dissimilar pieces.

I get a call from Isobel a couple days after that, asking for a hand.

"A hand? A hand with what?" I ask.

"I'm moving out. Like right now. Like right this minute while Brian is at work."

"Brian doesn't know?"

"No. I haven't told him."

"What happened?"

"I thought of what you said. About thinking better of myself. I think I'm going to try it out."

I hold the phone to my ear and smile. "Okay, should I bring anything, like boxes or something?"

"I don't know. If you have some garbage bags. I'm just throwing what we need into those."

I find a few garbage bags and ride over on my bike. I help her place her and Jazzy's things into the bags and then I pile them beside the door.

"I feel like we should be wearing ski masks," she says. "It would make it a lot more fun, like we're robbing the place."

"Right. I don't see any ski masks. But maybe this."

I hand her a winter hat and I take one of Jazzy's. We pull them over our faces and keep stuffing everything we can find into the bags. I hold up a toilet plunger and she shrugs and then nods, and it goes in too.

Even though this is just another thing Isobel has to deal with, we are cracking up so much my sides begin to hurt. We get all the bags down to my sister's Corolla hatchback just as her imaginary boyfriend shows up. I think about punching him in the face and then remember how I cannot do two pull-ups in a row.

My sister looks over at me and asks, "Can you take her, please?" and I get Jazz in the backseat.

I turn and see my sister and her ex shouting from down the block. He has what looks like a recent black eye. I walk over and he wordlessly hands me a box of Jazzy's toys. My sister is silent and incandescent. It's like you can't stand beside her, she's so powerful in this moment. She ignores whatever her ex-boyfriend is saying and then gets in the car. I put the box in the back of my sister's hatchback and close the trunk. I wave at her through the back window and she drives off.

We watch her car disappear down 95th Street. Her ex-boyfriend looks over at me and says, "I don't know if I'll ever love anyone like this again."

I look at him and shake my head once before riding away.

I sometimes imagine my family as four different record players all playing different kinds of music, all as loudly as possible, all at exactly the same time, classical, jazz, pop, seventies, me, my mother, my sister, my brother, and then there's Jazzy, another record player playing its own music as well, and I begin to understand why someone might feel overwhelmed by all the noise sometimes, all the different personalities, why someone might prefer silence.

Someone knocks on the door in the middle of the night. I come down and Benny is there with his van parked in the driveway. "I need your help, kuzyn," he says. He nods at the white van idling in the driveway. I yawn and throw on my sweatshirt. He opens the back doors and I am not sure what I am looking at, at first. At first it looks like a lot of human arms and legs. Then I realize it *is* a lot of human arms and legs all made out of plastic. He holds three or four to his chest and begins unloading them into our garage.

"What are these?" I ask, lending a hand.

"For missing limbs. These are prosthetics. Made in the Soviet Union after the Cold War. Very historical. Very good resale value."

"Where did you get all these?"

"Friend of a friend. No problem. Why worry? There's money to be made."

I hold several of the plastic body parts to my chest and carry them into the garage, wondering why this is the part of history my family always has to contend with.

On Monday, the next day, Isobel calls to say she has to work late and asks if I can please go watch my niece in the school play for Casimir Pulaski Day. I put on my headphones, pull up my hood, and go through my CDs, looking for the right composition.

Be it a riot, Mozart. Having your throat cut, Beethoven. Be it the beginning or end of the universe, Bach. Getting your nose broke, Wagner. Having your head stomped, Mahler. A knife in the back, Bartók. Death by drowning, Hadyn. Blunt-force trauma, Grieg. Slow poisoning, Puccini. Blown to pieces by cannon fire? Brahms. A car accident with multiple fatalities? Stravinsky. Strangled to death by someone you know and love? Strauss. Overdose? Liszt. Suffocation? Handel. Internal bleeding? Ravel. But what symphony do you play while riding your wobbly bike across the southside?

I go with Rimsky-Korsakov, turn on my Walkman, and take off on the ten-speed.

Fortunately, the southside ignores me as I pedal beneath its out-of-date signs, some in English, some in Spanish. I do not get jumped looking like a reject from Eastern Europe. I pull up to the elementary school, lock my bike, and hurry inside.

Someone's mother kindly hands me a Xeroxed program but I'm too nervous to look. I take a seat in the back of the auditorium. A boy dressed as George Washington is kneeling beside a fatally wounded Casimir Pulaski. Jazzy's in the background—I think she is supposed to be an owl of some kind or maybe a bluebird. She stares out at the sea of faces and folds her hands in her armpits while the other kids sing a song about how Casimir Pulaski's body magically disappeared. I can see Isobel has made Jazz's costume out of whatever happened to be on hand—wire hangers, a bathrobe. Another song starts and Jazzy begins to dance like she is in a music video, owning the moment in her teal leotard.

The orchestra—all first and second graders—carries on uncertainly. The cellist and pianist seem ready to cry. I send them both positive thoughts. The performance goes on unremarkably, the music carrying everyone along in its wide wake. I don't hear much of it because of the size of the room and the drone of the parents who keep whispering to each other.

In the middle of the third song someone in the front row makes a comment about my niece's lurid dancing. I look around and see my sister is nowhere to be found. I realize then that she hasn't been able to get off of work. I collect Jazzy from the cluster of brightly dressed kids after the final act and we ride over to Cupid Candies on 95th. Both of us stare at each other from over our bowls of ice cream.

"You want another?" I ask.

She shakes her head. Two empty bowls sit before her as she works on a third.

We get back to where Isobel is staying with her friend Molly, and realize Jazzy's wings have been lost somewhere along the way. Molly is at work as a nurse at one of the many drug rehab centers that have popped up over the last few years. Isobel and I get Jazz ready for bed in the spare bedroom, Isobel helping her out of her clothes in that strange sleepwalk dance they do, where Jazzy holds her hands up and my sister tries to pull on her pajamas for her.

My sister asks, "How was the play?"

"Long and kind of boring," Jazzy says.

"Sounds like I didn't miss much," Isobel says.

"You didn't," I say, trying to convince her.

Then Jazzy collapses into the small bed and we turn off the light.

Later my sister is sitting cross-legged on floor with a glass of wine and the lights down. Nina Simone is playing from a clock radio, also on the floor. Isobel has a long piece of pink thread held out before her and she is deftly sewing the holes in four or five pairs of Jazzy's socks, all of which are purple.

"Only purple," I say.

"Only purple. She won't wear any other kind of socks. I'm worried. I think I passed on all of my personality defects."

"No way. She's an awesome kid. You're doing great. Seriously. She's fearless."

"Look at me. I'm sleeping on my friend's couch. My kid is using a sleeping bag for a blanket. And she'll only wear purple fucking socks. I mean, I threw out some of her paper elephants the other day and she freaked out until we made some more."

"I know it looks bad right now. But you're one of the most interesting, smartest people I know. You're going to figure everything out."

"Everybody keeps telling me that. But what if I don't? What if I keep thinking I'm going to figure everything out but it never actually happens?"

I go by the no-name convenience store for a Yoo-hoo on the way home. When I come out, the same four southside thugs are telling the same Polish jokes I've heard since I was in elementary school. One tries to get me in a headlock but I shimmy free. All of them roar and laugh as their jokes reach a crescendo. When I rattle away on the ten-speed, I imagine it as an incredible piece of music appearing before me:

No.6 Op.53

How did the Germans conquer Poland so fast?

They marched in backward and

the Poles thought they were leaving. How do you stop

a Polish army on horseback? Turn off the carousel. How do you

know   if you are standing in front of   a Polish firinig squad? They

are   all   standing   in   a   circle.   What   happened   to the

Polish   National   Library?   Someone   stole   the   only   book.

* * *

Back at home, I find my mother asleep in bed with the blue typewriter at her feet. I look at what she has written that day:

GEORGE CLOONEY

Tom, you're making a terrible mistake by divorcing Nicole Kidman. She is the love of your life. Your mother, Julia Roberts, and I agree.

I go back downstairs to listen to one of my grandfather's Georges Bizet records. An hour later a strange thumping resounds from the basement. I do not know if I am actually hearing it or not. I go take a look at the furnace. I don't know anything about furnaces but the sounds coming from it makes it seem like it's trying to escape. Outside it is twenty-two degrees. All I can do is stare at the metallic faceplate and silently pray, tell it that all of our fates rest on its reliability and kindness.

As I'm climbing back through stacks of old boxes of children's books, I come upon something like a recognizable face—Isobel's cello, sitting in its case, resting beside some Halloween decorations. I put a hand out and can almost hear my sister's bow striking the strings. I remember our father saying my sister played in the European style and I played like a Russian, her with too much emotion and me with too much intellect. Her reply was to blaze through an exquisitely difficult piece by Ravel that left all of us in awe. In the shadow of the furnace, I think: *What happened? Where did those people go? What are all these amazingly beautiful sounds now?*

On Wednesday, Isobel asks me to go downtown with her for

a follow-up appointment at Cook County. We sit in the sad waiting room, trying to name as many eighties child stars who have died of overdoses as we can.

After she gets called into an exam room, she comes back out in a blue paper gown and asks me to wait with her. She spins on the doctor's stool for a while and then looks at a box of latex gloves and says, "We should totally steal these."

"For what?"

"For scientific experiments."

"Oh yeah. What kind of scientific experiments?"

"Rogue experiments. On small animals. To see if we can finally locate the soul."

And then she starts shoving latex gloves into my coat pocket, dozens of them.

When the doctor comes in, he says he needs to perform a short examination to see how everything is healing, and my sister says, "I'm so sorry. I didn't know I was going to have visitors. It's a complete mess down there," which I think is completely inappropriate and so I go back out into the waiting room as quickly as I can.

I sit on the vinyl seat and feel the ball of pink latex gloves in my pocket pressing against my side, and decide, then and there, through force of will or magical thinking, my sister will be all right. Eventually, I decide, all of us are going to be okay, even though all evidence so far is completely against this.

On the train ride home, Isobel leans over, refusing to look me in the eye, and says, "It was inconclusive."

"What was?"

"The biopsy from the surgery."

"So?"

"So no answers. I have to come back down here in another week for more tests."

I look over at her but all she does is stare straight ahead. Not even the noise and hum of the train can save us from our endless thoughts and feelings.

CHAPTER FIVE

BACK AT COMMUNITY COLLEGE: I TURN IN A HUMANITIES ESSAY about the history of Balkanization and the war in Jugoslavia. I have worked on it all week, pulled quotes from different articles and wrote the essay in such a way as to show how Bosnia was conquered again and again, using different-colored fonts—to make clear how it is a collision of cultures, ideas, and overlapping identities, often in conflict with each other. While a film on the end of the Ottoman Empire plays, the prof sits in the back grading the essays. After class he tells me he believes the paper has been plagiarized.

It goes exactly how I thought it would go: badly. I try to explain to the prof, to the dean, even to his administrative assistant—who writes everything down—that I borrowed the excerpts and built something new, but none of them are having it. I tell them how Stravinsky borrowed the opening of *The Rite of Spring* from a Russian folk song and how all of old-school hip-hop is based on sampling. In return, I am told the college has a strict plagiarism policy and that I am to be expelled immediately. I don't want to blame history but it is hard not to think how it might have gone if I had written about fencing or soccer, instead of doing something that mattered to me. But in that moment, it feels like my need to be clever has once again ruined me.

When you get kicked out of community college, when you fall down from a place you already considered to be so low, who are you going to run to, who are you going to complain to? *Our wills and fates do so contrary run, that our devices still are overthrown; our thoughts are ours, their ends none of our own,* or so Shakespeare once said.

After my downfall and all its attending shame, I ride over to the water-reclamation plant and conjure up a new composition as the wind blows pink vapor into my face. AMAZING COMPOSITION #198. Improvise a silent sonata. Klaxons, flutes, cellos are all quiet while the only orchestrated sound is the wind, vibrating at different frequencies like a whistle, like a single instrument describing the perilous whims of fate.

Isobel stops by a few days later and we get slightly high in the backyard, sitting in some icy folding chairs, ignoring the late-March snow. We pass a joint back and forth, looking up at the whitening sky. Jazz lies in the snow like she is dead, completely motionless.

Isobel turns to me and says: "I think maybe I gave her the wrong name."

"You do?"

"At the time it seemed like a good idea. But now I'm worried no one's going to take her seriously. Like her only career option will be an exotic dancer."

"I think her name fits her."

We're silent for a moment and then she says, "It's worked out for you. Having a unique name."

"Did it?"

"What do you mean? Look at you. You're doing okay."

"Look at me. I'm twenty and I don't have shit. I was hoping to finish community college and go to a real school, but that doesn't look like it's going to happen anytime soon."

Both of us turn and glance over at Jazzy who is rolling back and forth in the snow, laughing to herself like a crazy person. Isobel glances over at me and sighs and then comes out with it: "I think we're going to be living here awhile. My friend Molly doesn't have enough room. Also, she's trying to run my life."

I look at her for a long time and say, "Isobel, I love you. Are you sure you're okay?"

She turns away, unwilling to answer.

Later we all end up lying together in the snow.

I drop Jazzy off at the institutional-looking Catholic school the next morning. I ask her, "Jazz, what are you going to do today?" and she says, "Own it."

She walks into the single-story building and I shout, "Wu-Tang forever!" and she quietly nods her head in assent.

I go by the record store on 95th Street to look for an original pressing of John Cage's *Quartets I–VIII*. It's a record I've been looking for over the past ten years, something my father and I used to do together. It's one of his favorite compositions. Even on the Internet it's impossible to find. I flip through the stacks, discover a foreign pressing of a Beethoven concerto, take it up to the counter, then remember I don't have any money.

I go into work and mop the entire auditorium. I spot a pile of untended computers sitting behind the red curtain and stare at them. There are ten or twelve monitors and PC towers, all unplugged and covered in dust. I wonder what my cousin Benny would say about these computers sitting here like that and how much one of them would even be worth.

I am mopping down the second-floor hallway when I see someone has taped a printed-out photo to one of the lockers. It is from the Illinois Department of Corrections website. It is a picture of me, from a moving-violation incident a few years ago. (There is not much to know. I found out Siobhan had slept with someone else, some southside dirtbag, and I was so broken up I got drunk with Benny. On my bicycle. I tried to ride home and fell off my bike and then a car honked at me for sitting in the middle of the street and I picked up my bike and threw it at the car. And then I sat there in the street and eventually the police showed up. And I got a moving violation even though I technically wasn't on my bicycle. But now it is on my record, which affects my employment opportunities. And apparently, also, is public information for ratty teenagers to use.)

I tear the piece of paper from the locker and crumple it up. A few feet away another piece of paper with the same photo has been taped. I find my stupid face all over again. I look down the hall and there are five or six more, all evenly spaced throughout the building.

I glance down the hall and see the two girls in fancy coats laughing behind their hands. I throw down the mop, then find Mr. McCluskey and tell him I will not be coming back. He asks if I want to keep my uniform and I tell him no thanks.

I go out and grab my bike from the rack and find another

piece of paper with my photo on it. Thank you very much, Internet. I get on my bicycle and try to outrun the sounds of laughter, to let the deafness finally take over, to get to a place of absolute, glorious silence, but find it is impossible once again.

I wake up in the middle of that night and turn over and see Daniel is gone from bed. I creep downstairs and find him at the kitchen table, sketching.

"What are you doing up?" I ask.

"Nothing. Just drawing."

"Drawing what?"

I look over his shoulder and see he has sketched Mr. Fantastic hugging Doctor Doom in front of what appears to be a see-through casket. Daniel looks up to see me squinting.

"It's Mr. Fantastic forgiving Doctor Doom at Invisible Woman's funeral," he says. "She had cancer, from all the rays she was exposed to, but because it was invisible, no one could see it. See here, Doctor Doom is apologizing to Mr. Fantastic. Look. They're hugging."

I study how these two figures are holding each other and can see how hard he has worked on it. "It's really beautiful. You did a really good job with their hands."

"Hands are the hardest."

"It's really good. Really. But also you need to get some sleep. You can work on it again in the morning."

He nods and I watch him climb upstairs. As he's going I almost say, *I'm proud of you,* but I don't because I know it will only embarrass him. I look at his drawing, and can't decide if his intelligence, his inability to leave anything unfinished, is a blessing or a curse? And what is the purpose of such intelligence if no one else cares, if you can't do anything useful with it?

Later that week a friend of a friend of a friend invites me to go see something called the Chicago Philharmonic Symphony, a volunteer orchestra of amateur and retired musicians. I ask Isobel if she wants to go and she shrugs. We drive downtown and feel like strangers in our own city, staring up at the skyscrapers that surround the Loop. The orchestra performs inside an ancient-looking Louis Sullivan–era building. They begin with a Strauss tone poem and then make their way through a difficult Bartók concerto. Sounds bounce off the parquet floors and I feel bad having asked my sister to drive me all the way down here as the performance feels very joyless and staid.

But then on the ride home, I can see something going on behind her eyes even though I am not sure what it means exactly.

I get back the next afternoon from looking for another part-time job and the phone is ringing. I pick it up—it's Jazz's teacher saying she has failed a test. I say, "It's preschool. She's three years old. She still has a lot to learn," and the teacher says, "I think there may be something wrong with her hearing."

I don't know about any of this. Isobel is at work at the Polish cocktail lounge and so we sit in the back of the house and I put on a record, something by Beethoven. Jazz is busy with a coloring book, adding pink elephants everywhere. I put the headphones over Jazzy's ears but she doesn't seem to notice at first. I watch her as I turn the volume up. It takes awhile before she seems to hear it. I can feel soft vibrations coming from the headphones. I turn the music down and both of us sit in silence then, the sound of her hands against the paper the only sound in the world.

I know we don't have money for testing, for hearing aids or whatever this person is going to need. But we have to do something because I'm tired of just making do. I read about hearing impairments on the Internet all night.

The next day, I drop Jazzy off at preschool. I watch her climb down from my handlebars and I say, "You go in there and show them what you know. Don't be afraid. You're as good as any of them," but she just gives me a blank look and wanders off into school.

I call around to see how much it costs for a hearing test without insurance. One place says three hundred, another tells me two fifty. But we don't have anything close to that.

The next afternoon I get off the bus and lock my bike up in front of St. John of God's. Before I even get into the class-room, I can hear some of the kids say, "Aleks ain't shit," or, "Aleks don't know nothing about hip-hop or writing lyrics."

Then the boys start in on my clothes every time.

"Yo, Aleks, you look like someone from the eighties."

"I wear these threads for you," I say.

"Yo, you look like a 1980s porn star."

Today I say, "All right, then dream time. Write a dream you had recently."

A boy named Malik, who is seventeen, looks up at the fading asbestos ceiling tiles as if the answer is written there and then starts to write. When it's time to share, nobody will make eye contact with me. I call on Wallace and hope he'll come through. He tells me about a recent dream he had, one where he could fly into space, and go back in time before he did the thing he did that got him incarcerated.

I look over at Maria, who frowns. After the session is over, she says, "They're moving Malik up. Next week's his birthday. He's turning eighteen."

I nod gravely.

Maria says, "Sometimes I think what we're doing, getting them to write and paint, it doesn't do them any good. What's the point of getting in touch with your feelings if you're going to get sent up and surrounded by grown men in general population? They need to be hard. The last thing they need is to be able to express themselves."

She tries to smile but then shakes her head.

"Our grant got cancelled. I can't afford to pay you anymore. The program's being discontinued. If you're serious about becoming a teacher you need to finish community college and get a BA. Nobody else is going to hire you. This place, it's got no future."

"I know. I am. I'm trying to."

As I walk out and flash my ID again, I count the money in our savings in my head. Fifty-five bucks minus this month's utilities. When I get out to the parking lot, two boys—half my age—are trying to steal my bike but doing a bad job of it. One has a pair of comically large bolt cutters.

I try to talk it over with them, say, "Yo, guys, what up?" but they seem to have other ideas.

I get the shit kicked out of me and then one of them takes off with my ten-speed. For some reason they leave my front wheel. I ignore it and hold my head, sitting down on the curb. Both my ears ring with an increasing intensity. Everything else goes blank.

* * *

I don't even know. I think I'd like to begin again. I have a feeling I'm going about this all wrong. It ought to be a concept album, or a symphony, or a four-act opera.

I come home with a black eye and go and wash my bloody nose in the bathroom sink.

I borrow Daniel's bike the next afternoon and go by my grandfather's apartment on Cicero to ask for some money for Jazzy's hearing test, but he does not answer the door at first. I can hear him inside playing the cello, his fingers struggling to find the right notes, but no matter how hard I knock, he does not answer. I realize this is how he has survived for so long.

I keep on knocking until, finally, slowly, oh so regretfully, he opens the door. He stares at me for a moment as if trying to place where he has seen me before and then waves me inside with a frown.

"Ah, Grandson. Let me get a look at you."

We sit across from each other in the ruined overstuffed chairs and he squints, as if studying some abstract painting he does not understand.

What do I see when I look at my grandfather? A past I know almost nothing about. I see a seventy-year-old man, my father's father, who first emigrated to the US in the 1960s, a classically trained cellist and an ethnic Croatian who felt Bosnia was no place for anyone who loved art that was not for the Soviet puppet state, a person who came to Chicago and dreamed of becoming a world-renowned musician but ended up at the US Steel South Works like so many other Bosnians.

What does my grandfather see when he looks in my face? I don't know.

After a long time he nods. "Oh yes. Of course. I recognize that look. I've seen it many times before."

Before I can even tell him what I've come for, he slowly stands and walks over to the closet and then takes out a dust-covered violin case, one that is banged up and covered in severe scratches. Slowly he opens the case and I can see the blue cloth interior and can smell the history, the mold trapped inside. But there is no violin. Instead it is full of old photographs. He lifts out a photo of a serious-looking young man and asks, "Do you know who this person is?"

I smile. "It looks like you. But the eyes, they're different."

"This is my uncle, Josip Fa. He was a musician, like myself. Like my father. Like you used to be."

I hold the photograph and nod, seeing the same uncertain expression in the eyes.

"Josip was born in Sarajevo, Bosnia, in 1897. He was a music student and lived with his family including his youngest brother, Nicolas, my father, your great-grandfather. This violin case belonged to Josip. Music was all he cared about."

My grandfather takes out a second photograph of Josip with an arm around his siblings. In the front is his younger brother, my great-grandfather. I recognize his slightly round face, his mischievous expression, right away. On the back it says: *1912*.

"You have to understand, Bosnia was a place where people had been dominated by one power after another for centuries. First they had been conquered by the Romans, and then the Ottomans, and for hundreds of years they were persecuted, their churches burned, their boys stolen and converted to Islam, forced to become soldiers. Both the Kingdom of Croatia and the Kingdom of Serbia tried to reunify the lost parts of their countries during that time. All of their fates were unclear until 1908, when the Austro-Hungarian Empire annexed Bosnia. When this happened, many people in Bosnia were unhappy. My uncle Josip, along with some other philosophy and music students, began to whisper in secret. They did not enjoy being under the rule of the Austrians any more than they enjoyed being under the rule of the Ottomans. And so, when a certain archduke came to perform military maneuvers, some of the other students, along with my Uncle Josip, made a plan."

He places a third photograph down on the table. It is of Josip, maybe eighteen or nineteen year old, with a pair of spectacles and oily hair. On the back it reads, *1914*.

"My uncle was to take the violin from this case and leave it with his family and then go stand near the Latin Bridge with a bomb in its place. He was supposed to wait there on the corner until the archduke came by in the motorcade and then he was to detonate the bomb and run away, going to hide in Croatia. But he was unable to do it. When the motorcade came, there was gunfire, the archduke was shot, and my uncle ran off with the violin case still in hand."

I close my eyes and for a second can hear the explosions. Perhaps it's a car backfiring outside, or only my imagination. My grandfather leans so close I can hear him breathing.

"My uncle panicked and he ran back home as quickly as he could to avoid trouble and then he gave the violin case with the bomb inside to my father to hide. My father buried it in a trash heap but by then it was too late. The assassination had occurred and the police were already rounding up those they suspected of being involved, who later revealed the names of their cohorts. Eventually the police came and arrested my uncle. By trying to run from history, by trying to run from his fate, Josip Fa did the one thing that cursed his family, one and all. Afterward, all of us would be doomed."

My grandfather lifts a book, a tiny ledger, out of the violin case. Apparently it is filled with the names of all the Fas who have come to a specious end. Those are his exact words. *A. Specious. End.* In addition to the list are other photographs of our relatives—cousins, uncles, fathers, sisters, aunts. *Hanif Fa. Imran Fa. Luka Fa. Traki Fa. Fa. Fa. Fa.* It goes on and on, photograph after photograph all sharing the same benumbed look, as if, even in the moment, they are unaware that history is bearing down on them.

Handing the ledger to me, my grandfather finishes his story by adding, "All of us are forced to choose our own fate." Then he murmurs: "I apologize but there will be no handouts for anybody."

As I am riding back I think of another AMAZING COMPOSITION: Why not a symphony of only beginnings, with the instruments having to start over and over, the way so many families from so many countries have? To begin again in a new place, in a different land, with a different language, in a different landscape, with a different sky hanging over your head, to be laughed at, joked about, mistreated, forced to live in a certain neighborhood, forced to work at a certain job the rest of your life. The joy and frustration and absolute silence of having to bend your life to fit into someone else's world? Where is the musical composition that describes all of that?

When I get home there is an envelope of money on the counter in the kitchen. Inside is one hundred and fifty dollars. I go upstairs and find Daniel at the desk, organizing his comics once again. I ask, "Is this from your comic, the one you were saving for?" and he nods once shyly.

"I also sold some of my *X-Men*," he says. "Never liked the artwork."

I lean over, give him a kiss on the back of his head, and he pushes me away, shouting wildly.

I look through some of my old records and do the same, going by a couple record stores, selling whatever I can. In the end, it's close to two hundred, which is enough to qualify for the payment plan.

On a Wednesday in the middle of March, I bring Jazzy in for a hearing test. It's not great news. We sit in a soundproof room and the audiologist makes sure there are no obstructions in my niece's ears, then she places a pair of headphones over Jazz's ears and plays a variety of tones. Later she asks Jazz to repeat a series of words that come through the headphones, but my niece only says one or two. We get shuffled to an exam room and the doctor—who is old, ancient in a safe white lab coat—explains something to us called *autosomal recessive hearing loss* and how her hearing loss is possibly genetic and most likely permanent and then discusses how hearing aids or implants would work and gives us answers to questions I hadn't even thought to ask.

I stay up all night on the Internet looking for information on how to learn ASL and decide even though I have been avoiding it for a long time, I will do this one small thing for my niece. I replay the video over and over until my eyes go blurry and I am no longer able to see.

In the morning I drop Jazzy off at school and feel the entire world shift as she hops from the front end of Daniel's bike.

I immediately miss the weight of her on the handlebars. I hold my hand out and show her the sign for *good*, by placing the fingers of my right hand against my lips, then dropping my hand into my left palm. She looks away, ignoring me.

"Jazzy," I say, "look."

I do it again and again until she glances back at me. I repeat the sign a fourth time and finally, unhappily, begrudgingly, she repeats the gesture before turning away and hurrying into preschool. When I ride off, for the first time in as long as I can remember, I have the feeling anything might happen.

MOVEMENT TWO

EVERYTHING STRANGE AND NEW

Adagio cantabile.

CHAPTER SIX

I COME BACK FROM PICKING JAZZY UP AT SCHOOL ONE afternoon and find something upsetting the air around my mother's house. At first I think it's my hearing. My niece slowly climbs from the handlebars and stands beside me as we both listen to a stirring single note, a high G, as it dangles somewhere above us. I hold my brother's bicycle at my side and I feel a series of odd vibrations along the back of my neck.

I pull open the front door and find Isobel in the back room, sitting on the corner of the sofa with her old cello between her knees, playing a complicated piece by Sibelius. I can see by the expression on her face how resolute, how confident the music is, as her bow travels gracefully back and forth across the strings. Moments later, she falters and an awkward note hangs between us, and then, a moment after that, she looks up and smiles, the spell suddenly broken. Jazzy stands wide-eyed, staring at her mother in wonderment. I don't know if she's ever seen my sister play cello before. It's scary how it affects us all.

Daniel whistles as he does his homework at the table. My mother magically gets out of bed and sits in the front room and begins to paint a gruesome-looking watercolor. Later she tells me it is a portrait of Nicole Kidman. Even though it is a pink nightmare, I tell her it looks amazing.

I go in search of silence every day after dropping Jazzy off at school. Ever since I quit my job, I've been riding around, building a library of different kinds of quiet. The sound of my brother Daniel silently snoring in A♭. The sound the L train on 95th Street makes just before it arrives, with the awaiting passengers shuffling back and forth, and then a glorious hum like a violin screech from Vivaldi as the first car approaches. The sound of my niece laughing on the handlebars of my brother's bike, which sounds exactly like a firework, loud at first and then imperceptibly soft, becoming a remarkable silence as she catches her breath. I close my eyes and try to imagine its color, its tone, its configuration. With my lost hearing, these silences have become more and more important to me.

Later that week I go to get an HIV test so I can work at a retirement home off of Kedzie Avenue. I am sitting in the small waiting room at this clinic and the tinny loudspeakers are playing Chopin and even though I am pretty sure I don't have HIV, I am almost moved to tears hearing the work of this Polish-born composer. I am not going to pretend anyone else will understand.

I come home and see my mother has baked some kolaches. I force two into my mouth, then a third. I find one of my brother's library books sitting open on the kitchen counter and notice that it has been underlined and marked up with pencil. I flip through the pages trying to understand what is going on in his phenomenally odd brain. Why has my brother destroyed this world-famous book? I do not know. I read through one of the passages and try to grasp what he's noted:

WAR AND PEACE
EPILOGUE CHAPTER ONE

Seven years had passed. The <u>storm-tossed sea of European history</u> had subsided within its shores and seemed to have become calm. But the mysterious forces that move humanity (mysterious because the laws of their motion are unknown to us) continued to operate.

Though the surface of the sea of history seemed motionless, the movement of humanity went on as unceasingly as the flow of time. Various groups of people formed and dissolved, the coming formation and dissolution of kingdoms and displacement of peoples was in course of preparation.

WHAT ABOUT WHERE OUR FAMILY CAME FROM? WHERE DO WE BELONG IN ALL THIS? JANOW IN EASTERN POLAND WAS ONCE PART OF RUSSIA . . . SO WHERE WE COME FROM DOES NOT TECHNI-CALLY EXIST?

The sea of history was not driven spasmodically from shore to shore as previously. It was seething in its depths. Historic figures were not borne by the waves from one shore to another as before. They now seemed to rotate on one spot. The historical figures at the head of armies, who formerly reflected the movement of the masses by ordering wars, campaigns, and battles, now reflected the restless movement by political and diplomatic combinations, laws, and treaties.

The historians call this activity of the historical figures "the reaction."

In dealing with this period they sternly condemn the historical personages who, in their opinion, caused what they describe as the reaction. All the well-known people of that period, from Alexander and Napoleon to Madame de Stael, Photius, Schelling, Fichte, Chateaubriand, and the rest, pass before their stern judgment seat and are acquitted or condemned according to whether they conduced to progress or to reaction.

According to their accounts a reaction took place at that time in Russia also, and the chief culprit was Alexander I, the same man who according to them was the chief cause of the liberal movement at the commencement of his reign, being the savior of Russia.

There is no one in Russian literature now, from schoolboy essayist to learned historian, who does not throw his little stone at Alexander for things he did wrong at this period of his reign.

"He ought to have acted in this way and in that way. In this case he did well and in that case badly. He behaved admirably at the beginning of his reign and during 1812, but <u>acted badly by giving a constitution to Poland</u>, forming the Holy Alliance, entrusting power to Arakcheev, favoring Golitsyn and mysticism, and afterward Shishkov and Photius. He also acted badly by concerning himself with the active army and disbanding the Semenov regiment."

Is this what any thirteen-year-old should be worrying about? I wonder. I put the book down and try to forget what I have just read.

Apparently, after another follow-up appointment at Cook County, my sister's blood count is slightly off and so there will be more and more tests. Isobel has to complete some additional paperwork about our family medical history, but most of the spaces are not filled in. I sit next to her as we try to answer the innumerable questions:

Have you or anyone in your family ever had heart disease?
Have you or anyone in your family ever had diabetes?
Have you or anyone in your family ever had cancer?
Have you or anyone in your family ever suffered from depression and/or some other mental illness?

Isobel looks over at me and asks: "Do you know if anyone else ever had cancer?"

"I don't know. Mom and Dad never mentioned it."

We don't have any records, we don't have any photos of these people, we don't know anything about their names, their birth dates, where most of them were actually born.

I think of the fate of the different countries my family came from. I look up some of these places on the Internet and find many of them don't exist anymore, the cities or even countries having fallen off the map. One great-grandfather, Joseph, was born near Janów, Poland, but like my brother noted, Poland was part of Russia at the time. And then Poland became part of the Austrian Empire and later Nazi Germany. My other great-grandfather was born in Korićanske stijene and moved to Agram, in Croatia, but that city later became known as Zagreb after World War I. I know my great-grandfather Nicolas was born in Sarajevo, Bosnia, just before it became part of the Austro-Hungarian Empire before World War 1. But then it was part of the Kingdom of Jugoslavia. And then it was part of the Third Reich. And then it became Jugoslavia. And then, eventually, after a decade of bloody conflict, Bosnia again. Imagine a blank map of Eastern Europe where the borders and names shift so often that it all becomes a blur.

On Wednesday I take all our clothes to Laundryland, separate the colors, force two loads into one washer, close the lid, put in some coins. I listen to the sound of all the washers humming together, which makes a lovely C♯. I tilt my head against the wall, letting the single note fill my ears. I am just about to put on my headphones when I look over and see someone in the corner reading a book—some kind of textbook about Gauguin. It is a girl with dark-blond hair that hangs slightly over her eyes in an attractive way. Those eyes—large, brown—make her seem improbably cautious. I look at her quickly but she does not seem to notice and does not look back once.

I sit and watch her read for the next half hour, trying to come up with something interesting to say. But I can't think of anything. I've always been better with music than words. Also, she never seems to glance up, not once, except to move her laundry from the washing machine to the dryer. She looks like she is my age or maybe a year younger—I begin to imagine she in in community college or nursing school. She is wearing a soft gray T-shirt, sweatpants, and ballet shoes, all of which make her seem approachable but still unreachable. Look at the freckles on her nose. I invent ten million different ways her laugh could sound before she gets up, pulls her laundry into a basket, and carries another armful of clothes over to the dryer.

One hour later, she gets up again and pulls the laundry from one of the dryers and begins putting it in cardboard boxes. It becomes obvious then—she works here. She's in school someplace, working to cover her bills. Or maybe she wants to go to school but can't afford it, which is why she is reading about Gauguin. Something in me leaps at this possible realization, that maybe we have something in common. Even though it's only the two of us, I don't bother to try to look at her again. I pull on my headphones, bop my head a little as I finish putting our clothes into the dryer, and forget to add the dryer sheets.

Every so often I see her writing something down. I jot some ideas for another AMAZING COMPOSITION in the little notebook I carry around sometimes. Later my pen explodes all over my hands. I look for something to clean myself with and then the girl is standing there, holding out some paper towels.

"Oh, thanks," I say. "Pen exploded."

She smiles in a shy, forgiving way and then motions to my cheek and I realize I've got ink there too. I rub my face and she looks at me, still pointing to a spot, until finally both of us seem to give up.

"Thanks," I say. "I think I'm just going to have to live with it for now."

Outside, as I'm unlocking my brother's bike, slinging the duffel bag of clean laundry over my shoulder, I realize I don't think I've heard her say a single word.

No one has called with Isobel's test results. I stand outside her bedroom that evening and ask, "Anything?" but she just shakes her head. She says she has called her doctor ten times already and is worried they are getting the wrong impression. "What's the wrong impression?" I ask. "Like one part of you isn't trying to kill the other?"

"Hilarious," she says. "That's exactly what I need right now. Your sad attempt at humor. Thanks so much."

As she walks past me, I realize I need to stop trying to be funny.

I go down the hall into my mom's bedroom and find Jazzy brushing my mom's hair like she is the Bride of Frankenstein. Jazzy has put makeup all over my mom's face, which seems like it might have been against my mother's will, as she is currently asleep. Even with the blue typewriter sitting unevenly on her chest, my mother looks beatified, like a painting of a saint who is about be beheaded.

I shake my head at Jazzy and rush her out of there and then go answer the sound of someone knocking at the back door.

Apparently some very questionable Serbians are interested in the fake arms and legs. Benny stands on the back steps and asks for help packing all the prosthetics into his van. I carry two or three at a time and fling them into the back. Seeing them lying on top of each other in disarray is completely horrifying.

We drive over to Bridgeport and two large, silent Slavic men begin unloading the appendages, carrying them into the back of a white delivery truck. When they're done, they lift something large and blue from the truck and lay it carefully in the back of Benny's van. I don't know exactly what it is, but it looks a blue metal bomb, or something shaped like a bomb.

When we get back inside the van, I turn to Benny and ask: "Is that an actual bomb?"

"It's an important artifact, from history. It's a practice bomb from World War II. They used them for target practice in the navy. Do you know how much this is worth?"

I shake my head.

"I need to keep it at your place for a while, if that's okay. My mother and father, they ask too many questions."

We get back home and Benny convinces me to bring it inside. We lug it up the back steps into the back room.

"It's too cold to keep outdoors," he says. "We don't want any accidents."

"You've got one week to get rid of it. Seriously. This is crazy."

He nods and Jazzy immediately begins drawing elephants on it in crayon.

Later Isobel comes home from work, looks at the bomb sitting upright in the back room, then walks away, shaking her head. I know what that expression means. It means she is too angry to say anything.

When I drop Jazzy off in front of preschool the next day, she turns and gives me a sign I don't recognize. I ask her to sign it again and she does. With my hands I ask, *What's up?* and she spells out a new word for me: *bomb.* Then she whispers in my ear that she's scared and I tell her I am too.

Back in our bedroom that afternoon, I put on one of my grandfather's records and my headphones and try to leave my body. At the desk, Daniel carefully cuts something out of a magazine and glues it into a black-and-white notebook. On the cover he has written, *The Book of 20th Century Tragedies,* in perfect penmanship. I get up and look over his shoulder, seeing a mass of bodies near an unmarked grave. It looks like it's from World War II but could just as easily be from the conflict in Jugoslavia.

"What's this?" I ask.

"I'm compiling an encyclopedia of everything bad that happened in the twentieth century."

"How come?"

"To see if there's a pattern. So I can come up with a kind of mathematical equation and find out if there's anything you can do to avoid it."

"Is this for school?"

He slowly shakes his head.

I say, "I don't know if it's good to focus on this kind of stuff. I mean it might be bad for your brain or whatever."

Daniel shrugs and then glues another photograph of a bomber in place.

When I go to pick Jazzy up from preschool the next day, one of her teachers comes out and introduces herself as Ms. Green. She looks like she is twenty-three or twenty-four, has sharp features, and seems to have the disposition of a very unhappy librarian. I wonder, how could someone so young be so uptight?

"Hello," she says. "You must be Jasmine's older brother?"

"No, no, no way. I'm twenty. I'm her uncle. I'm just helping out."

"Oh, sorry about that."

"No problem. And also, we call her Jazz."

"Well, as you know, *Jazz* has had a hard time acclimating to some of our classroom routines. I feel like she's struggling to find her place."

"Yeah, she was at this day care before and they let her go wild. To be honest, it was like a prison movie over there. They had them like lifting weights and making shivs, banging out license plates, that kind of thing."

The young woman just blinks at me.

"That was a joke," I say.

"Of course. As I was saying, it seems like she's struggling. Have you or her parents thought about putting her in an immersion program for hearing-impaired students at a different school?"

"No. I mean I don't think we knew something like that even existed. We're still just trying to figure everything out. We just found out she has some hearing issues."

I look over at Jazz and frown. I see she is hitting someone with a stick. I quickly end the conversation and get her on the handlebars before any other serious traumas occur.

As we ride off, I tell her, "You really need to stop hitting people," but it doesn't seem like we reach any kind of agreement.

On a Tuesday, Isobel gets a promotion at the bank because they say they appreciate her service. She is now a level-two bank teller. They even give her a button to wear: *Valued team member*. But what does it mean to take pride in something you know you are better than? The promotion means more hours, which is both good and bad; she will now qualify for basic health insurance.

We decide to go to Olive Garden to celebrate: Olive Garden, the place where you go if you feel like giving up! Olive Garden, the restaurant for people who have stopped believing in themselves or anything meaningful! Olive Garden, with its fake décor, never-ending breadsticks, and phony Italian cui-

sine! Olive Garden, when you don't think you deserve anything better!

Regardless, we all have a blast. Beneath the clamor of the
restaurant I have a hard time hearing what anyone is saying,
but I can tell everyone is joking and in good spirits. I have
never seen Daniel eat so much in his life. Isobel doesn't even
touch her glass of wine, even though there was a whole thing
with the waitress checking her ID and then spilling some of it
on the table. I can see that faraway look in her eyes, like she's
trying to think of an escape plan, looking for the nearest exit,
some other way out.

As we're leaving, she sits at the table alone and says, "I
never thought I'd be working at a bank for two years. I never
thought this was how things were going to turn out."

"But you're good at it. So who cares? I mean you have
a neck tattoo, Isobel. Think about it, you're lucky anybody
hired you at all."

She looks up and says, "If I have to work there another
year, I'm going to seriously kill someone."

"Cool. Thanks for sharing," I say.

On the following Monday, Isobel finally gets the test results
from her oncologist at Cook County. There is no sign of any
tumor or elevated white blood cell count, shifting her diagnosis back to stage zero.

She takes off work the next day and asks if I want to do
something fun and so we drop off Jazz at preschool and end
up going downtown to the Art Institute. We sit in front of the
green iron lions and do the thing we used to do in high school,
before each of us came up against something overwhelmingly
difficult. We go inside, we don't pay because technically you

don't have to, and then we run through the entire building as fast as we can, like we did two or three times before, with hundreds of years of art flying by in a matter of seconds. We end up out of breath in front of the Marc Chagall windows where I ask how she feels about the test and if she is happy and she just shrugs, which is her way of telling me she doesn't want to talk about it. So we don't. Instead we stare at the opaque blue and gold stained glass, and watch strangers go by. Someone points to the windows and says, *Look, Monet,* and Isobel rolls her eyes. I try to read her thoughts from the face she makes as another group of people pass, but it's impossible. The blue light obscures the shape of her eyes, making her appear more distant than ever. So we sit beside each other in silence, two members of an imaginary unnamed country who believe themselves to be better than everybody else, or perhaps exactly like two animals about to become extinct.

I look over and say, "The czar of Russia's family getting murdered."

I see her smile. "The czar's family getting murdered. First they're shot, then they're drowned, then forced to listen to extremely sad stories, and then fed to a couple of Russian circus bears."

I grin and then, out of nowhere, she says, "I want to play the cello with an orchestra."

"Are you serious?" I ask, but she does not answer.

CHAPTER SEVEN

Every day I wake up and go search for new signs on the computer to try with Jazzy, each a different movement, each a different shape. *Bird. Elephant. Ghost.* I even try to do some finger-spelling, which is a whole lot harder than it looks. Usually Jazz just ignores me as she eats her sugary cereal, so I decide to look up a few curse words and try those out too. For some reason she seems to learn those words much more quickly. And so we eat our breakfast, aggressively flashing obscene words and gestures at each other and laughing obnoxiously. As we do, the house slowly begins to come awake with music, as Bach's *Cello Suite No. 1* echoes from the other room.

For days and days, Isobel does nothing but go to work and play the cello. While she sits perfectly stiff, her bow carefully glides back and forth, fingers moving soundlessly along the strings, a small yellow box of rosin resting at her feet. It's more than just remembering. It's as if she is attempting to locate all the missing pieces of her life from the last twenty-two years, and through the incredible fierceness of her playing, it's like she's trying to force all these different pieces back together.

The sounds coming from the back room are powerful but also somewhat frightening and so we finish breakfast and ride off to preschool in a hurry.

As I ride back home, I conjure up AMAZING COMPO-SITION #218: what about a symphony staged in an aviary full of various species of birds, or better yet, a forest with each animal standing in for some instrument, with the conductor nodding to a skylark for a flute, a wren for a violin, a sparrow for viola, with all of them taking flight at the end?

I come home and look up more ASL videos on the low-speed computer. I find an immersion school for deaf children which is forty-five minutes away and costs twenty thousand dollars a year.

I finally get the HIV test back a few days later and it is thankfully negative. I start working at Pine Hills, the retirement home on Kedzie. I don't get to see a lot of the beauty of the world at that job. I mop and clean the hallways and take out the trash mostly. There is an odor of mortality, it's everywhere, gets on everything. But the part I like best is conversing with the inmates. It's a little like a funhouse, people talking to themselves, singing, crying, ramming their bodies into corners with their wheelchairs, other people leaving strange stains on the carpeted floor. I call them inmates because it's definitely like jail. I know you are not supposed to call them that, but that's exactly what they are.

I wear my headphones when I mop, put on some old-school hip-hop, and if I am passing someone like Mrs. Barbara Sheryl in the hall and I see her snapping her fingers and pretending to dance in her wheelchair, which is something she does, I lean over and gently put the headphones over her ears for a moment or two and play Lil Wayne. The expressions she makes, the mischief in her eyes, are like nothing you've ever seen. She has a tattoo of a tiger on one shoulder and a blotchy portrait of her ex-husband on the other, which is just about all you need to know about her.

I come home after work and find the bomb in the back room is gone, just like that. There is a mark on the rug from where it has been standing for the last week. I stare at the circle for a while, enjoying it absence. Even the room sounds different. As I am contemplating the bomb's sudden disappearance, I hear a strange buzzing coming from somewhere inside the house. I run up the stairs, afraid something is wrong with my mother, and find Benny in our bedroom, sitting in a chair at the desk, giving himself a tattoo, while Daniel holds up a mirror.

"I traded the bomb for this tattoo gun," Benny says. "It's in really good shape."

There on Benny's narrow upper arm is the evidence of his apparent intellectual limit: *BENNY.*

I look at it, look at it again, and then shake my head. "Benny. You tattooed your own name on your arm."

Benny just shrugs and gives a happy, self-assured smile.

"Get rid of this. Right now."

Benny dabs at his sore arm with a piece of paper towel. He grumbles a little and picks up the machine—which somehow consists of parts of a soldering gun and a car battery—then puts it in a dirty brown box and carries it downstairs.

I look over at Daniel who is unwilling to meet my eyes. I tell him, "I expect more out of you. I thought you were supposed to be some kind of genius."

He nods, eyes blinking, which is what he always does to keep himself from crying.

"You're thirteen years old," I say. "You need to start acting like it."

He nods again.

"Get your homework done if you didn't already."

"It's done."

"Then do it again," I say and close the door.

On the way to work the very next day, I see Siobhan smoking in front of the no-name convenience store. She looks fearsome and lovely. As I ride past I notice the bruises on her arms, see the purple-glitter eye shadow over her eyes even though it is only a Tuesday.

I don't bother to stop as she curses me out, calling me every name in the book. For a second the sun catches her face and I have to look away because of how attractive she is. When I ride past her, she curses at me with such beautiful ferocity, it almost becomes a different language. She looks like someone else now. The fumes from the paint factory where she works with her brothers have made her face hard, expressionless. She spits out her words and peers through me like I don't even exist. I have begun to think maybe she is right.

I get a call from my old high school friend Chris KRS, who I used to play in the marching band with and who now goes to art school downtown. We haven't seen each other in months. We meet up at one of the record stores on 95th. She has on one of her trademark ball caps, which she's customized with some of her artwork: a gold microphone under her tag, *KRS-KRS*. I pass her a copy of a Monteverdi opera and she shakes her head and hands me an album by MF Doom. Then she tells me all about art school.

"I'm seriously thinking about making it official and becoming a lesbian," she says. "I mean, you should see some of these females at school. The way they dress, with their hair all kinds of different colors. They're wild. All you got to do is tell them you're a visual artist and ask them to model for you and then *boom*. It's a little too easy."

I hand her the record back. "It sounds cool. I envy your ability to change your identity like that—you know, to actually decide who you want to be."

"Ha. Well, you should've paid attention in school."

"I can see that now," I say. "I made the mistake of believing in some future that never came, and by the time I figured it all out, it was too late."

"Well, you're missing out now," she says, putting a hand on my shoulder. "You're never going to find anybody worth your time in this neighborhood."

I come home and see that Isobel is once again practicing the cello. This afternoon it's a piece by Haydn. Jazzy and I sit in the kitchen and listen for a while before Daniel walks in from school. He tilts his head toward the music and asks, "Why do you always play music from countries that conquered all the places our family came from?"

I ask him what he is talking about and he says, "All you ever play is music by Germans or Austrians or Russians. All the records you listen to, all the pieces Isobel always practices. Don't you think you're just letting yourselves be humiliated over and over?"

I ignore him and go upstairs. In our bedroom I find my brother has added to his notebook of tragic horrors. Page after page features a never-ending list of events from the twentieth century with a numerical value for each.

12. Hiroshima. -1000.
45. 1969 Santa Barbara oil spill. -500
83. Cuban Missile Crisis. -135

I continue flipping through the notebook, puzzled by some of his calculations. Many of his mathematical values seem entirely reasonable, while others, like, *115. The end of The Beatles -100000,* are much more arbitrary.

I look through all the gruesome photographs and drawings he has glued in place and come to see the pattern he has traced over one hundred years. Everything we think is important or unique about ours lives means nothing in the face of history. Even our tragedies are entirely ordinary.

Jazzy's preschool teacher calls our house later that afternoon and asks if maybe we have given any thought to her suggestion of putting Jazz in an immersion program for children with hearing impairments.

"We have," I lie. "We've given it a lot of thought and have done a lot of research and are still debating all the finer points."

"I really think Jasmine could do with some more inclusive one-on-one attention."

"For sure, but what kid couldn't?"

Ms. Green, who I know is only a few years older than me, laughs condescendingly. "I know this must be hard for you."

"It's not hard for me at all. It's hard for Jazzy. We really appreciate you looking out for her, but right now there's not a lot we can do. The closest school that has accommodations for deaf kids is forty-five minutes away. And it's really expensive, so it's not going to happen. Besides, she's eventually going to have to live in a world where people can hear, even if she can't."

A few days later, I pick Jazz up from school and look at some of her papers. I see where she has scrawled her name in blue crayon. Everything else looks wrong: the spelling of all the words is abysmal, and most of her numbers are backward. On a math sheet about counting is a drawing of elephants in place of any answers. I turn the sheet over and find more elephants. I don't tell my sister because I know, at the moment, there's nothing else we can do.

After everyone is asleep, I go on the Internet on the old computer and find a free ASL class at the park office on Tuesday afternoons.

On Tuesday, I ride up there with Jazzy and sit and watch a woman with slim fingers give a new shape to the universe as I've come to know it. In that room, I do not feel embarrassed or self-aware about my deafness.

Later that evening, we have a contest, Jazzy and I: who can do the signs for certain words the fastest, who can go through the alphabet letter by letter. It becomes our own secret language, a way to share our thoughts, another exceptional kind of silence.

On Wednesday, I ride to the laundromat. It is breezy and mild, and the sun suddenly acts like it has not forgotten us. The green smoke from the nearby plastics factory has changed color, faint pinks, blues. I ride with two bags of laundry over my shoulder, and by the time I get to Laundryland, I am covered with sweat. The glass windows and doors are all humid and foggy. I lock up my brother's bicycle and go inside.

The young woman with the book about Gauguin has her feet up on a plastic seat. She is paging through her book and also glancing up at a reality dating show on a small television on top of the dryers. I nod at her as I enter.

Once I finish loading two washing machines, I take a seat on the other side of the room and put on my headphones, trying to summon an air of mystery. But I can't keep still. I keep glancing up to see what this other person is doing.

I get up, put a dollar into the vending machine, and out come two cans of orange soda. I look at the perfectly cylindrical cans, beaded over with moisture. I don't even like orange soda, but everything else is out. I definitely don't need two. I head over to my seat, then stop, and meekly advance toward where the girl is sitting in blue cutoffs. I offer her one of the cans of soda. "It gave me two," I say.

She looks up as if, until that moment, she had no idea I was there. I do not wait for a reply. I put the can down on the little table beside her and walk back to my seat, then slip on my headphones. Later I watch her pull wet clothes from four or five different washers and shove them into an industrial-sized dryer.

I put all my family's clothes into a dryer and realize it has been months since I washed my hooded sweatshirt, so I take it off and wash it by itself. I put in a couple of quarters but the machine begins to rumble and shake.

The young woman sets down her book and comes over. Without saying anything, she opens the lid, shakes her head, and says, "It's off-balance. These machines, you can't just put only one thing in there or they will not work properly. I can put it in one of these if you still want to wash it." She points to a smaller machine, already filled with laundry.

"Sure," I say. "That'd be great."

I hand it back to her and she shoves it in with someone else's laundry.

"Thanks."

"It'll be an hour, if you want to come back."

"No, it's good. I don't mind waiting," I say, both of us standing there, several feet from each other.

"I don't drink soda," she says, pointing to the unopened can. "But thank you for offering."

"You don't drink soda?"

"I don't like how it feels on my teeth."

"Got it. No orange pop for this person."

But then, just then, she cracks open the can of soda and takes a sip. I don't know what to think.

Somehow I end up standing near her as I am folding my family's clothes and shoving them in one of the duffel bags. I gesture toward her book. "Are you studying for something?"

She nods and then shakes her head. "No, I just like to read."

"So you just work here then?"

"It is my parents'," she says. "They came here from Poland in the 1990s."

"Oh, really? That's amazing. I'm part Polish."

"Have you ever been there?"

"No. But my mother, her parents were Polish. From Poland." I look around and try to think of something else. "I'm Aleks. With a k and an s."

"Halina," she says. "With an H."

It is quiet for a while. I look over at her again. "So it'll be another hour for the sweatshirt?"

She nods.

"Do you ever get to go outside?"

"What?"

The question is so fantastically dumb, I know she can't

help but laugh. And so then I ask it again: "Do you ever get to go outside or do you have to work all the time?"

"Of course I can go outside. I go outside when I go home."

"Is that the only time?"

"No. What kind of a question?" she says, shaking her head.

"Do you ever go dancing?"

"Sometimes."

"What about going for a walk? Do you ever walk anywhere?"

"You ask some very weird kind of questions."

"It's feels like summer outside. I was thinking we could maybe go for a walk?"

"To where?"

I can see her cheeks going pink from the question or from the heat of the dryers, I don't know. "Anywhere. We could just pick up our feet and go for a walk."

She talks to herself a little in Polish, and then takes a sip from the can of soda. The orange pop makes her lips red.

We end up walking together down 111th Street all the way to the overpass, where evening traffic roars by forty feet below. It's like a silver river, the closest we can get to anything romantic around here. A fence and concrete barrier prevents anyone from jumping. All you can see are the headlights becoming one solid blur of color. Both of us stand there and watch the cars flying past in both directions. It's almost impossible to be heard, especially with my hearing, so we have to stand closer than we otherwise would.

"I like to come and watch," she says. "I like all the sounds."

I nod.

"I like the way the light looks, all the cars going together," she says.

I stand beside her, our hands up on the fence. In the distance, the narrow shapes of towers, spires, skyscrapers demarcate the other realm of downtown. It's only a few miles but might as well be a thousand.

"I can't wait to leave this place," she says.

"You don't like the southside?"

"No. I'm ready to go somewhere else. I've been here ten years. I see the same people on the bus, every day. I would like to see something different." Then she says something I don't catch and I don't feel like explaining I'm having a hard time hearing. So both of us stand there and watch the lights streaming beneath our feet.

"I never came up here before," I say. "I like it. I like talking with you. I like your accent."

I think about kissing her but see I have said the wrong thing. Her face goes red beneath her eyes and she lowers her hands from the fence.

"I'm sorry, I shouldn't have mentioned it, I was just . . ."

"I have to go back," she says.

Later, as I unlock my brother's bike beneath the yellow sign and sling the duffel bags over my shoulder, it's like we've never spoken.

Isobel has been getting up earlier and earlier before work to practice the cello. She says there's an audition for the citywide symphony coming up in May in two weeks. As I lie in bed, listening to the house reverberate with the same concerto, I look over at Daniel and wince. There's no way she'll be ready in time, no matter how much practice she puts in. Still she plows ahead, charging through Bach and Wagner, as if they are ex-boyfriends she can push around.

Once when I come up the front steps and hear her soaring

through Sibelius's *Symphony No. 2*, each phrase sounds effort-less, full of a kind of stupefying grace, and I begin to think maybe she can actually do it.

Benny comes over one night in the middle of April, very late, looking upset. His pale face is blotted red. Someone has bro-ken into his van, he says. One of the back windows has been smashed. Together we go outside and cut a piece of cardboard and fix it in place with black electrical tape.

"Do you have any idea who did this?" I ask.

"It could be many different people. I have made a lot of enemies with my enterprising spirit," he says, and I wonder what he has gotten himself, and us, into.

The following evening, I go by Laundryland and Halina is sitting in a pale-blue chair reading a book about Degas. When I pull up on my brother's bike, she regards me as if she is making her mind up about something. It is seven thirty p.m. When I walk over to say hello, she does not look up at me, only takes my hand. She turns the sign on the door to *CLOSED*, leads me outside, locks the door, and then the two of us walk around behind the strip mall to where there is an enormous parking lot that is entirely empty. She walks me over to a bumpy-looking Honda, her brother's car, she tells me. We go in the backseat and start kissing. By and by we take off each other's clothes. She has on gray sweatpants, which she pulls down quickly. As we are fumbling there together, she looks like she's upset so I stop and ask, "Are you okay?" but she only nods.

I realize we are behind a dollar store and a laundromat and the light is less than romantic. But there is something sad and lovely about the way she closes her eyes and how she is half smiling, half frowning. Her ambivalence is strangely attractive. I hover over her, wishing I could stay in that moment forever, capture how both distant and lovely she appears to be. Somehow I can almost hear the neon from the sign out front buzzing above us, but maybe that is the tinnitus or just my imagination.

Before anything else happens, there is a knock on the window. A cop with a flashlight shakes his head, tells us to move on. So we take her brother's car and go and fool around in the grass near the pond by the community college. We do what our bodies tell us to do. Afterward, my left ear rings for several hours.

Even in those moments I know I do not deserve the attention of someone so beautiful, so kind, so willing.

One night, after it is all over, after we have fumbled around in her brother's car, we share an orange soda in the light surrounding the front of Laundryland, sitting on two plastic stools. When I go to hold her hand, she moves away. I ask her what's wrong and she says, "Kacper is coming back in a few weeks."

I don't know what this all means. I look over and see the glass door to the laundromat has been propped open and I can hear one of the machines vibrating in F♯. I hand her back the soda. "May I ask who is Kacper?"

"My boyfriend."

Everything becomes a pinprick of light then. I almost fall off the stool. "Your *what*?"

"My boyfriend. My husband, I mean."

"Wait, you're married?"

"I was married when I was eighteen, back in Warsaw. But I'm not married here."

"I don't know if that matters. I mean, I've been seeing you for a couple weeks."

"I thought we were just having fun," she says, and I catch her accent again, but this time it sounds harsh and distant.

"We *are* having fun. But usually people mention it when they're married."

"I didn't know if I was married anymore. I didn't know if he was coming back." She looks away for moment and then adds, "We can keep meeting until he does."

Inside the laundromat, I look over at the television and see someone has crashed out on the game show *Press Your Luck*. Both of us stare at the lights over the parking lot as if they hold some answers. Even as I get up and walk toward where Daniel's bicycle is locked, I can hear the applause from the television. I try to remember what the ASL sign for goodbye is. I know I know it but am unable to remember it in that particular moment. I turn to her and have to improvise, making the shape of a bomb exploding over my heart.

CHAPTER EIGHT

THE BOOK OF 20TH CENTURY TRAGEDIES, MY BROTHER'S EPIC tome, gets larger and larger each day, filled with maps, scraps of papers, and photographs. Sometimes I flip through it like I am reading a novel or the newspaper. Every week he adds more and more horrible events which slowly go beyond the scope of the twentieth century. Almost unwillingly, he seems to have begun reinterpreting history, revising certain descriptions or adding completely imaginary details.

327. Second Boer War. A strange mist from a valley near Pretoria puts all the combatants to sleep.

445. Battle of Austerlitz. A flood prevents the crossing of the Rhine, drowning all of the French army before the battle begins.

530. Crucifixion of Jesus and two thieves. The association of thieves arranges for all of the crosses to be built with faulty nails. The two crosses collapse at night and the thieves help Jesus escape into the wilderness, where he grows to old age in hiding.

The book becomes a place where his imagination almost always triumphs over grief, where fantasy overtakes the awful record of reality. But what I wonder is, what if history isn't so easily forgotten or amended? What if it's a part of your blood, part of how you think about yourself, what if it's something you can't ever escape, no matter what you do?

I am coming home from work later that week when I hear someone scream. There is a flash of pink as someone yells, "Suicide attack!" and I see it is Jazzy rushing full speed at me on her Big Wheel. She crashes hard into my ankle and we fall together onto the front lawn. I almost have a stroke but I see she is giggling so hard, there is nothing I can do but roll on the ground beside her, joining in her fantastic shrieking.

In that moment, I see all our history, hear it all remade in the sound of her relentless laughter.

A few days later, Isobel asks if I want to accompany her to the audition for the citywide symphony. I can see how nervous she is by how quietly she asks. So together we drive downtown again, where we are both strangers, feeling intimidated, undereducated, inferior, because downtown has always loomed large as someplace both complicated and foreign. Even our somewhat-intellectual parents, even our mother the librarian, seems to believe this part of the city is off-limits.

We enter the grand concert hall and go and sit in plush red chairs while we wait for Isobel's number to be called. Onstage, an older African American man with enormous bifocals and large shoulders plays the French horn miraculously. It sounds like a recording, completely flawless, the music unspooling like some great silver ribbon. Isobel looks over at me, her eyebrows going wide, shaking her head in disbelief.

A young Asian American man, no older than eighteen or nineteen, sits with his mother until his number is announced. He climbs onstage, sits down, and plays a gorgeous étude on the violin and the entire recital hall goes still. This kid clearly does not belong here. Is it for a college application? I wonder. He makes all the other players look like beginners.

Isobel looks stricken. "I just realized I can't do this with you here," she murmurs.

"What? You asked me to come."

"I know. I'm sorry. But can you go outside please?"

"Why?"

"If you stay, I am going to cry."

Just then, someone calls my sister's number. I give her a nod and watch her walk over and slowly carry the cello up the steps, then see her take a seat in the folding metal chair onstage.

I go into the hall and find a bench to sit on next to the door. I close my eyes and attempt to listen. Isobel begins to play. The music is tentative at first, not a definitive shape or color. It feels like the notes have not decided what they want to be yet. Then the music becomes a bold bright-yellow triangle, and then it flashes to orange, then purple, shifting to a pink circle at the end. I open my eyes, amazed, just before it all comes crashing down. Somewhere near the end of the composition, she misses a phrase, then another, then gets lost, her confidence fades, and she starts thinking, you can hear it in the music, like a large red trapezoid blocking all the other notes, and then all the shapes she has made fall to the floor. I don't hear much after that. Moments later she comes out into the hall, dragging the cello on its small metal cart.

After that we sit in her car. I see her hands on the steering wheel, see that they are still trembling. I turn on the radio and she immediately turns it off, letting the silence of our complicated history fill the air, forcing us to face a disappointment both of us fully expected. After some time I put my hand on one of her hands until it is no longer shaking.

Jazzy turns four in May. We have a party with colorful paper hats and a small cake my mother seems to bake in her sleep. We all gather around and watch Jazzy blow out the candles. The sound of laughter peals around the room. In that brief moment before her exhalation, I try to remember the silence, the pause of all of us holding our breath and smiling at once. Malcolm, Jazzy's father (I think of him more as an anonymous sperm donor), sends Jazzy a bike from California where he is in graduate school, getting his third or fourth engineering degree.

I go outside and Jazzy shows me the bike, a beautiful yellow Schwinn. Watching her ride up and down the block, I listen to the sturdy sound of the training wheels and study the silver streamers cutting through the air. On the bicycle she looks old, like she is somehow already becoming her own person. I feel a tinge of regret as she blurs past, realizing at some point in the near future she won't need me as much. And then what will I be?

Another hospital bill comes due a few days after that. I ride my brother's bike beneath the signs for *European Music School* and *Bilingual Waxing* and pull up to my grandfather's apartment on Cicero. I knock and my grandfather, my only living grandparent, opens the door and takes a seat in his chair, drinking vodka from a jam jar, and begins talking about Dvořák like they are contemporaries.

I get right to the point and ask him for two hundred dollars to help pay for a portion of my sister's ongoing medical bills. I tell him the collection agency will not let up. They've been calling nonstop. He nods and sips his liquor from his jar and then tells me a story about his father instead.

"As you know, my father Nicolas was born in Sarajevo in 1910. This is your great-grandfather who we're discussing, yes? After the assassination of Franz Ferdinand and World War I, the Bosnians were forced to be part of the Kingdom of Jugoslavia under King Alexander, who was then assassinated in 1934. All those years, my father Nicolas grew up with stories of his older brother, who had been arrested and who, during the war, disappeared. Killed by the Austrians, no doubt. All my father had left of his older brother was the violin, which he played every day. As a young man he scraped together a meager existence as a musician. When he was twenty-two, he was thrown out of the musicians' union for failure to pay his dues. As a Bosnian Croat in a mostly Serbian part of the city, he was often mistreated by landlords and shop owners. Even the mongrels on the street snarled as he walked by. So that in the end, the only possession he had in the world was the violin that his older brother had left him.

"Enter this young man—worse, a young musician—into the madness of Bosnia, at a time of great change. My father made a living assisting an embalmer and playing Croat dirges at wakes where the dead would be laid out on the kitchen table. In 1935, at one of these funerals, the world unexpectedly turns. At a Serbian wake, where a very tall man was lying on a too-short sideboard, he met a girl, Jozefina, who came from a farm near Livno, where her family raised horses. She is a Croat too, in the employ of the Serbian household where Nicolas now finds himself improvising melodies on themes of distress and longing. Jozefina is fair-haired, shy. Later that same week he convinces her to go for a walk by the river."

"Which river?" I ask.

"What river? It doesn't matter what river," my grandfather says. "You're missing the point," and he leans forward in his chair. "The young man brings his violin on their walk and plays some grand aria for her, they kiss, embrace in the moonlight. Weeks later, there is a rushed marriage and they have two kids in quick succession, first is my older sister, and the second is me, born in 1937, given the same name you happen to have. As the father of a small family, he has to make do at a time of great upheaval, my father plying his trade as an embalmer's apprentice, playing music when he is paid to."

I politely nod and look for an opportunity to discuss the hospital bill again.

"But here is the moment, here is the part everything's been leading to," my grandfather announces. "War breaks out when the Germans and Italians invade Bosnia in 1941, which at the time is still known as the Kingdom of Jugoslavia. Once again the bombs begin to fall, first from the Germans, and much later from the Allies."

I close my eyes and can almost hear the bombs coursing through the air, colliding with the soft earth, buildings and overturned carts tumbling in a wake of destruction. I open my eyes and all the sounds fall away. My grandfather stares at me with his sharp hazel eyes.

"After the fall of the kingdom, the Germans put a radical Croat in power and he enforces a regime of terror and eth-

nic cleansing against the Serbs, Jews, and Muslims, called the
Ustaše. Some Bosnian Croats join the ranks of the Fascists,
while other Croats take the side of the Communists and Partisans. A civil war soon divides a nation that has already been
divided time and time again. Faced with the insistence of history, my father does as his older brother once did. He attempts
to run. He sells the only possession he has of any value, the
violin, gathers his family, and takes the train to his wife's farm
far away in Livno, placing their papers in the empty violin
case. And there my family attempts to hide for the rest of the
war. It was on that farm that I grew up as a boy, surrounded
by open fields and horses, which were sold to the Ustaše and
the Germans and, after the war, the Communists. My father
never talked about fleeing Sarajevo and the decision he made,
giving up his life as a musician in exchange for collaborating
with the Fascists, choosing his family over fate."

He leans forward then, placing a hand on my knee. I feel
him studying my face. "So you see, it is the curse of history,
that similar circumstances are doomed to repeat themselves.
Each of us has the exact same decision to make when we face
it, all on our own."

When my grandfather is finished speaking, he slowly
stands and removes a book from his enormous bookshelf. "All
I can give you is this," he says and hands the book to me. It is
a collection of poems by a Bosnian poet and historian named
Izet Sarajlić.

I go outside and unlock my brother's bike, thinking of my
grandfather and his life. I put the book of poems in my back
pocket. I pass under the business signs in Bosnian and Polish
and Ukrainian. I think about what it could mean, to be cursed
by history, by the place and situation into which your family

was born, and how that history carries on, even as you escape from one country and begin your life again in the next. It becomes part of your origin, part of your culture, part of your life story, something which can't ever be changed, no matter where you end up.

I think about my own father, my sister, my brother, myself, all of us, and realize we have done exactly what our family has always done: we have tried to run from trouble, run from our fates, run from ourselves, all with the exact same consequences.

Later that week, I drag our laundry down Western Avenue on the back of my brother's bicycle. I don't go to Laundryland anymore because of Halina. I go to a different laundromat, carrying everything in two duffel bags which I balance on my shoulder. After I've sorted and folded, I come up our block and see Jazzy sitting on the front porch. She looks like she has been crying, her cheeks glistening with discreet silver lines.

"What's wrong?" I ask. "What happened?"

"Someone took my bike," she says.

"What? Who took your bike?"

"A boy."

"Wait, what boy? What did he look like?"

"That one boy. The one with the mask."

Recently there's been a boy who rides around the neighborhood with a George W. Bush Halloween mask. He lives with his mom and grandmother a few blocks away on Clifton Park. Both of his parents were police officers and his father died a few years back, I think. I think the kid is maybe fourteen or fifteen, rarely goes to school, and is known to break into other people's cars and garages. It is odd and startling, to see a kid with a George W. Bush mask riding around. Sometimes the boy wears a T-shirt that says, *Nuke 'em all,* with an American flag floating behind the words.

Only once have I seen the kid's actual face, and then it was only for a few seconds. It was in front of the no-name convenience store last summer. The boy was drinking milk from a bottle, was chugging it and had the mask pulled up. His face was pale with freckles and there seemed to be something slightly wrong with his eyes. I don't think I've ever seen anyone drink that much milk all at once. When he was done, he pulled the mask down over his face and then rode away, leaving the bottle of milk on the curb.

There are stories about the kid, that he has been to juvenile detention, or that he stabbed his father, or that he beat up one of his teachers and got expelled. I believe all of them, and so when Jazzy tells me that the boy with the mask took her bike, I am more than a little afraid.

I call Benny to see if he can come help me find Jazzy's bike. Although he often talks about how hard it was growing up in Warsaw, I have never seen him in a fight. But I think maybe he could talk his way out of it, if he had to.

Benny hops on the back pegs of my brother's dirt bike. First we go by the elementary school. Sometimes, late in the afternoon, you can see the kid with the mask sitting at the top of the slide on the playground, terrifying the younger kids who are trying to use it. But no one is at the playground now. There are three or four high school girls up in one of the trees, still in their uniforms, passing a joint around, their legs dangling from the limbs, looking exactly like nymphs.

"Hey," I call up.

"Hey yourself," a smart-mouthed girl says, and all the others laugh.

"We're looking for someone," I say.

"Nice floods," one of them says. "What is it, 1980?"

"I know you," one of the other girls says. "You're the janitor from school. Hey, everyone, this is the janitor. Where have you been, janitor? We haven't seen you in a while."

Because I feel my face getting red, I decide it is better to let Benny talk. He asks if they have seen the boy with the mask.

A girl in a jean jacket with glossy black hair nods. "I saw him about a half hour ago over by the convenience store. I think he was taking some little kid's candy."

We thank them. Benny even bows, I think, and then both of us ride over to the no-name convenience store on Kedzie. I pause when I immediately see my dad's white van parked in the lot. I check the rear bumper and find the Bosnia sticker placed there.

"It's my dad."

Benny nods. "Do you want to go talk to him?"

I think about it: I think about going inside and talking to him, telling him what we are doing, but then decide against it.

As far as I know, my father has been fired from at least two different factories: once for shoving a lineman and another time for sitting in his van and refusing to go into work. Apparently he just sat in his van blaring classical music until they told him to go home. Benny, whose mother is my mom's cousin, and who stays after Catholic church to gossip every Sunday, told him everything and he passed it on. Unfortunately, she was like CNN, very dramatic but only right about half the time. Recently she told Benny that my father had gotten a job as a security guard at one of the steel plants that had closed, and was seeing some woman in the neighborhood.

I don't know what to believe, don't want to think about it, after all that is going on with my mom—the depression, the antidepressants, the dialysis, the play she is writing, lying in bed night and day. Knowing he is okay is more of an insult than I can handle at the moment. I put my hand against the side of his van, feel it sitting there idle, imagine the shape of the silence it makes, and then move on.

There are no signs of the boy with the mask or my niece's bike. Two ten-year-old boys sit on the curb and one of them is crying.

I ask, "Have either of you seen that kid with the mask?"

The two boys look at each other in panic. One of them nods slowly, wiping his face with the back of his hand.

"He stole our candy. And then he took our Slurpees and threw them against the wall. Both of them." The kid points to the side of the convenience store where a red splash looks exactly like a murder scene.

"I'm sorry to hear that. Do you know where he hangs out? Where he goes?"

The boy itches his nose. "By that one garage," he mumbles.

"What garage?"

"The one by the park. The one with the curse words all over it."

"Got it." I reach into my pocket, find a dollar in quarters, and hand them to him. "Not enough for a Slurpee but maybe you two can split a candy bar."

The boy takes it, looking a little ashamed, and then Benny and I ride off again.

* * *

Both of us trade Jay-Z lyrics as we head down 99th Street over to Circle Park. We never find the garage but we do see a strange figure passing along the side of the park on a dirt bike. Benny points. There is the boy in the George W. Bush mask, holding a second bike by its handlebars. Somehow he is riding both. I don't know how; the physics of it all seems impossible.

At first we follow him at a distance. Finally he goes down a gravel alley and stops in front of a rickety-looking garage, which is covered in graffiti. He glances around once, then again, and reaches down and pulls the long, rectangular door open. Benny hops off the back of the bike and we slowly walk up.

Inside the garage are ten or twelve bicycles, mostly little-kid ones. The boy is in the back of the garage, locking the newest one he has stolen to a stack of another four or five bikes. I see Jazz's yellow Schwinn with its training wheels and nod to my cousin.

Benny makes himself tall. "Hey, kid," he says.

The boy turns and looks at us from under his mask, glances from Benny to me, and sees he has nowhere to run.

"That's my niece's bike," I say, pointing. "We just want it back."

The boy backs away, looking around for a weapon, I think. Benny steps forward. I have no idea what is going to happen. The boy grabs a small metal screwdriver and holds it up.

"No," I say. "We don't want to fight. Put the screwdriver down."

Benny holds out his hand calmly. "See this?" he says and points to his gold necklace. "This is a charm. From Poland. I can use it to bestow the evil eye on you. Nobody wants that. The evil eye can wreck you badly. So please put the screwdriver down."

The boy tilts his head and slowly sets the object on top of a pile of boxes.

"We just want his niece's bike," Benny says. "We don't care what you do with the other ones. We're going to take it now."

Benny carefully walks over and lifts Jazz's bike from where it is leaning. The boy in the mask inches backward. Benny holds his hands up, the way you would to a frightened animal. He gets Jazzy's yellow bike by the handlebars and walks it over to me, and in doing so, turns away from the boy.

The kid in the mask takes this opportunity to jump onto Benny's back. Clearly this boy has never attacked anyone before. The saddest, strangest physical struggle of all time ensues. My cousin and the boy spin in circles as the kid tries to get his arm around his neck. I don't know what to do. Benny is turning around and around with the kid on his back, and I am trying to pull him off. Somehow the kid ends up kicking me hard in both shins and I fall right over.

Benny eventually stumbles forward and both he and the boy go to the ground. Benny then sits on top of the boy and tells him to calm down.

The kid shouts, "I'm a minor! I'm a minor! You can't do this! You can't do this!"

Finally Benny lets the boy up and the kid grabs a beat-up silver ten-speed from inside the garage and pedals off. I sit on the ground for a while and then help my cousin to his feet. He has had the wind knocked out of him but is somehow laughing.

"Why are you laughing? That kid just kicked both our asses."

"Because," he says, still catching his breath, "we faced certain death and both of us survived."

"Oh yeah? George W. Bush is certain death?"

"Yes. We have faced the absurdities of history and now we will be invincible. Who else among us can say that?"

I roll my eyes and wonder if everyone in Poland has such an odd sense of humor.

I stand there and think how I have tried to do what any other adult would have done, what I believe my father would have done. I think about my grandfather's story. If this is history repeating, if we are all doomed, at least let us be doomed together.

I grab Jazzy's bike and Benny takes my brother's. I pull down the garage door and both of us ride off, even though my ankles are sore. Benny shouts a Tupac lyric at me and I do my best to follow along.

CHAPTER NINE

ONE DAY IN THE MIDDLE OF MAY, I GO TO PINE HILLS AND lock up Daniel's bike in the back and see they are bringing out a black object on a silver gurney and it takes me a moment to realize it is a body bag, like on a police show, with black plastic covering the recognizable shape within. An ambulance pulls up and I look over at one of the nurses from Pine Hill, Sheree, but she won't look at me. Her eyes are runny with mascara. I know it before she even says it. I go down the hall and see Mrs. Barbara Sheryl's room is a mess—her sheets torn off the bed and there are clear plastic wrappers that cover disposable medical instruments left all over the floor. I stand there and don't bother to take off my headphones. I leave everything. I go through the back door, unlock my brother's bike, and ride off without saying a word.

Things are bad enough that I just can't handle people dying around me. Besides, with my mom being constantly ill and my sister's ongoing issues, it's just too much.

A few hours later, I ride my brother's bike up to the back entrance of Pine Hill, buzz the door, and explain the situation to Sheree. She looks at me and nods, puts a latex-gloved hand on my shoulder, tells me to come collect my check at the end of the week. I do something strange then. I ask Sheree for a hug. I am so grateful that she's not going to yell at me, and even stranger still, the way she hugs, patting me on the back, is the same way my mom used to. I don't know why but it chokes me up. I have to turn away quick before the tears begin to show.

One day Isobel asks me to go to a follow-up appointment to get the results of another biopsy. I meet her at the clinic on 95th Street after she gets off work and find her sitting in the waiting room, staring at one of the high school math books I placed on her back steps months ago. For a second she doesn't see me and I watch the expression of joy on her face as she works through a problem. Sitting in the vinyl chair with her legs crossed, she has her tongue in the corner of her mouth, crossing out figures in the air. I haven't seen that gesture in years. I take a seat beside her as she starts another problem, enjoying the fierce look in her eyes with its stillness and momentary satisfaction.

A nurse calls Isobel's name and she looks over at me and nods. I nod back, mumble, "Good luck," and then she disappears. I sit in the waiting room and page through a *Highlights for Children* for forty-five minutes. Finally Isobel comes back through the waiting room, looks at me once, and then hurries outside, all without saying anything. I find out in the parking lot that she is okay, that her tests have all come back negative. For now there are no new cysts and the threat of cancer is at a minimum.

I say, "This is great news. Why are you so upset?"

"I'm not upset," she says. "It's just that I hate not being in control of my own life. She could have told me I was dying and there'd be nothing I could do about it."

I shrug, not really understanding.

"And anyway, I have to come back in another two months so they can keep monitoring me," she says. "I don't feel like I'm ever going to be done with this fucking thing." She takes a pack of cigarettes from her purse and places one nervously in her mouth.

I ask: "So are you actually going to smoke that in the parking lot of a medical facility?"

"I'm celebrating," she says. I nod. I won't begrudge her this. She offers me one and I shake my head. As she lights the cigarette, I can see how badly her hands are shaking.

"You seemed really scared in there. Are you sure you're okay?" I ask.

"No, I'm trying to tell you. I'm not okay. I am definitely not okay. I keep waiting for everything to be okay and it just doesn't seem to be fucking happening."

"You have to try and keep a positive attitude," I say.

"Aleks, I appreciate it, but you don't know shit about this, okay? Can you just be a brother for once and please, please stop talking?"

I am forced to agree at the moment and so I don't bother to ask her what being a brother means.

When things like that happen, I miss being able to play the piano, so I go by the music store on 95th Street, which is run by the irate elderly Italian couple. Usually if it's slow, they'll let me sit in the back and sound out a few compositions on one of their used pianos. Our old yellow upright still sits in the corner, with its nicked-up sides. It's a steal at seven hundred bucks, but I know there will be no time when I have enough to buy it back.

Other items, possibly stolen, appear mysteriously inside our garage over the next few weeks. Benny stays busy throughout the spring. One day, it's a rack of women's dresses, all XXL. Another day, stuffed animals that look to be from a fire, covered in mildew and dust. One night, fifty or sixty child-sized crutches. I put my brother's bike against a stack of them and don't even bother to ask.

One evening Benny calls and cheerfully says he has read, in the newspaper, that a sporting goods store has burned down and asks if I want to come help. We sneak past the boarded-up entrance and end up with ten or so singed basketballs and a bow and arrows with dull metal tips. As we're unloading everything in my mother's garage, he hands me the bow and says, "This is for Daniel. It will be good for a boy his age."

When I come back from work the next day, I find Daniel up in a tree in the front yard, aiming the bow and arrow at a large orange cat. I shout his name and he frowns, climbing up even higher so that he can't hear me. I notice then he has his book bag with him. He gets near the top of the tree and then takes out his black-and-white composition notebook and begins writing something in it, glaring down at me.

I come home from playing the piano at the music store one evening and find Isobel has invited some friends from the bank over, people I have never seen before. Some of these people are smoking and drinking in the kitchen. In the bathroom I find two people cutting lines of coke on the cover of a Rachmaninoff symphony. I have no idea where Jazzy is. I immediately begin tossing their beer cans away, purposefully making a racket and pushing past them. Isobel notices and completely ignores me.

I go to the back room and find Jazzy passed out on the couch with some cartoons playing. I turn the television off and carry her upstairs to bed. The way she looks, asleep with her mouth open, it makes me tender-hearted and angry at my older sister all at the same time. I come down and find some numbskull looking through my classical records, not treating them with the respect they deserve.

Finally I say something, finding my sister laughing in the kitchen: "Jazzy has school tomorrow."

Isobel gives me a sharp look, blowing smoke out of her nose. "I appreciate your concern. But she's going to be okay."

"But should you even be partying right now?"

She grins sharply and I see the corner of her dogtooth. "I don't need you looking over my shoulder, Aleks. I'm the one who's looked out for you your entire life."

"I don't really know how well that worked out," I say. "Anyway, I thought you just had a tumor removed."

"I think you need to mind your own business."

"I'd really love to. But then please don't ask me to look after your kid."

The false smile disappears and I know what I've said is a mistake. I look at this person, my sister, and can only see the abstract shape of some person I don't recognize anymore standing before me, daring me to continue the argument. I walk off, to go keep a watch over my records. Later I find my sister making out with some imbecilic person I have never seen before on the back couch. I go upstairs and walk past

Daniel reading comics in his underwear and put my headphones as loud as they will go until the ringing fills both
ears.

A few days later Benny comes by, knocking hard on the back
door. Something's happened to his face. He sits down in the
kitchen holding a balled-up shirt up against his eye. The shirt
is covered in dark blood.

"What happened?" I ask.

"I don't know," he says. "Someone jumped me. I was getting into my van and someone hit me from behind. I think
it was with a brick. I don't know. I came here because I didn't
want to upset my mother."

I take a towel and fill it with ice and hand it to him. "What
are you going to do?"

"I am going to have to start watching my back. Or think
about some other business opportunities."

"Benny, I'm worried about you."

He grimaces, putting the ice against his eye again. "I'm
worried about me too."

Later that same evening Jazzy's teacher from preschool calls
again.

"Hello," she says in a slightly irritated tone, "this is Ms.
Green."

"Wow. Hi. We have to stop talking like this," I joke.

"Excuse me. I don't think I . . . ?"

"Nothing, I was just . . . Sorry."

There is a long pause and then she says, "I wanted to share
some good news. I talked to our principal, Mrs. Vickers, and
she said there is a grant we can request to help provide an in-

class aide to work with Jasmine. There's some paperwork, but I'm willing to do it, if it's okay with you."

"If it's okay? It's amazing. I mean, who are you anyway? Are you one of those angels from one of those shows on the Hallmark Channel that takes the form of preschool teachers? Like Michael Landon maybe?"

"Excuse me?"

"Or like the light people see after they have cardiac arrest?"

"I don't think I know what you're talking about."

"I don't think I know either. Sorry. I just . . . I really appreciate what you're doing for Jazzy. It means a lot."

Afterward, I hang up the phone and stare at it awhile, trying to convince myself the conversation actually happened.

After everyone has gone to sleep, I flip through the book of poems my grandfather gave me. I find he has copied something out in his oblique penmanship on a blank page near the front of the book.

The etymology of slave *contains some of its history, which explains why slave and Slav appear to be related. Slavs inhabited Eastern and Central Europe and were considered the "barbarian" enemies of the Greek Empire. In the ninth century, Slavs were forced into slavery under the Holy Roman Empire and sold to Muslims in Spain. Under the rule of the Ottoman Empire, which began in 1463, many Christian children were separated from their families and were raised to be part of the Ottoman military corps. Slave appeared in English in 1290, first spelled as* sclave, *based on the Medieval Latin* sclavus.

I wonder why, of all things, my grandfather has taken the time to copy this out and why he insisted on giving me this particular book. What is he trying to tell me? What does he expect me to do with this?

A few days after that, another medical bill comes in the mail, then another, and then a third. One is for my mother's dialysis, two are for Isobel. I look at the totals of what we owe but the numbers don't seem to make any sense. I think about throwing them out, but know it won't do any good. The thing is, we really don't have anything of value left. Even our television, which is from the nineties, seems like more trouble than it's worth. I think and think, and for some reason, I remember all those unused computers sitting in the back of the high school auditorium where I used to work. I slowly put a plan together and then tell myself how ridiculous it is.

Later, when I go into my mother's bedroom, I find her smoking a menthol. Literally, she is sitting up in bed, smoking, waving her hand back and forth to try to disperse the smoke.

"Dang, Mom," I say.

Daniel is sitting beside her and the two of them are watching some violent suspense thriller. Blood fills the screen. I turn to my brother and ask him what the heck and he tells me my mom asked for the cigarette nicely.

"It doesn't matter if she asked for it nicely. You know she's not supposed to be smoking. Where did you even get these from?"

"Benny," Daniel says. "He's been selling them to middle schoolers. He's got a couple of cartons hidden in the garage."

"Jesus," I groan and take the cigarette from my mother's

hand. Daniel shrugs. I go back down to the kitchen and see somehow a fourth medical bill has shown up. I pretend to draw up some numbers, monthly expenses, bills, but none of it adds up to anything. I end up sketching pictures of famous dead composers all over the bills instead. Bach is frowning. Beethoven cries openly.

I think and I think and I think. I listen to an opera by Brahms and see the answer sitting right there in front of me, in its singular and irrefutable symmetry.

On a Saturday evening, I take my old keys from work and go into the school. In the back of the auditorium are the stacks of outdated computers, some with keyboards dangling, others piled high on top of dust-covered monitors. I call Benny and he helps me carry one of them down the street, both of us taking turns, as if this is a thing people do, walk around their neighborhood in the dark with a computer. We lug it through the back door and into the back room of my mother's house.

On the side of the computer monitor, in stenciled blue paint, are the words, *PROPERTY OF ST. JOSAPHAT SCHOOL*. Our criminal actions ring out like a dazzling harp.

Isobel stands with her arms folded, immediately recognizing something is not right. "Where did you get that?" she asks.

"Nowhere. They were just going to throw it out," I lie.

She looks at the large stenciled letters on the side of the computer and then stares at me hard. I have to look down. "You're so stupid. They're going to know it was you. I don't want to be here when the police show up to cart you off."

I frown, still holding the computer against my chest, my arms growing weak, knowing she is absolutely right.

Out of inertia, the computer stays exactly where it is for

the next couple days. I don't even try to turn it on to see if it works. I can't find anyone to buy it, and neither can Benny. It just sits in the back room like an enormous weight, like an invisible anvil hanging over all our heads.

When, a few days later, my sister asks when the computer will be gone, I don't know what to tell her. When she says, "What do you think Jazzy thinks? She's not stupid. She knows you stole it," all I can do is look away.

A few nights later Isobel's strange new boyfriend comes by for dinner. He has the appearance of a Sunday school teacher or a podiatrist or maybe a dentist. His hair is slicked back and he has a long nose. Worse, we find out he was the assistant principal at Isobel's high school a few years ago and that they saw each other at the bank and so on and so on. He's like ten or fifteen years older. Kevin, her new boyfriend, asks us to say grace before dinner. You should hear all the chuckles. Isobel gives us a fearsome look. Daniel raises his eyebrows in alarm and the rest of us mouth along. All Kevin talks about is exotic pets—he has a chinchilla—and sweaters and church. Seriously, he talks about his own sweater. Throughout dinner he never, for a minute, stops touching my sister. Hand on knee. Hand on shoulder. Brushing her hair out of her eyes like she is a child.

She keeps laughing at his lame jokes. *Ha ha ha. Tee-hee-hee.* I look at her and feel an unending sadness and wonder, what is happening here?

Later, after he goes home, I ask Isobel, "Are you for real? What are you doing with this guy?"

Jazzy is asleep on the couch, dangling precariously near the edge. Isobel shrugs. "I like that he thinks I'm smarter than him." She says this and then exhales cigarette smoke through her nose, blowing it out the back room window.

"Okay, but let me ask you one question: Is he married? Is he divorced? Does he have kids? Kids older than you?"

She rolls her eyes and ignores me.

"I don't get it. I mean, what are you doing hiding out, working at that ridiculous place, dating people like Kevin anyway? You should be working for NASA or something. You should be running MIT. Not hanging out with some paunchy middle-aged assistant principal."

She blows twin barrels of smoke from her nose, still ignoring me.

"Anyway, you know you're not supposed to be smoking in here. Mom's sick."

"Mom's been sick for a long time. Who died and left you in charge?"

Both of us laugh because of how funny it isn't. Then she turns her sharp smile on me. "And I don't know why you think you have the right to tell me how to live. You're a child, Aleks. You've never even left home. I don't think you'd make it a minute on your own."

"I don't really think you're in a position to offer criticism. Considering, you know, how things have turned out for you."

"You can be such an asshole."

"Agreed."

She glares at me. "You think you're so smart. I'll tell you one thing: you need to get rid of that computer or I'm telling Mom and she's going to toss you right out."

"See if I care."

I go to blow off some steam after that, smoke a cigarette I have stolen from my mother on the hill overlooking the reclamation plant. I take in the sound of the great circulating basins and pumps, imagining the shape of the noise they make. I see the pink steam rise from the pools of untreated filth. If you squint at the sun behind it, it almost approaches beautiful.

All the other people who live in my house are gathered around my mother's bed when I come back home. It looks like someone has called a family meeting or maybe someone important has died. I think for a moment: *Is it me? Am I a ghost?* But then Isobel looks at my mother and back at me before giving me the news that I'm being kicked out for bringing a stolen computer into the house.

Before the words are even out of my sister's mouth, my ears ring from anger.

"Okay, are you serious?" I ask. "Are you even for real?"

I am standing in the doorway, stunned. Daniel and Jazzy sit beside my mother's bed, staring up at me as if I have betrayed everyone. And for once my mother's eyes are clear. She looks at me as if to say—*You know the rules.*

"Mom," I say, "Benny has had every kind of stolen object in our garage for the last four months! How is this even fair?"

She looks right through me and says, "I am not Benny's mother. I didn't raise you, I didn't read to you, I didn't play music for you to become a thief."

I look at each of them for a moment, especially Isobel, who refuses to make eye contact, then nod and go grab my backpack and throw some things inside.

On the front steps, I try to come up with a plan. But I can't think of anything.

Daniel comes out. "You shouldn't have done that, Aleks. You really shouldn't have stolen that computer."

"Daniel," I say, "I love you. But mind your own fucking business."

I get my brother's bike out of the garage, sling my backpack over my shoulder, and begin to ride away even though I have no idea where I'm going.

Eventually I end up at Benny's house. I sleep in his basement and listen to his parents fighting in Polish nonstop, stomping around on the floorboards above me, even though I can't hear what they are saying. I need a full-time job more than ever so that I can afford an apartment of my own. I go up and down Western dropping off applications everywhere I can. I do the one thing then, the one thing I never thought I would do: I go by the remaining factories on Pulaski, then on Cicero, then onto Central. I go by Modified Plastics, I go by Thermal United, I go by B and B Tool, and I feel more and more ashamed as I fill out each application because I always thought I was too clever, too smart for factory work. There is nowhere on the application for your high school GPA, for the books you read, the poems you memorized, your dreams of classical music fame. You aren't even a number to them, just a body, a back, a pair of hands.

Then nothing happens. Once you find yourself lowered to the place you did not think you could go, you find they don't even want you—that you're not good enough for the kind of work you beheld for so long. Then you have to think about that, about what it might mean.

You sit on the hill by the reclamation plant and wonder how. How can any of this go on? How will it all continue? How will it end for everybody?

Someone is blowing off fireworks on the other side of the

plant. Or it could be a domestic dispute. Or maybe they are gunshots. With your hearing, it is hard to tell. Lights flash upon the surface of the sky and you realize you are so tired you are seeing tracers, images from the day reflected upon the inside of your eyelids. No, it's the fluorescent lights of the streetlamps. You slip on your headphones and put off thinking about tomorrow.

On the hill, you feel like you are falling into a wide, black hole.

CHAPTER TEN

I DON'T SPEAK TO ISOBEL FOR SEVERAL WEEKS, EVEN WHEN I GO pick up my niece for preschool on Wednesdays and Fridays. One day I write a Post-it note to my sister because I don't feel like talking to her:

I don't know if you know this but Mozart composed some of his best work when he had syphilis. So being kicked out of the house is nothing. Also, just so you know, I don't have syphilis. I am just comparing two similar situations.

I leave the note on the passenger-side window of her car when I go to get Jazzy. I look for a response when I bring her home but there isn't any.

Over the last week of May, I make my way once again down Central Avenue on my brother's bicycle and drop off as many applications as I can, stopping at every factory, every plant, handing in résumé after résumé, until my fingers are blue with ink from having to write my address so many times. I come to hate my ridiculous name all over again and start to abbreviate it, until it is only a series of nonsensical initials.

I go on to the next factory, the next plant, Verdi screaming from my headphones, and ask to see the manager or assistant manager, then go on to the next, going down as far as 55th Street. On the southside, the directions are sometimes reversed. Going *down* Central really means going north, toward downtown. But going down can also mean going south, which is why so many people in the neighborhood seem lost. It's a place that is its own universe, with its own physics in which clocks and watches and compasses don't always seem to work.

But now the southside isn't anything. After the collapse of the manufacturing and steel industries in the 1980s, all the jobs went away, and now the plastics and adhesive factories are the only ones holding on. Or you can be a cop busting someone's head, or a nurse, or a public school teacher, or you can work at a check-cashing place, or at Taco Bell, or, if you're lucky, you can do oil changes for six dollars an hour.

I pause on Central near the bridge by the refinery and enjoy the silent plume of violet smoke erupting from its towers. Then I get an application. One of my friend's parents worked there and died of cancer at the age of forty-two. Another friend's sister got leukemia. I see, by the loading docks, workers wearing plastic suits, lifting drums of petroleum by-product onto trucks. I decide life is too short and drop the application into a trash can and then pedal back toward my cousin Benny's.

I go with Chris KRS to a hip-hop show at the Congress Theater on the northside to try to forget some of my problems.

We get up right in the front row and let the thrum of the bass knock us both senseless.

Here's what it's like going to a hip-hop show with hearing loss: amazing, because the low end of the music booms through your chest and the movement of the crowd and the people singing is so loud I am able to become completely lost inside the sound.

Afterward, Chris shows me her dorm and we meet her roommates who giggle when we shake hands and then she asks if she can draw me.

"Draw me? What are you talking about?"

"It's for this series of sketches I'm working on," she tells me, and so I take a seat in one of her chairs and she positions my head a certain way and I sit like that for an hour, and when she is done, I see she has only focused on my left ear, the bad one, and I don't know how I feel about any of that.

I go to Laundryland the next day because the laundromat near Benny's place is closed and also I am hoping to catch a glimpse of Halina. I am unloading my laundry from a washer when I look up and see her cleaning the circle-shaped windows on a row of dryers. She looks over at me and smiles without smiling, such an Eastern European expression. And then things begin to happen without us even talking.

Once she is done folding the pile of laundry on the metal table before her, I follow her outside around the corner to a blue stucco apartment building that looks like a motel, with outdoor stairwells that connect the different apartments. I follow her up to the second floor, lock up my brother's bike, enter the apartment, walk past a sleeping grandmother in a blue nightgown, and enter a bedroom in the back. It is small and white and there is a collection of Polish nesting dolls on a dresser. Several pairs of ballet shoes. A poster of a Polish pop star with silver makeup hanging above the bed. We lie back and it feels like falling into an ocean, collapsing into a hole at the bottom of the world, a place of complete darkness. Whatever we do doesn't count because it's only our bodies that are present and not our minds or our hearts.

When it is over, and it is over before long, Halina sits in a chair, in her T-shirt, brushing out her hair. She hums a faraway-sounding song to herself and I can't make out the exact words but it is like I'm not even there. She ties her hair in a knot and then puts on a gold leotard. Without looking up, she plays some electronic music on a boom box, something that still sounds vaguely classical, and begins doing calisthenics or gymnastics or a kind of dance, I'm not so sure. In a moment, she is flying around the room, doing tumbles and kicks, and it is like something out of the Olympics. Her face is completely expressionless, and when she is done, she is posed on the ground, as if she is before some invisible, enrapt audience. I can see how hard she is breathing from the way her back moves and heaves. I clap and she seems to ignore me.

In some ways, seeing her do that is more interesting than the part where we were fooling around. In that moment, I wonder why you have to go through all the trouble just to get to that place, to some act of wonder, and I worry if maybe there just isn't some other, easier way.

At the very end of May I get a call from a Chinese restaurant asking if I'm interested in delivering food. I go everywhere on my brother's bike within a five-mile radius, but when I knock on the door, I know people are disappointed to see me, a Polish Bosnian person. I think they are expecting someone Asian and there is this strange moment of disbelief where they look at me and, even though I am holding their food, it's like they don't believe it's really happening. I end up ruining the mystery maybe. I think this is reflected in their neglectful tips. I didn't imagine ever having the capacity to disappoint strangers the way I do.

I think about calling Isobel but I don't. I go by and pick up Jazzy from school once or twice a week, but when I drop her off, I don't go inside, don't ring the bell, don't talk to anybody, just give Jazzy a hug, show her the sign for *See you soon*, and then ride off.

Sometimes, when I drop my niece at home, I can hear Isobel playing the same piece by Liszt, over and over. Sometimes Jazzy and I stand on the front steps and listen together. At first my sister sounds unsure and then, slowly, she finds her footing, and leaps from one intricate phrase to the next. Usually, somewhere in the middle, she stops, frustrated, and I can hear a screech, which immediately changes the color, the mood, the outlook of the entire neighborhood. Birds whirl from the telephone line overhead and go hide in far-off trees. A baby being pushed in a stroller on the other side of the street begins to cry.

Today I look down at Jazzy and sign, *Good luck.*

At the beginning of June, I get a call at Benny's house. I find out that Daniel has also been kicked out. Apparently Isobel caught him huffing model glue and gave him a warning, and then a few days later she found him doing it again. Also, apparently, he passed out in his underwear and got model glue all over the carpeted floor.

"Can I come stay with you for a while?" he asks over the phone. I know there is no way we can both crash in Benny's basement, so I go looking for a place, a studio or one-bedroom, somewhere cheap. I have maybe a hundred and fifty dollars to my name, which is not enough to rent an apartment with.

I find a small one-bedroom not too far from Midway Airport, where Daniel can have some space of his own and where I can sleep on the couch. It is three hundred and fifty dollars a month. I get away with only putting a hundred dollars down when the landlord sees the St. Elijah medal, the patron saint of Bosnia, on my necklace, given to me by my father before he moved out. The apartment building is called Hidden Terrace. I can lie on the couch with my feet pointed toward the window and watch the streetlights come on, can hear the evening traffic moving two stories below, can see the people shambling at all hours from their part-time, minimum-wage employment, well past midnight. Nobody is at Hidden Terrace because they want to be. It is like an emergency room. It is exactly like limbo.

One morning I hear Daniel leave for school. I get up and go into his tiny bedroom and find some comic books, some dirty gym socks left on the floor. There, hidden partly under the bed, is his black-and-white composition, *The Book of 20th Century Tragedies*. I open it and find it is now completely full: an encyclopedic history of awful events that spans decades, pages cut from history books, comics, *National Geographic* magazines, full of assassinations, bombings, the *Hindenburg* disaster, Chernobyl. There is no end to the horror. Over a century, it seems to be the one constant. But he has changed most of these events, rendering them odd, surreal, completely lacking in suffering.

Somewhere near the back of the book, I find a picture of my brother and sister and my mom and dad and me from about ten years before at one of our cousin's weddings. My father's head has been cut out, though his shoulders and the rest of his body remains. In pink marker, Daniel has written:

> . . . *After this photograph was taken, the family went on a long vacation to EuroDisney*

. . . which is something that did not actually occur. I sit down and look at the picture and sigh. I am afraid his inability to accept reality, his desire for escape, is only going to lead to more heartbreak, but who am I to say?

I leave another Post-it note on Isobel's car window a few days after that:

> *You think you're so smart. But so are a lot of other people. So what good has being smart gotten you? All kinds of people make mistakes.*

And then I run out of room.

Later I ride down Cicero to check up on my grandfather though he doesn't answer. I knock and knock. I find his key under the mat and go in slowly, afraid I might scare him. His two feet are sticking out from under his bed, and it appears like he's hiding.

I ask, "What are you doing?" and he says he is looking for something.

"What are you looking for?"

"History," he says, and I sit on the bed and shake my head.

Eventually he climbs out and goes to sit in a chair in the front room. After that he puts on a record and refuses to speak.

Over the next few days, I go by Halina's apartment a couple more times. I don't know if her grandmother is blind or deaf but she doesn't seem to see me. I think she might exist on some kind of provisional astral plane, somewhere between the present and the past, United States and Poland, the living and the dead. She just sits there wearing enormous plastic sunglasses over her bifocals, staring at game shows on the television screen that have gone off the air decades before.

I go and take a seat on Halina's bed and do not ask any questions. But I can't stop thinking about her grandmother who seems to be able to look right through me. She knows that I know that what we are doing is completely wrong.

In the second week of June, I get a call from Modified Plastics asking me to come in for an interview. The interview is five questions read by a large woman with white hair who looks like she has more important things to do.

One question is about previous experience, another is about drug use.

"I don't do drugs," I say. "I can't afford any."

The woman—someone's grandmother I'm sure—looks over the top of her glasses at me.

"Sorry. I don't do drugs," I say. "I was just joking."

After the exam, a man named Rick—who looks immortal, ageless in a blue uniform, he could be thirty or fifty—shows me around the plant, asks if I have any questions. There are thirty or forty assembly lines, all of which produce cheap plastic toys, the kind you get inside a plastic bubble in a dispenser at a supermarket or bowling alley, the kind that usually cost a quarter. The factory pays a dollar and half more than the retirement home did, offers limited health insurance, and can even give me forty hours a week. "Your uniform—blue hat, three blue shirts—will be deducted from your first paycheck," Rick says.

At the end of the tour, Rick shakes my hand and goes to yell at some workers who are awkwardly loading boxes onto a pallet. I go outside and unlock my brother's bike. The sunlight through the trees seems like something my English teacher back in high school would call *sublime*. I ride back toward the apartment and I realize there are no thoroughfares, no boulevards named after any Bosnians or Croatians in Chicago. Where is the statue of some ancestor, someone like us astride a bronze horse? I do not let it get me down.

I start work the next morning at seven a.m. on a line that produces small, pink plastic elephants. I steal one for Jazzy, cupping it in my hand. The foreman—an overweight woman with powerful-looking forearms—looks at me and rolls her eyes. Even with my hearing loss, the fearsome hum of the presses is hard to take.

On the news that evening, someone's talking about derivatives and falling housing prices. I listen as I help Halina fold clothes at Laundryland. Some people in Florida are getting kicked out of their own homes. *Underwater*, they call it, like it's not a manmade disaster manufactured off the greed of some bankers living on the East Coast, and I wonder if something like that could happen here in Chicago.

Later we go over to her apartment and I follow Halina into her room and we fool around again but it isn't anything, it's just a couple bodies fumbling against one another in order to avoid sadness, nothing more than waves crashing on a beach. Both of us would probably rather be alone but it looks like we're just not strong enough.

When we're done, I take out a CD of a Rimsky-Korsakov piano concerto from my Walkman and play it for her. I tell her it's one of my favorite pieces of music of all time. I lie beside her and, after a few minutes, she looks over and shrugs and says, "It's different," and I say, "Different how?" and she says, "It's classical," and I frown.

After a few more minutes, she says, "Kacper is coming home next week," and I look over at her again.

"And then?" I ask, but no one wants to answer.

I come home from work and find my cousin Benny sitting on the concrete steps leading up to our apartment. He is moaning. His face is whiter than I've ever seen it before, which is saying something.

"Benny? What happened?"

He shakes his head and points to his thigh. There is a gash in his stonewashed jeans above his knee, which is covered entirely in blood.

"Jesus, Benny, what happened?" I ask.

"I think I maybe need to go to the hospital."

I try to help him stand. "Where are your keys?"

"They took my keys," he says.

Together, step by step, we make our way down the stairs.

"I don't know how to do this," I say, trying to get him on the back of my bike.

"You pedal and I'll sit on the seat."

What is this madness? You should see the two of us trying

to balance, his leg stuck out at forty-five degrees, me standing on the pedals. It takes forever to get to the hospital on 87th. By then, the whole right leg of his pants is soaked in blood.

As we sit in the waiting room, Benny turns to me and winces, trying to smile. "I think I was too enterprising."

"Jesus, Benny, aren't you worried they're going to come after you again?"

"No. I gave them my solemn oath. I told them I was going to pursue other career opportunities. They said they thought this would be a wise decision. It ended with a very polite exchange. Even the one who stabbed me apologized and said it was too bad it had to go this way. They were Russians so they understood."

I shake my head.

On the waiting room television, some factory in Michigan has gone out of business, and another one in Ohio has closed its gates. Factory workers with angry faces stand outside long wire fences demanding their pay. Soon a nurse calls Benny's name.

On Friday I take my first check, cash it at a check-cashing place, and buy a used silver ten-speed. It's the end of June, but the weather still has not changed. Everything is cool and wet. I end up pulling my hood up as I ride, just like I did all winter.

I go by the laundromat to show off my bicycle. I see Halina inside folding other people's laundry. I watch her for a while before she finally looks up. I don't know how to describe the way she smiles other than feeling it is a rare, true thing. She comes to the door of the laundromat and watches me do figure eights.

I ask her, "Can you get away for an hour? An hour is all this will take."

She nods and turns the sign on the door to *CLOSED* and locks the lock and I put her on the front of my handlebars and the two of us roll forward unsteadily. At first we are a disaster. Eventually, though, we find a kind of almost-musical balance.

Over the next hour, I show her all the things, all the places I love about the southside. I ride her over to Kedzie where a King Kong statue stands towering above a muffler shop. I go by Rainbow Cone where they give you seven layers of ice cream on a single cone which both of us quietly share. When we kiss it is cold orange.

Later I take her by an old movie theater that closed down a few years ago after the manager was shot during a robbery. I explain that's where I used to go to the movies when I was a kid, where I first saw *Bambi* and *Star Wars* seven times, where I began to imagine the world outside my neighborhood. She only stares at me and blinks. Over on the hill by the reclamation plant, I point out the pink-and-purple fumes and tell her how, at the moment, I don't have anything else in my life except my little brother and my niece. I tell her how I think we can maybe make this work if she is willing to try. She can break it off with her boyfriend or husband or whatever. She can start over if she wants. I tell her all this in my own words, but even as they come out, I realize how ridiculous it all sounds, can already see what the answer is. I look at this girl and know that she doesn't have the capacity to believe in anything so preposterous. It's what you get being the son or daughter of someone from some other place. I see the entire neighborhood through her eyes and recognize there is no room for beauty, no room for poetry or music, anything imaginary.

I drop her off in front of the laundromat later that night, see her climb off the handlebars too embarrassed to look me in the eye, see her turn to go back inside. Before she's gone I call out her name. I find the pink plastic elephant in my pocket and put it in her hand, knowing in that moment it will mean nothing but doing so anyway. I ride off as quickly as I can and don't glance back.

When I am a block away, I turn and see she's still standing there with a look of puzzlement on her face. It's a marvel, with the parking lot lights shining down upon her face, the best thing I've seen in ages, and in that moment I know we won't be seeing each other again.

The phone is ringing in the apartment when I get home. I answer, certain it will be more bad news. It is the assistant principal from Daniel's school. He tells me there was an incident. Daniel tried to bring the bow and arrows to school. When the assistant principal said he was not allowed to bring them inside, Daniel ran off and never came back.

"Daniel?" I call, but he doesn't answer. I open the bedroom door. There is a pizza box, library books, an old Atari, and the bow and arrows in question, all sitting on the bed, but no sign of my brother.

I sit there for a while, in the middle of all the mess, and wonder where he is. I hold one of his dirty gray socks like it is a relic, a small, holy memento.

I write another note and leave it on the driver's-side window of Isobel's car when I go to pick up Jazzy for school the next day: *I guess I was just trying to help. I know I messed up. I'm sorry.*

One day that week I am coming out of the convenience store

a block from our apartment when someone in a white Ford Escort yells something at me. Along the bumper is a sticker of the Polish flag with its white two-dimensional eagle. There is rust along the car's rear wheel well and from the look of it, the vehicle's been in more than a couple accidents.

There are a few people in the car—all young men, all with shortly cropped hair, some with beards. I pause. The passenger-side window is rolled down. The guy in the front passenger seat looks at me and points.

You, he seems to be saying. I see the shape of the word even though I don't hear it.

I stare at him and understand who he is. But then nothing happens. We just look at each other and I see how ashamed, how sad he appears. He is younger than I thought, with dark hair, looks like a boy really. *Kacper.* I think of his name and then immediately push the thought away. I watch him continue to point at me, holding out his finger, and then he nods to the driver, and the sad car and sad person both pull away. I realize it's less of a warning than an agreement, a plea. I go over to my new used bicycle and see both tires have been slashed.

I come home and Daniel is sitting on the couch, eating cereal, playing video games with his headphones on. He sees me and nods his head. I look at the answering machine blinking, think it might be Benny, and press play.

It's Isobel and it's bad. Apparently she had a follow-up with her oncologist but she got some other doctor instead and this person ran some other kind of blood tests and didn't like what she found and so Isobel had to get another round of biopsies and the results were not good. It turns out that the cyst that was removed may have been cancerous and may have spread. Her doctor believes she might have ovarian epithelial cancer and so she has now been given a stage two diagnosis because she has an elevated white blood cell count and there is some evidence of malignancy in one of her lymph nodes. This new oncologist says Isobel is going to need either radiation or chemo or both.

I stand there and listen to my sister's recorded voice twice and realize how even though we are not talking, somehow we are always talking, how you are never able to completely sever yourself from the people you love. I turn to my brother and say, "You and I need to have a word. Stay here until I get home," and then go back out into the dark.

I ride over to my mother's on my new used bike. Before I am even off the bicycle seat, I can see Isobel sitting on the back steps, smoking. I can't tell if she is crying. I go over and give her a hug. Tears are stuck to the ends of her long eyelashes. We don't need to speak, or to say anything really, so we just stand there, a couple of worn-out young people. We see how long we can go without talking and then finally she says, "I used to be so much taller than you," and both of us laugh and then she says, "I could really use your help," and we become silent because neither us has any idea what happens next.

MOVEMENT THREE

COMPLETE ÉTUDES

Allegro molto.

CHAPTER ELEVEN

THE BOOK OF 20TH CENTURY TRAGEDIES CONTINUES TO EXPAND prolifically throughout the month of July. Without school, my brother has nothing else to do and so it spills into a second notebook and, later, takes up two walls of his bedroom. At some point he starts putting up drawings and photographs that he has whited out with Liquid Paper.

"What's all this?" I ask after coming back from work one afternoon.

"I'm blanking out everything bad that ever happened," he says. He tapes up a photograph of a World War II bomber in place, except the bombs falling over its target are now mysteriously missing.

"Why are you doing this?"

"Because. Because I'm tired of our family being from places that are only famous for getting conquered. So I'm changing it. I'm coming up with an imaginary history for everything."

After he goes to bed, I flip through one of his notebooks and see it's filled with famous images—the assassination of JFK, the San Francisco earthquake—all with strange shapes and holes cut out, a collection of assorted historical absences, interruptions, and alterations.

I wonder: *Who is this person and how will he ever survive in a world where bad things are constantly happening?*

I don't tell him anything about Isobel's new diagnosis. I don't tell him about her latest test results, about her upcoming chemotherapy, about the fact that her chances for a full recovery have now gone down drastically.

I go by my mother's neighborhood a few days later and pause before Circle Park, finding an endlessly interesting dissonance ringing out from over the fence—whistles howling, tympani pounding, strings screeching exactly like something out of Mussorgsky. Kids fight and play and laugh and scream, jumping from the top of the slide. I can't hear exactly what any of them are saying but it is an overwhelmingly joyful noise.

I find Isobel waiting on the front steps. I ask if she is ready and she nods, then tosses me her car keys. We drive the hatchback over to the hospital on 95th Street in a long, anticlimactic silence, the opposite of any kind of happy sound.

As expected, Isobel makes fun of the music playing in the waiting room. After her recent biopsy, she was told she would have to complete four cycles of chemotherapy to be sure all the malignant cells were destroyed, using a combination of drugs none of us know how to pronounce. It is amazing to see how chemotherapy changes her personality. She becomes quiet, vulnerable in a way she's never had to be before. She lets me ask how she is doing without giving me the evil eye. But when a song by Celine Dion comes on, she shakes her head and groans out loud.

When it's over, she looks completely exhausted. They offer

her a wheelchair and she instinctively refuses. I admire her even more in that moment. Later, as we are crossing the parking lot, she puts a hand out on somebody's car and says, "I'm not feeling so hot."

"Okay. Let's get inside the car and take a rest."

"Aleks, I'm really not feeling so good," she repeats.

I hold her under her arm and then dump her in the passenger seat. I even help her with the buckle. I think I should try to get her back to my mother's as soon as possible.

As we're pulling out of the parking lot, she says, "Don't you think it's weird for a person to be getting chemo at the exact same hospital where they were born?"

I tell her I haven't thought about it, but it is a strange feeling. It's a little too coincidental or poetic, like none of us have actually gone anywhere, like all of our lives will be defined by this one hospital, by this one neighborhood, by this one unimportant place.

Everything takes on a ridiculous air of nostalgia because I am driving my sister home from chemotherapy for the first time. Here is the restaurant where we go to get pancakes. The ice cream shop. The library where my mother used to work, etc., etc. I don't say any of these things out loud because I know Isobel will be furious with me.

After we pass Kedzie, she says: "I'm not feeling so good. I'm actually feeling pretty nauseous."

I try to roll the windows down but both of them are stuck. I tell her, "No, no way, you're doing great."

Moments later she begins to vomit. I quickly pull over but it is too late. Vomit is everywhere. I run around and open the passenger-side door and try to get her out but it is all over the front of her shirt, her seat, her shoes, the rest of the car. I lift her out and sit her on the curb and try to clean up using a box of tissues.

"I think I'm going to be sick again," she says. She apologizes and then vomits once more between her legs, then again all over a fire hydrant for good measure. I have a suspicion this fire hydrant has probably seen worse. I don't think I've ever heard her apologize so much and all we can do is laugh once we get back in the hatchback.

Later I drive the foul-smelling car to the car wash and try to clean it out but the odor is not going anywhere. People stare at me and seem to back away. "Rough night," I say. I go inside and buy three tree-shaped air fresheners.

The man behind the counter gives me a funny look.

"I like blue spruce," I say and hang two from the rear-view mirror and one around my neck, but as I am driving back home I realize the manufactured odor is almost as bad as what it was meant to hide. I think maybe this is a metaphor for something—pain, shame, regret, mortality, Eastern European history, American expansionism—but I am not so sure. If only my ineffective humanities professor from community college was there to explain it to me.

I go to work the next morning and try not to think of my family. You were probably forced to read *The Jungle* in high school or maybe *Working* by Studs Terkel. You maybe thought those places didn't exist anymore but they do. You've got eighteen-, nineteen-year-olds without high school diplomas working the line in manufacturing, in shipping, you've got workman's comp and rough, mangled hands. You've got young people ending up in the same jobs their parents were forced to take a generation, two generations before, who thought their children, their grandchildren would end up somewhere else. Because college does not seem realistic for most people I know. Some people can't even afford the application fee, let alone room and board. So the same kids from the same kinds of families end up going to college and the entire system starts over and over. As I work pulling malformed animals from the line, I end up reciting all the lyrics to Ghostface's *Ironman*. I wear the hairnet, keep the earplugs in, go to a different spot every two hours.

The line never stops, not for human error, not for an injury, not even when something catches on fire. Here, no one can hear properly because of the nonstop presses and also everyone wears earplugs, and when I realize this my heart swells. Everyone around me is also deaf, at least for as long as they are working. It makes me want to sing so I do. Sometimes it's a few of the hip-hop lyrics I have memorized, sometimes it's just the melodies to Bach and Beethoven. Sometimes I just watch the colorful plastic animals moving before me like they are floating, part of some musical parade. Then something somewhere starts on fire, a person in a hazmat uniform appears, sprays the area down with nontoxic, flame-retardant foam, and then the whole process starts up again, like a messed-up merry-go-round, an off-kilter amusement park.

At the end of the line, at the end of the day, what remains is hundreds of thousands of small plastic animals, a jungle, an ark, the sum total of all our hearts and labor, indistinguishable from one another, each as flawed and as featureless as the next. I make toys that aren't really toys, only simulacra of real gifts that kids would actually enjoy. I make substitutes, placeholders for parents who can't afford something better, the false, almost shapeless figures—antelope? tiger? elephant?—as forgettable, as disposable as the plastic bubble containers they come in. By the time it's over, by the time I can step out into the sunlight again and take the orange earplugs out, all I can see are the lurid neon colors going past me when I close my eyes.

I try to make up AMAZING COMPOSITION #319 as I unlock my bike at the end of the day, but it all turns out wrong. I imagine a choir, like the one in the fourth movement of Beethoven's ninth, singing lyrics that become more and more ridiculous as more plastic animals appear:

The presses
The plants
The places where things get made
The places where people all turn to smoke
Those are the places that ending up manufacturing other
people like me . . .

I am twenty and I realize I have been doing this for less than three months and am already bored to death. The long-term implications are not so good.

At the beginning of August, I am riding home from the plastics factory when I spot Benny's van parked out in front of the liquor store on 87th. I see Benny behind the driver's seat arguing with someone, some other young man with hair that has been cut short. This other young man also looks Slavic or Russian; you can almost see the ingrained sense of disappointment on his face. I wonder if this is one of the men that have been threatening him. I slow up on my bike and wait and watch, and get ready to jump in if I have to. The sounds of night birds and humming insects add a menacing quality to this already tense moment.

But all they do is talk. A few moments later the other young man climbs out and slams the door closed. I watch Benny frown and punch the steering wheel with one hand, then the other. I feel a flash of panic, wonder if his life is in danger. I think about riding over and asking him if he is okay, then realize whatever it is, he probably would not want me to know what I've just witnessed. So I back up and pedal off, the humidity weighing heavily upon the air.

In the middle of August, Jazzy starts kindergarten at the underfunded Catholic school on 103rd, where apparently even the nuns have lost faith and are allowed to wear gym shoes and no one seems to know how to do the sign of the cross properly. My sister and I have no idea what is going to happen—will Jazzy have an amazing teacher like Ms. Green last year or will it just be a nightmare? I ride her on the silver ten-speed's handlebars, which she does not seem to enjoy so much since getting her own bike. I help her down in front of the unkempt school and adjust the backpack on her shoulders. I can tell she doesn't want any help from me, wants to pretend we do not know each other, that I am only her mode of transportation and nothing else.

I sign to her, asking if she is all set, and she shows me a sign of her own invention—some kind of hand gesture like an object taking flight. Then she joins the line of other kids and makes her way inside. I wait with my silver bicycle by the curb for her to turn around to see if I am still watching, but for the first time since she's been going to day care or school, she doesn't look back. *Jesus*, I think. *This kid is seriously independent.* The glass doors close and she vanishes inside and it's like I have been punched in the gut. I nod to myself and ride away, feeling a collision of heartache and pride.

I carry that feeling around all day as the small plastic animals come my way, each slightly flawed, an imprecise figment of what it's supposed to be. One of the lines begins producing green giraffes that afternoon so I grab one for my niece. No one seems to notice.

A few days after that Daniel starts eighth grade. For the first week, he gets up on time, packs himself a lunch, and rides his bike to school, all on his own. He comes home mostly happy, does his schoolwork at the kitchen table while the television plays from the other room, and tells me he is going to try out for the Academic Bowl team this year.

"What's that?"

"Each semester they have these academic competitions. Like a tournament, with teams from all these different parts of the city. But I have to make it on the team first. Tryouts are in November."

"I'm proud of you showing so much initiative," I say, rolling out the dough for potato pierogies. It is the only Polish food I know how to make. I glance over at him doing his homework and feel, for the first time, the two of us are doing okay on our own.

Sometime after midnight, Daniel comes and sits at the end of the couch and says, "My condition is worsening."

I sit up and rub my eyes and ask, "What condition? What are you talking about?"

"I don't think I want to be who I am anymore. I'd like to start over. As someone other than myself. As a complete blank."

I say, "Daniel, no one gets to start over. Go back to bed."

He sits there for a moment longer and eventually wanders

back to his room. I lie awake for a while, feeling worried, listening to the sounds coming from Hidden Terrace, my ears playing tricks on me the entire time.

I go by my mother's house later that week to see how Isobel is feeling after her second round of chemo. I find a number of strange people standing on the front steps. I push my bicycle into the garage and excuse myself as I walk past.

My amazingly irresponsible sister is having another party. I march into the kitchen and see her sitting on someone's lap. She is smoking and using a beer can as an ashtray. I do not bother to be polite or diplomatic.

"Isobel, what's going on?"

She looks right past me as if I am not really there.

"You just had chemo like four days ago."

"I'm feeling fine."

"I'm pretty sure you're not supposed to be smoking. Or drinking. Or getting high." I shake my head and look her hard in her eyes.

She purposefully looks away. Then she says, "I want you to meet Billy," tilting her head toward the guy whose lap she is sitting on. Billy has dark hair and four red stars from the Chicago flag tattooed on the side of his neck. I've seen men like him my whole life. Knuckleheads in high school who eventually became cops, bouncers, security guards, drug dealers. Something about the wideness of his shoulders, the grip he has on my sister's leg, and his confidence—all suggest more than a passing familiarity with violence.

I nod at Billy and ask, "Where did you two meet?"

"A friend of a friend," she says, and I immediately realize this is the guy she's been buying illicit substances from.

"And what happened to the assistant principal? You know, the guy you were dating a few weeks ago?"

I see the anger in her eyes for a second before she gives me an icy smile. "I keep telling you that you should stop trying to be funny."

I look over at the beer cans accumulated on the kitchen counter and ask, "Where's Jazzy?"

"Asleep."

I go upstairs and find Isobel's bed empty. I nudge my mother's door open and find Jazz sleeping beside my mom. My mom has her arm around Jazzy's shoulder and both of them are breathing at the exact same time. Their faces look tranquil and calm, as if downstairs certain self-centered, self-serving people aren't making infinitely ridiculous mistakes.

I go back down and find out Billy served in Iraq, lost his leg in Fallujah. He now works as a welder and sells pain pills on the side. Later he asks if anyone wants to see his fake leg. He rolls up his pants to show where the lifeless beige plastic meets the scarred remains of his knee. When the plastic foot is passed to me, it's hard not to run off with it, to get him as far away from my sister as I can.

After all these people go home belligerent or drunk, I look over at Isobel and ask, "Are you serious? What are you even doing with that guy?"

"I like him," she says. "I like that I can see what's wrong with him from a mile away." Then she exhales a cloud of cigarette smoke through her nose.

"You really shouldn't be smoking in here. What about Mom?"

She completely ignores me, turning away as she continues to clean.

"I've got to go. Daniel is probably waiting up for me."

* * *

On my ten-speed, I pedal off without looking back. I sneak past the landlord's first-floor apartment, go up the stairs, and find Daniel sitting in front of the television wearing what appears to be someone else's clothes. He has on a too-large black tracksuit and pink flip-flops, something you'd wear to a beach or the pool.

"What's this? What are you wearing?" I ask.

"Nothing."

"Where did you get all this stuff?"

"Nowhere." And then after a long pause, he says, "The airport."

"Which airport?"

He only shrugs.

"Did you take someone's bags?"

He shrugs again.

"Did you go to school?"

"For a while."

"For a while? What do you mean *for a while*? What's wrong with you?"

He only turns up the television and asks, "What, are you going to throw me out too?"

I have to keep reminding myself that all these setbacks, all these failures are only the beginning stage of success. I've been putting inspirational Post-it notes on the refrigerator, beside my alarm clock, on the bathroom mirror each day. I read them as I get ready the next morning:

Wolfgang Amadeus Mozart died at the age of thirty-five. His last three compositions were all considered musical failures.

After reciting a few affirmations like that, I ride to work. As I lock up my bicycle I see the factory standing before me like a hulking mass of disappointment, one completely despondent shadow upon another completely despondent shadow. I put the orange earplugs in and go to face my fate.

I get home from work that afternoon and find Daniel on the couch wearing a beekeeper's outfit, the whole getup: boots, gloves, suit, mask. He is sitting in a beekeeper's outfit, playing video games like this is nothing out of the ordinary.

"What's up with this?" I ask, standing before him with my arms across my chest.

"I found it," he says.

"Let me guess: at the airport?"

He nods, apparently bored by this conversation.

"You are messing with other people's lives," I tell him.

"You don't know that," he says.

"I do know that. I know if I worked all year and only got two weeks off and I went to Chicago and someone stole my luggage from the airport, I would be pretty angry."

"I'm not bothering anyone," he says. "Anyway, it's just clothes."

"But what are you even doing with them? I mean, how many suitcases have you stolen?"

"Seven."

"Seven? What is wrong with you? Are you seriously crazy?"

"I don't know. Ask Mom. Ask Isobel," he says.

"Maybe I will," I say and walk outside to sit on the concrete steps as there is nowhere else to go.

* * *

When I'm not working or worrying about my sister or brother, I go to spoken word readings and hip-hop shows with Chris KRS. Or I go to the record stores on 95th, looking for old-school hip-hop to add to my collection. I'm still on the lookout for John Cage's *Quartets I–VIII*. But all I ever find is Mahler covered in mold.

One evening I am lying on the couch with the radio on my chest, listening to the classical music station, when I hear a Mozart sonata and think of my father. I realize that I have not spoken to him in over four years. Four years is way too long, even for Eastern Europeans who prefer every kind of silence.

After work the next day, I carry my bike up the concrete stairs to my father's apartment and think about what I can talk about. I knock on the door, wait, knock again, but there's no answer. It's eight o'clock at night. I see his van parked below. I look around, reach above the doorframe, find the hidden key, and hold it in my hand. All at once, I am too afraid to put it in the lock. I realize I have nothing to say to him. I put the key back above the frame and carry my bike back down the stairs, hoping no one has seen me.

I get a coffee from the corner store on the way to work the next morning and see the headlines screaming across all the newspapers. "Financial Panic," one of them says. "Financial Crisis," says another. Another says: "Apocalypse Now." I have no idea what this means. It seems like it's only a problem for people with money, and have no idea how bad it will be.

At work I try to leave my body but it almost never works. Even with earplugs, even though my hearing is terrible, the thrum of the plastic presses keeps bringing me back, my hands scrambling to remove the malformed giraffes as they hasten by.

* * *

Benny calls and says he has gotten a job at CVS on Kedzie, stocking shelves. They make him wear the little red vest, which is humiliating. When I go to see him, he frowns and says he can't talk. He is in the parking lot, busy wrangling shopping carts into some kind of manageable order. I tell him I can wait. He frowns and shakes his head again.

As I'm riding off, I see a blue car with a custom muffler and chrome wheels pull into the lot. Benny looks around and climbs inside the passenger seat, then closes the door behind him. The sunlight blocks my view. I have no idea what he is up to but I am certain it's not good.

Later that same week, I get called into the health office in the middle of my shift. Immediately, I think Daniel has gone crazy and has been shot robbing a bank. Instead, a doe-eyed nurse hands me a form to fill out and says, "We need a urine sample. You're being tested for drug use."

"I can tell you right now I don't do any of that."

She clicks her teeth, looks me up and down. "We still need a sample."

"No problem," I say.

She hands me the plastic cup and I head into the little bathroom and try to go, but can't. I sit in there for like ten minutes, until the nurse knocks and asks, "Are you all right?" and I say, "I don't know. I don't have to go," and she says, "Well, I need a sample," and I say, "Well, nothing's happening," and she says, "Well, that's going to be a problem," and I say, "Maybe if you stopped talking," and she says, "I can wait all day," and I ask, "Can I just go back to work?" and she says, "Not without a sample," and I think, *This, this is how they are*

going to get us. I will be fired for not being able to go to the bath-
room on command and my brother and I will be evicted and our
belongings tossed into the streets and I will have to work at Mc-
Donald's and he will become a drug addict and I have dealt with
everything else but they are going to overthrow us because of this?
but already I have begun to go to the bathroom and outside I
can hear the nurse clapping.

The drug test comes back negative, which it should because I have not done drugs in a few months, but for some
reason I am sure I am going to be accused of something. I
decide we need to celebrate.

So my brother and I go to Taco Bell and order one of
everything off the menu. I've never seen Daniel eat so much.
He's talkative, he's telling me about school, about Greek mythol-
ogy, about the latest issue of *The Fantastic Four.* We could sit
in that hard plastic booth for hours, I think, with the fake
plants, the off-kilter lights. We have a hot sauce–eating contest
and make ourselves sick draining the tiny packets. I put my
arm around him and it's like nothing will ever defeat us.

Then, the very next day, I get a phone call from Midway Airport saying Daniel has been picked up trying to make off with
someone's suitcase. I go down there, pull the anxious, squinty-
eyed security guard to the side, and say, "I'm going to level
with you. Both our parents died in a plane crash last year. It's a
mental thing for him," and the guard ends up apologizing for
the whole incident.

But when I get back to work, the floor manager, Rick, asks
me to come into his office and tells me I am on probation for
taking time off without prior approval. I explain the situation,
tell him about my brother, tell him it is a family emergency.

He nods and folds his fingertips together in front of him. I can tell that he is listening but that he doesn't have a choice in the matter. I get sent home without pay for the rest of the week.

When Monday comes around again, I ride over to the factory on my ten-speed and see a long line of people standing outside, all in their uniforms. The metal doors have been locked with chains. One person says that the bank the company uses has run out of money. Someone else says the factory has defaulted on its loans and cannot make payroll. *Financial crisis*, I think. Some of the workers bang on the windows. One woman, Rosie, who is in her late sixties, pounds hard on the glass. Someone puts an arm around her shoulder. I come back to the apartment and find the electric bill stuck under the door. One hundred fifty dollars.

I call my mother, I call my sister. I apologize to both of them and ask if Daniel and I can please, please come back home.

Isobel tells me she's amazed we made it this long.

Isobel comes by in her car and picks us up, like we are two orphans. It's sad to see how few objects we actually own. Everything fits in the rear compartment of her hatchback. I look back from the passenger seat at Jazzy in her car seat and she seems gloriously happy. For no good reason she is in a witch costume of some kind.

On the way we have to stop by Billy's. Like many of us, he too lives at home, in a ramshackle little A-frame, which is humbling for a purveyor of illicit substances. It actually makes him seem a little more human. He leans in through the car window and kisses my sister and all of us look away. I try not to notice what he places in the palm of her hand. But when she starts driving again I am relieved to see it is only a photo. A Polaroid, of himself as a boy. She said she asked for it. I roll my eyes.

I go in and say hi to my mom in her bedroom. She is busy typing on her little blue typewriter. She ignores me at first. I don't think she has entirely forgiven me. Finally she looks up at me briefly and nods.

"How's the play coming?" I ask.

"Better. I'm at the part where Tom Cruise and Katie Holmes get engaged and then a few months later, they announce she's pregnant."

"Big turning point."

"Exactly. But all of it seems a little suspicious, even if it isn't, because of how rushed it is, which may be the saddest part of all."

Back in our old bedroom, I put on my headphones, play one of my grandfather's Puccini records, and stare up at the ceiling. I imagine all the missteps, all the mistakes, all the failures of the past few months hanging over our heads like musical notes. There are a lot of them, when I think about it, more than a few. I try to appreciate each one, to think of what went wrong, to see something beautiful in them, to understand they are only part of a much larger composition. But it's pretty hard. Some of the mistakes are just mistakes after all.

I look over and see Daniel, in his underwear, reading a library book about submarines, mouthing the words to himself. I realize then, regardless of our age and the problems that have beset us, each of us is still hiding from the world, all of us are back at home, exactly like the children we are.

CHAPTER TWELVE

I COME BACK FROM DROPPING JAZZY OFF AT SCHOOL AT THE beginning of September and find my brother dressed in some kind of European fencing uniform, complete with a mask, sitting on the back couch, playing video games. At his feet is an empty yellow suitcase. I almost have an aneurysm I am so mad. "Stop being selfish and go to class!" I shout.

I grab him by the shoulder and force him out the back door, shoving his backpack against his chest. He puts the backpack on and then rides off on his bike, still wearing the outfit. Even in that moment I have very little hope he will actually end up at school.

I go to pick Jazz up from kindergarten a few hours later and she comes out crying. I look over at her teacher, a red-haired young woman, and then lean down and sign to Jazzy, *What's wrong?*

She shakes her head and buries her face in my shirt. I tell her to wait by the bicycle and then go over and introduce myself.

"Hey, I'm Aleks. I'm Jazzy's uncle."

The teacher is busy helping other kids get dismissed and seems to have no time for small talk. "Yes. Can I help you with something?"

"It seems like Jazzy had a rough day."

She finally looks over at me. "I'd be happy to talk with you on the phone or over email."

"Okay, but both of us are standing here right now."

"I'm sorry. I'm just not able to discuss this at the moment," she says as she helps another kid get matched up to her sibling.

"Okay. But maybe you can tell me why she's crying?"

"Jazzy seems to be having a hard time keeping up. We're just not able to develop individualized learning plans for every student."

"Is there a way she can get some help, like last year?"

"Unfortunately, we don't have the resources to support every student in that way. You are more than welcome to look into any grants you think your family or Jasmine are eligible for. Again, maybe we could discuss this at another, more appropriate time?"

I look at her and nod.

Jazzy has no interest in riding on the handlebars that day and so we walk home side by side in silence.

I go to a bookstore downtown near UIC, looking for a book of poems for my grandfather's seventy-first birthday. But all the poetry books seem to be by someone named Rūmī. I walk up to the counter and a young woman—some college student, I'm guessing—is working there. I tell her what I am hoping to find.

"Let's take a look."

This young woman is a year or two older than me, maybe twenty-one or twenty-two, part African American possibly, I don't know and it doesn't matter, except to say she has beautiful dark hair and a few freckles on her nose. I keep glancing at her as she searches through the bookshelves.

"I guess you're right," she says. "It doesn't look like we have a lot. Were you looking for some poet in particular?"

"I don't know. It's for my grandfather. He likes European poetry. I thought I could get him something contemporary. From this country."

"I'm taking this cool poetry class this semester. We've read some great modern poets but it doesn't look like we have any of them."

"Too bad."

"Do you know Matthew Zapruder?" she asks.

"No."

"His poems feel really modern and funny."

"Anybody from this century would be great."

"Okay." She kneels down and retrieves a thin book by Tracy K. Smith called *Duende*. She hands it to me. "This one is about America and race and class. She's African American. It's one of the best books I've read in a long time."

I flip through a few pages. "Yeah, this looks great. I really appreciate it."

I follow her up to the counter and fool around with my money.

"Here," she says, staring at me. "Just take it."

"Wait, what? Really?"

"This place is closing in a couple months. Nobody knows it yet."

"Thanks. I . . . I really appreciate it. My grandfather will too, but . . ." I pause near the counter and say, "Are you like a poet or something? You seem to know a lot about poetry?"

"I'm an English major. I'm a junior. What about you?"

I frown and look down at the book of poems. "I'm not in school right now actually. I was. I'm taking some time off. I'm still working everything out."

She seems to remember something. "You know they have poetry readings here. Every first Saturday of the month. You should bring your grandfather." And she hands me a purple flyer.

"Okay, cool," I say. "I'll look into it. Thanks."

I hold the purple flyer and hurry off, feeling embarrassed for some reason. I guess it is the first time in a long while I admitted—out loud—that I am probably never going to finish college. That, and the fact that she gave me the book and the way she spoke, how lovely she was. I pedal away as quick as I can before I make an even bigger fool of myself.

Obviously, by now, I have to do what all the unemployed young people in my neighborhood do. I go and fill out an application at the cemetery. Within hours, there is an automated call telling me when and where to show up for an orientation the following Monday. The automated voice is shrill and hard to understand. It feels like a false victory and not even that.

I go to the poetry reading on Saturday, just to see if this person will show. There she is, sitting in the back of the room in a yellow sweater the color of a lemon drop. When she sees me she smiles, which is something almost no one does anymore. We wait through an hour and a half of freestyle poetry from two middle-aged professors before everyone politely claps. When it is over, everyone makes a run for the free cookies and punch. I walk over to her and say hello.

"Hey," she says. "I'm really surprised to see you here."

"I'm really surprised to be here," I say and don't know what to add after that. We drink clear plastic cups of red, artificially flavored punch, which is apparently what they serve at upscale, collegiate poetry readings. I follow her over to a corner of the bookstore that's more secluded and quiet.

"Did you like the reading?" she asks.

I try to arrange my face into some kind of passable expression. "I like coming down here. I like looking at people listening to poetry. I also like a lot of the adjectives those two guys used."

The young woman chokes a little on her punch, laughing. "Where are you from?" she asks.

"The southside," I say, as nonchalant as possible. "Around 99th Street."

"Is that . . ."

"Over by Beverly, in Evergreen Park."

I can see from how she's staring at me that she doesn't know where that is. "I'm from over in Hyde Park," she says.

"Hyde Park. Wow."

I suddenly imagine this young woman growing up in a tony high-rise, overlooking the posh University of Chicago, all tree-lined streets, adults wearing monocles and ascots sipping Chardonnay, while laughing about Proust—the opposite of my neighborhood.

"Do you go to school over there?" she asks.

"I do. I mean I did. I'm trying to save money by getting all my gen-eds out of the way. I'm actually taking a break from my studies at the moment."

"I wish I had done that. My parents are mad at how many courses I took that don't go toward my major."

"Oh, dang. I thought it all counted."

"It does. But usually just as electives."

"Electives," I say. "Right."

Her smile shifts as her eyes become slightly more inquisitive. "And you seem to like poetry?"

"I do. My parents, they always played music for us when we were kids. Me and my sister and brother. And they read us poetry. My grandfather too. He's always reading poetry from Bosnia. And I go with my friend Chris to spoken word, hip-hop shows. I guess music, poetry is what's informed me most as a person." I itch the side of my nose. "I can stop talking if I'm talking too much."

"No. It's cool. Bosnia is really beautiful. I got to go there in high school."

"Really? That's amazing. Where else have you been?"

"I don't know. Greece and France. And England once."

"I've never left the country."

She smiles and it gets awkward then. The apparent distance between us becomes clearer. She nods, sips her fruit punch very demurely, both of us trying to think about what else to say.

I ask: "So what about Hyde Park? I never met anyone from Hyde Park. What was it like growing up over there? Was it fancy?"

"No, it's not fancy. My father is a professor and my mother is an architect."

"And you go to school at UIC? Why not University of Chicago?"

"It's complicated."

"Oh yeah?"

"I didn't get in, actually. I didn't exactly try all that hard. I also felt like I needed to get out of Hyde Park."

"Too many monocles?"

"What?"

"Nothing."

"I just wanted to see what I could do on my own."

I nod.

"I'm an RA this year, a resident advisor. I like it but it's a ton of work. It's kind of like being a parent."

"I hear that. I have a niece I spend a lot of time with. I like her better than anyone else in my family."

"I think the idea of family is overrated," she says with a little frown.

"I completely agree."

She smiles then and it is almost too much, too warm, too beautiful. Another long silence intervenes. I look up and see the room has begun to empty. She glances down at her shoes and seems to be searching for something else to say.

"Sorry to be weird. It just got really personal all of a sudden," she says.

"Yeah, no, maybe I should go," I say.

I head outside and unlock my bike. She comes out, holding open the door, and says, "Maybe next time you'll tell me your name."

I grin and say, "Okay, but why don't I tell you now?"

"Okay."

There's a long pause and I say, "I'm Aleks. What about you?"

For a while I cannot read her expression. She squints, as if deciding something, and then says, "It's Alex," and after we exchange phone numbers, I know I'm in trouble.

The following Monday I go to the orientation at the gigantic cemetery with ten other young people. All of us are given three green shirts and three green pairs of pants, just like we are entering prison. No one asks my name. A supervisor points to a pair of hedge clippers and motions to a hedge that seems to go on for miles and miles. He points to his watch and then walks off. I shrug and start clipping, having no idea if I am doing it right.

At some point I sit down and take a break just to feel the sun on my face. All around me, history, the dead, stretch out in every conceivable direction. I find an entire Polish section and wonder why all these people chose, even in their death, to be separate from everyone else, to be buried among their own countrymen. I fall asleep and the foreman kicks me awake. I tell him it was from sadness, from seeing all the Polish graves and also I have low blood sugar. He only looks at me and shakes his head.

I come home from the cemetery and find Isobel fighting with her boyfriend Billy on the front lawn. They are yelling at each other, Isobel on the steps, Billy pointing at her angrily. I throw my bike down and quietly try to intervene.

"Go inside," I tell my sister.

"You go inside, Aleks," she says. "And please mind your own eff-ing business."

I haven't expected any response, to be honest. I stand there a few seconds and then shrug and pick up my bike and put it in the garage.

Later neither of them are around. Billy's black car is gone, and when Isobel comes back, she is tranquil and happy. I cannot tell if she is high or if she is just happy from having sex. I do not want to imagine either scenario. On the couch, she reads Jazzy a storybook before bed and I listen with suspicion.

* * *

One afternoon in the middle of September I go to the record store after work and look through the classical albums. The covers don't ever match the music: Shostakovich's *Symphony No. 5* is drab white, Mozart's *Piano Concerto No. 11* is red, Beethoven's *Diabelli Variations* is some modernist nonsense. At the back of the stack I come across a sooty Dvořák reissue and a slightly damaged John Cage record. I lift the Cage album up and stare. I recognize it so quickly that I don't even see it at first. It is black and nearly silver, the photograph of John Cage looking timeless. *Quartets I–VIII*, a record I've spent the last ten years looking for. The cover is worn, and it looks to be a foreign pressing of some kind. First composed in 1976, John Cage borrowed melody lines from other musical compositions including *Lift up your heads, O ye gates, Judea,* and *Christ the Lord is Ris'n.* I gaze at the liner notes and realize I should go by father's place and listen to this with him. I pay for it quick, eight dollars, put it in my bag, and bring it over to my dad's.

In the parking lot I see his white van, see the empty disposable coffee cups piled up along the dashboard and across the passenger seat. I carry my bicycle up the concrete stairs, lean it against the metal railing. The black paint on his door is peeling. I knock once, then again. No one answers. When I turn the doorknob, I discover it's locked. I reach up, find the key over the doorframe, and open it.

On the couch, I can see the shape of my father, his rounded cheeks, his head nearly shaved. It's eight thirty at night and he's already asleep. Has he been drinking? Benny told me he was working the night shift as a security guard but maybe it is an off night. The television is on, a documentary about Finnish music, but the sound is turned off, something my father always liked to do. His black work boots have been placed by a pile of magazines, *Scientific American, National Geographic*. On the floor there are a few Chinese takeout food cartons. I stand there in the tentative light and see an electronic keyboard placed on some milk crates and in the corner a cello.

There is a Philip Glass record on the glass coffee table. I turn it over and study it. Apparently, all my father ever listens to anymore is eighties European experimental, records no one in their right mind would ever want to listen to. I stand there for a moment and hear him breathing. I don't know if I should wake him. After about eight minutes of thinking about it, I carefully reach into my bag and place the John Cage record on the table. Outside, I lock the door, carry my bicycle down the stairs, and ride off into the dark. For the rest of the evening, no sounds seem to follow me.

Two days after that Daniel gets busted for not going to school. I get a phone call at the cemetery. One of the supervisors comes and pulls me from where I am mowing beside one of the many crematoriums. I can barely fake my way through my embarrassment and anger as the assistant principal asks if I know where my brother is. I tell him Daniel's home sick in bed and that I'm sorry for not calling but I have to go.

When I get back to my mom's house, there's no sign of my brother, nothing but a crushed milk carton and an empty box of cereal in the trash, and a stack of library books beside his bed.

Around nine thirty that night he comes in, trying to unlock the back door as quietly as he can. He is holding another suitcase. I stare at him and shake my head.

"No. No way. You didn't. Tell me you're not going to the airport again."

He frowns, then itches the side of his nose.

I'm so mad I don't even know what to say. After a few seconds of us staring at each other, I finally find some words. "Daniel, if I find out you went back to that airport again, I'm telling Mom. Then you'll be out of here again, on your own. Then you can see how long you make it. Now go to bed."

He glances down, nods once, and then hurries upstairs. I am so angry that my hands shake and so all I can do is go sit and pretend to play the invisible piano, put my fingers over the empty air where the keys will likely never be again. I let the hearing loss take over, don't try to fight it, just let the ringing in my ears become its own kind of quiet.

Alex and I begin talking on the phone almost every night. Nothing serious at first, just short conversations like *How was your day? What kind of music and films do you like?* and eventually Alex begins reading lines from some of her favorite poets to me, William Carlos Williams and Lucille Clifton and Emily Dickinson, and in turn, I play a few parts of some of my favorite compositions for her, holding the phone up to the silver stereo.

One evening I go out to the garage to put some air in my bicycle tires and find Daniel kneeling over an enormous piece of black PVC that he is sawing in two. I stand there for a few seconds and ask, "Daniel, what are you doing?" and without looking up, he says: "Building a submarine. For my impending escape."

I look over his shoulder and can tell from the different parts he has gathered that he is not joking around. He has some blueprints sketched out in a notebook on the ground beside him.

"Someone posted these instructions on the Internet. You can do it without welding, just using screws and glue."

I watch him work for a while from the blueprint and then wander back inside, content in knowing exactly how my brother is going to die.

Exactly like some occupying force, Billy spends more and more time at our house throughout the month of September. Some of his friends come by at odd hours, playing loud music in the kitchen. Some of them smoke marijuana in the basement like the basement is not a part of the house. Billy takes over the back room, stretching out on the couch. There's no room for anyone else to sit. Sometimes Isobel gives him long massages on the sofa, which is disgusting. You can hear the two of them laughing, no matter where you are. He likes to take long showers and shows up to breakfast without a shirt on. Then sometimes he leaves his prosthetic lying around. It's very disconcerting to see what appears to be a human foot sitting unattached beside the tub. I watch Jazzy watching him at breakfast, her small dark eyes becoming momentarily like an animal's. I see her silently growling over her bowl of cereal and try not to smile to myself.

At the end of the month, I ride down Cicero and knock on my grandfather's door to see how he's been getting on and to give him the book of poems. I put my ear to the door and can hear his feet padding across the floor and then the sound of the lock being unlocked.

He doesn't even look to see who it is, just turns and quickly shuffles away. He goes and sits on his bed in the bedroom. I can see he is only wearing a stubbly bathrobe and it looks like he hasn't shaved in weeks. I ask him how he has been and he only shrugs.

"I have a present for you. For your birthday," I say and hand him the book of poems.

He looks down at it and gently touches the cover. "Very thoughtful. Very nice," and immediately he sets it down without looking at the poems inside.

"Okay, well, that's it," I say. "Just wanted to come by and see how you are."

He seems to ignore this and says, "I need your help with something, Grandson." He waves me over to the closet, which he keeps shut with three different kinds of locks. One by one, he unlocks each lock, the first using a combination he seems to struggle to remember, the second a dial, and the third with a small key he keeps on a silver chain in his bathrobe pocket. Once the closet is opened, I see it is full of suitcases of all sorts, stacked one on top of the other, from the top to the bottom, all wedged inside like a kind of vertical puzzle. On the top is the infamous violin case and beneath it are suitcases of every size and shape. I immediately think of my brother but, from the amount of dust and grime gathered along their edges, I can see these particular suitcases have been sitting in the closet for a long time.

"All the past, all our history," is what he mumbles as he points to a gigantic black valise at the very bottom. I sigh and begin to remove the other suitcases, carefully restacking them on the floor. Finally, I am able to get the black portmanteau free and lift it onto my grandfather's wire-frame bed.

I begin to unlatch its golden hinges when my grandfather

shakes his head. "Not yet. At first, this is only for you to listen and try to understand. As you know, I was born in Sarajevo in 1937, just before the start of the Second World War. My father took my mother and my older sister and myself to my mother's village to wait out the war. He was a musician, as I said, who learned to sell horses to the Fascists and later the Communists. After the war, he never returned to music. Something in him had been broken, perhaps, or maybe he felt he was too old. I don't know. He never spoke of it."

My grandfather puts a single hand on the black valise just then. "When Josip Tito, one of the Partisans, rose to power after the war, Jugoslavia became a Communist nation, protected and yet somewhat independent of the Soviet Union. Tito was famous for his personality and also for his ability to play the piano. He thought Jugoslavia's strength was its collision of distinct cultures. He believed culture could be a powerful force in the twentieth century."

"I don't know any of this," I tell him. "My dad never talked about it."

"These are stories even your father doesn't know. So I am telling you. Where was I? Oh, yes, as I was saying, my father, having been a musician, was also a great believer in the idea of culture and music. He thought it might be a way for our family to prosper. So when I was seven, he found a way to get me into the Children's Conservatory in Sarajevo, mostly through bribes. I went without question. You have to understand, at the time, all I wanted was to please Father and my teachers. So I learned how to play the cello and did not ever question what was being taught. After that, my cello, and the other students, became my family. I rarely had the opportunity to venture back home. In some ways I was like you, wanting to be on my own, to be my own person in the world, to find my own place."

I give him a smile.

"When I was twenty, I played in one of the national symphonies and was beginning to take on students of my own. Sometimes I was asked to play at important political gatherings, meetings of the cultural ministers. Once I even played before Tito himself at a lavish party. He put his hand on my head and said, 'This boy is the future of our country; he will make all of Jugoslavia proud.' I thought I had found myself, where I belonged. Everything I wanted was within my grasp."

He turns away for a moment, as a shadow seems to pass over his face. "There was a girl, Maja, a flutist, whom I was deeply in love with. By then, there was much political discussion, some criticizing Tito and others questioning communism. She was the center of many of these discussions. Although I felt as she did, that something needed to change within the country, I did not have her sort of courage or conviction. Again and again, she wrote letters to the cultural ministers, wrote essays for an underground newspaper, even made posters in her dormitory, which could be searched at any time. This was 1960 now and the sense of change felt great. We saw what was happening in France and Czechoslovakia and we wanted the same things for ourselves, for our friends, our families. Some of the other music students became radicalized, talked openly about revolution. One even planted a bomb in a post office to protest how mail was being censored. But I was not ready to risk everything—my life, my career, the respect of my family—for the world Maja imagined. Instead of following her, I choose to leave, to find a way to escape."

Here he resettles himself on the bed, his face now looking

disturbed and drawn. "One of my friends, Peter, who played French horn, had been permitted to travel throughout Europe and the United States as part of a cultural exchange program. The postcards he sent, about life abroad in the States, about the sense of freedom and prosperity, I admit, they seduced me. I knew at some point Maja would be arrested and silenced. I had seen what had happened to other musicians, journalists, anyone that questioned the government too vocally. So I thought if I could get a visa as part of the cultural exchange, I might make a life built around music in some other place. I thought I could bring my family here eventually. But, of course, I was wrong about that and almost everything.

"I made plans to leave on a cultural exchange visa but I told no one. I did not even tell Maja that I would not be coming back. I carried all my photographs and letters inside my uncle's old violin case. For seven months, I traveled across Eastern Europe and played with all the great symphonies of the Eastern Bloc, even performing in St. Petersburg. After that, I took a train to Norway and then the United Kingdom and eventually a plane to the United States."

Now he looks down at his bare white feet. "Once I arrived in New York, I immediately applied for citizenship, I went straight to the offices in downtown Manhattan. I had nothing but a small suitcase, some sheet music, a book of poems from my father. I knew I would not be permitted to return. Like my father, my whole life had been reduced to what I was able to carry in my hands."

I see his palms are upturned, like he is searching for something.

"After the government back in Jugoslavia found out that I had fled, my family suffered terribly. Within a year, they had lost the land where my mother's family had raised horses for almost a century. The horses themselves were dragged out of their stables in the middle of the night and shot. My older sister was cast out of a public service job. It became difficult to communicate with any of my family as my letters were never delivered. I always had to write friends of friends of friends. Everyone was the worst for my decision to leave. Even me. Once I was in the States, I moved to Chicago where a second cousin lived, and began working where he worked, at one of the steel plants. I was not taken seriously as a musician here because I could not speak the language, and worse, I believed I was a better than I actually was. So I gave music lessons to children in my cousin's apartment and worked at the plant. Later I met your grandmother at a dance at the Croatian Catholic church. We got married without my parents or my sister being able to attend. I was never able to see them again in person because of my decision."

He looks away, his face turning to stone. "I gave up everything for a life of insignificance. As my father did. You see, I figured it all out a little too late: fate is family."

I sit there silently. I do not know what he wants me to say. I think about putting my hand on his but cannot work up the nerve.

"Only when Tito died in 1980, after the amputation of his left leg, did I finally receive this suitcase in the mail. It turns out my family had sent it nearly ten years before, but the bureaucrats, the customs officials, whomever, refused to send it. I had no idea what it could be. You have to imagine how terrified I was to open it at first."

"What's inside?"

"It's all I have left of the past, of my country. All my history."

I look down at the enormous black suitcase, afraid to open the golden latches.

"Go on. Open it. It's your inheritance now," he says and pats the top of the suitcase. Small flecks of dust rise into the air.

"Is it someone's body part or something? Because I don't know if I want to see anything like that."

"Go on and open it and find out."

All I can see is the smooth plane of the top of the suitcase. It feels like a black hole, like there's something sinister inside. I perseverate. I pause. I stall. "I just remembered," I say. "I forgot. I've got to go pick up Jazzy, Isobel's daughter, from school. I should go. I'm sorry. I'll come back and check this out later this week. Happy birthday."

Before he can respond, I get up, close the front door behind me, and hurry down the stairs.

On Tuesday I get pulled from work as I'm cutting the grass on a sloping hill. Another phone call from Daniel's school. It's the assistant principal again. He says Daniel has already accumulated enough absences to receive a failing grade for the semester.

I tell my supervisor, ask to punch out. He looks at me and says he's sorry for the family emergencies, but if I leave, I should not plan on coming back. So I leave. I pull up my hood and ride around, looking for Daniel. The weather has turned again and it feels more like the middle of October than the end of September.

I go by every place I can think of, Circle Park, the no-name convenience store, the library, but he's not anywhere. I come home and put a classical record on, lying down on the sofa in the back room. I put the speakers beside my ear, turn it up so loud until all I can hear is static.

Hours go by and still no Daniel. I look outside and see it's gotten dark. I get up, put on my sweatshirt, get on my silver ten-speed, ride off again. The cold outside is fiendish, personal. The air makes the street feel hard. Every crack in the pavement is a jolt. My nose is running. It looks like I'm crying but I assure you I'm not.

On my bike, I go by the arcade on 79th. I go by Circle Park again, by the no-name pizza place, but he's nowhere to be found. Around and around the neighborhood. Eventually the airport rises ahead of me and I decide to go inside and take a look.

In the B terminal of Midway, I see my brother sitting on a bench, wearing his blue stocking cap and staring at a family talking in German, all of whom are hugging each other. I watch him for a while and try to think what he must be thinking. I watch him smile for a second, studying this other family, see how he studies these people who have been reunited, happy to see each other. I suddenly realize this is why he has been coming here. I go and sit beside him for a while, neither of us saying anything.

Outside, above us, planes continue to take off and land, disappearing into the dark. I think of all the comings and goings, all the beginnings and endings we have already faced, and realize I ought to be thankful for all of them, to have family I can count on. I will tell him about it sometime whenever he wants to talk. After a while I leave him there to watch the planes by himself and go out and pedal back into the dark.

One way or another, I know this year is not going to break us.

CHAPTER THIRTEEN

I IGNORE ALL THE GHOSTS HOVERING ALONG THE STREET AS I get Jazzy from school in October. I find my niece waiting with a group of other kindergarten students by the east door. Immediately, from the color of her face, I can tell she has been crying. I ask, "What's wrong?" and when I go to take her hand, she turns and runs away. The backpack trips her up at first and so she drops it and cuts across someone's front lawn. I have to stop and put the bicycle down and grab her bag and by the time I try to follow her, she's gone.

I call out her name again and again but there is no reply. I rush back to the bike, put her tiny backpack over my shoulders, and pedal past all the Halloween decorations in windows and placed on lawn after lawn. She is four and I have no idea where she is. Finally, just as the sun is beginning to set, I see her sitting on someone's front porch, holding the hand of a grinning plastic skeleton. I don't even bother to ask her what happened. After we get home, I open her backpack and find all her school papers have been balled up or torn apart.

* * *

Alex asks if I want to do our laundry together. I don't know why, to be honest. It's her idea so I go with it. She comes by in a beautiful 1980s cream-colored Mercedes, which has a good deal of rust creeping along the rear bumper, but is still a marvelous-looking vehicle. She says it's her father's but he lends it to her whenever she wants, which sounds like it's actually hers but she has a hard time admitting it.

We go to a laundry place on Rockwell. Both of us fold our clothes at the exact same time. A long stretch of time goes by without us talking, but it doesn't seem to bother her. I like how quiet, how thoughtful she is.

On the television at the laundromat, someone is explaining how the banks no longer have any money. *Good,* I think. *Let them know what it's like to try to survive. Let them eat cereal without milk for a couple of weeks.*

I look over at Alex and she smiles, demurely folding a sweater. I realize how you almost never meet someone like her on the southside. She seems like she has herself together. She wants to know more about me, my neighborhood, is not afraid of going to fast food joints or just hanging out at Circle Park. So we meet out a few times during the week, go get some fries at Pop's, then on a Friday night she invites me to her dorm room and I fall asleep there and after that things begin to get much more serious.

Alex makes out like she means it. The sex is something, and that's all I will say. We sit in her dorm room where she is an RA, in our underwear, and listen to records. Alex has a *Miss Saigon* poster on her wall. She says she loves musicals and has a wall of classic novels that she has read multiple times, all highlighted, with different notes in the margin in different colors from each time she has gone through them. She is smart and funny and nothing like the girls on the southside who fight each other in the parking lots of bars. I pick a book of poems by Rilke from a bookshelf and flip through it. I feel her watching me before she asks: "Do you ever think about going back to college?"

"I think about it all the time," I say. "I had to take a break for financial reasons. I'm taking care of my brother and niece and mom. And also my sister, I guess."

"What do you mean taking care of them?" She sits up to listen as if she is genuinely interested. She has a little black sleeveless T-shirt on, with nothing underneath.

"I mean I'm living with them and helping out. My mother's been sick. And my sister's in chemo."

"But you're twenty. How do you do that and work?"

"I do okay, actually. I mean I had a job, had two jobs at one point. And my sister has a job. Everyone contributes when they can. I guess I'm looking for work again."

She turns and faces me, leaning on her elbow. I can see her glorious neck, the shape of her shoulders. "Do you mind me asking how old were you when you lost your virginity? I'm just curious."

"How old were *you*?" I ask.

"I was eighteen," she says. "It was freshman year. First semester. Some jerk I never saw again."

"I was fifteen."

"Wow. That's young."

"It was. I wish I could go back and do it with somebody I liked. All I did was feel bad afterward. Because another guy I knew was with the same girl that same day, I think."

"Really? That's kind of trashy."

"It is. Some of the people in my neighborhood are trashy. A lot of them, actually. I have a lot of mixed feelings about it."

"Your life and my life have been pretty different," she says, and it seems like it is maybe the understatement of the century.

I check my watch and say I have to go. "I've got to be back to take my niece to school in a couple hours."

As I'm getting dressed, I watch her in bed reading a book of poems by Auden. She is chewing gum and then blows a giant pink bubble. Outside the sun is just coming up. It's six in the morning and the sky looks distant and cold.

I get my shirt on and point at the book. "I know that writer but I never read him. My mom, I think she actually used to read us some of his poems when we were little."

"Who, Auden? He was kind of one of the first out poets."

"You mean gay?"

"Yes, gay."

"Is he any good?"

She nods.

"Maybe I can borrow it sometime?"

"All you have to do is ask."

I stand there not wanting to leave, looking at the books, the posters, this entire new world, and I say, "Okay. See you in the funny pages," then close the door on the realm of higher education behind me.

On the train it's easy to forget I'm losing my hearing. Everything is so loud, the sound itself seems to carry everyone along. I carry my bicycle off at 95th and ride over to Western. The sun is rising behind me, making my neck and the back of my head feel warm. There is dew on the windshields of cars up and down the street. I pass the parking lot across from Benny's house and am just about to speed through the stoplight when I see someone sitting in the front seat of Benny's van. It is the shape of two people actually, and it takes me a few seconds to understand that I am seeing two humans embracing in the half-light of the streetlamps, which have not been switched off yet. Another moment passes and I see my cousin holding another young man with short blond hair, the one I saw him talking to a few weeks ago, and like the third movement of a symphony, I watch all the separate pieces fall in place.

In the third week of October, Isobel goes for another cycle of chemotherapy and it isn't much better. This time she asks me to wait in the car. I ask her why and I know it's because she doesn't want me to see her looking weak. I tell her I don't think I can just wait in the car and it turns out I'm right.

When they wheel her out after her appointment, she looks to have aged about ten years. She refuses to even glance up at me. I get her across the parking lot in the wheelchair and drag her into the passenger seat. In the car, she is silent and I can imagine how hard she is trying not to vomit, not to cry. When we get home, she rushes inside and I sit on the front steps, wondering if I should follow or give her some space. I opt for the latter.

When I go inside later, she is nowhere around. Like some kind of injured animal, she has gone somewhere to hide. For some reason I suddenly find myself admiring her even more.

I go upstairs and check on my mother and find she's typing with a pencil stuck between her teeth. "How's the play coming along?"

She takes the pencil out and says, "I'm on the part about

Katie Holmes having to give birth in silence, according to the Church of Scientology. It's because they're afraid loud sounds can cause trauma and they don't want the baby to suffer spiritually."

"I don't know if any of that makes sense. I guess it kind of does, in a way."

"I think it's a nice idea, even if it's not true. But it became just another thing for the press to criticize them for. I mean, think about it, here she is giving birth and everyone is poking fun at them."

"I like how much you really think about them, like they're people you know."

"It's an extraordinary story. It's about triumph and failure and how none of us, even celebrities, can avoid misfortune." She puts the pencil in her teeth and goes back to typing.

I take Jazzy to school the next morning and find a pink foreclosure notice plastered to the door when I come back. I call the mortgage company and find out my mom's house is worth 47 percent less than what she and my father paid for it twenty-two years ago. It went from being something to being nothing, but believe me, the bank, the same bank where my sister works, keeps calling anyway. Later, as Isobel's washing Jazzy's hair in the bathroom, she tells me that 31 percent of the houses in our neighborhood are overmortgaged or underwater, meaning their houses are worth a lot less than what the owners originally paid for them. It's like living in a neighborhood, a city, that's sinking, collapsing, but ever so slowly.

I go by Alex's dorm room whenever she asks, a couple nights a week. She likes to read the books she's been assigned out loud to me. I put my head on her lap and she reads some novel or a book of poems to me but does it with an English accent, though not on purpose, it's just something she does, and as she is reading, I close my eyes and wonder about my future, about my family, about my sister and brother and her, and then, all of a sudden, I'm not thinking of anything.

One night I finally tell her about my hearing loss. The moment I choose to relay this important information is when we are sitting in the front seat of her father's car in the drive-through of a Taco Bell near the UIC campus. She gives me a sad look and then kisses the side of my face.

A few nights after that, we are at a stoplight and I tell her how I actually got expelled from community college for plagiarism on an essay about Bosnia. She just blinks. I think maybe she sees this as a challenge. She doesn't even sit there and offer some modest yet false kind of understanding. She just keeps looking at me like I am an actual person. Then she whispers something in my ear and I don't have the heart to tell her I can't hear it. But I can tell it is important from the way it feels against my cheek.

Later, we are parked in the corner of the university's parking garage and I can feel her studying my face like she is still making up her mind about something.

"Okay," she says, finally coming to some kind of answer.

I follow her up to her dorm room and we lie in bed looking at each other for a while, and then we begin to undress each other, carefully at first and then with more and more intensity.

Afterward, with the light from the streetlamps coming through the windows on our faces, she tells me she lied about going to Europe. "I'm sorry. It's something I do when I'm nervous. It's a bad habit."

I laugh. "It's a really funny thing to lie about."

"In high school, other kids would go to all these different places and so I just started saying we went on all these different trips too. My father, all he ever does is write and read. Once he took us to Arkansas. That's about it."

"That's too bad, because the only reason I was interested in you was because you were so worldly. So I guess we have to stop seeing each other."

She snorts and says, "I guess," and then someone starts laughing and then someone begins touching someone.

I come home from visiting Alex downtown and hear someone shouting from down the block. I pull up to the house on my ten-speed and listen to the windows rattle. Isobel and Billy. I notice that the cold has turned the grass white. It's quiet for a few moments and then someone shouts again and then I hear someone pounding the wall. I open the door and go to the kitchen to where Billy is sitting at the table eating a bowl of cereal like nothing is happening and Isobel is yelling at the back of his shaved head. Jazzy is also sitting at the kitchen table, coloring in her coloring book. I walk over to the table and say, "Jazzy and I are going for a walk."

Even though it's dark, we head over to Circle Park. I push her in the swings. Jazzy says she's too old for me to push and wants to do it herself so I let her, watching her struggle. Eventually she asks for a push. We wait at the park until our hands get numb.

When we come back, Isobel is picking up a broken bowl with her head down. It looks like some cereal has been tossed against one of the kitchen walls. "One of us is moving out," she murmurs with her back to me. "Either him or me."

"I don't think he was supposed to be living here in the first place," I tell her. "You need to focus on yourself. On taking care of yourself and your daughter. Jazzy needs you right now. She's having a hard time at school."

"I don't know if I can take care of anybody right now," she says.

I go to put a hand on her shoulder but she pushes it away, angrily.

Later we sit on the couch and watch a cop show. I look over and see how messed up she is. I look at her face and see a history of suffering, the Bosnians, the Poles. I know she is so much smarter than the rest of us and how frustrating it must be. I know she could have done something amazing, could still do something amazing if she only believed. But now it seems all she has is anger and I don't know how to help, what to say. In the middle of the program, she ends up getting up off the couch, grabbing her coat, and then disappearing through the front door into a rectangle of vivid light. As she does, I feel like all I can do is look away.

One day I get a call from my friend Chris KRS asking if I'm still looking for a job. I tell her I am and she tells me to meet her at what appears to be an abandoned day care facility on 79th and Western.

I pull up on my bike and put my face to the glass, placing my hand over my eyes like a visor, trying to see inside, but the windows have all been soaped out. There is a bootleg mural of recognizable cartoon characters—Mickey Mouse, Bugs Bunny— playing together, but the paint has chipped a long time ago.

Chris pulls up on her ten-speed and unlocks the front door after giving me a hug.

"How's art school?"

"Crazy. They let me paint naked women all day. I actually get credit for it."

I laugh. "That is crazy. So, what is this place?"

"My aunt owns it. They had to close down because of some insurance thing. But they need to put someone on the lease who doesn't have a criminal record. So I thought of you. Have you ever been to jail?"

"No," I say.

"Didn't think so. Here." She hands me a set of keys. "You're an assistant manager now."

"What do I have to do?"

"Don't worry, my aunt will handle everything. You can make your own schedule, but usually that means covering the shifts the other workers can't make."

"Is this legitimate? I mean, is this place actually legal?"

She looks at my signature and says, "It is now. There's all kind of money to be made in day care, man. Places like this can get grants from the state, all kinds of payouts, all you got to do is keep your nose clean."

"But what are my individual responsibilities?"

"Listen, it's day care," she says. "All you got to do is read them stories, change diapers, that kind of thing. You're not supposed to change diapers, but you're going to have to change diapers. You got a brother and a sister, right? You know what to do."

"Okay, but I'm not licensed or anything."

"No one is. It's day care. In Chicago. Nobody's licensed."

I look over and see there's an orange sticker that's been unsuccessfully peeled off the door, calling for the business's closure with a number of citations.

Chris puts her hand on my shoulder. "Also, look out for my aunt. She's half Filipino. She doesn't mess around."

I go by Alex's dorm that night to tell her the good news. She seems a little skeptical at first. Then she puts down the book she's reading and stares at me.

"Have you ever actually worked with kids before?"

"I mean, I have to take care of my little brother and I watch my niece all the time. And I did this creative writing thing with these kids on 55th Street up until a few months ago. I'm kind of looking forward to it."

I take a seat beside her on the bed. She's reading *Black Skin, White Masks* by Frantz Fanon.

"Is that book any good?"

"My father sent it to me. He's a history professor. He's a big deal in his department. He has this whole thing about race theory. He's written some books on it and everything."

"Oh yeah?"

"Like one of his theories is that without the concept of race, the United States couldn't exist. It needs race to maintain its economic conditions. It's why things don't really ever change. Cities like Chicago, they kind of depend on racial hierarchies in order to maintain order. So that white Europeans can keep their power and money."

I feel my face go flush. "Wow, I don't know," I say. "I mean, my grandfather came here in 1961. Back in Jugoslavia he was a musician, but here he had to work in a steel plant. He didn't have anything. No power, no money."

"But he was still able to find work. And save money. And buy a house. Lots of Black people weren't allowed to do that."

"I guess. I really don't know that much actually."

"I don't know that much either," she says, leaning her chin on her hands, "other than what my father tells me. He's an overachiever and so we all had to be overachievers too."

"I know what that's like. My parents had me playing piano when I was three."

"My father had me learn French from the time I was two. Believe me, having a father like him was way worse than anything you can imagine. All he ever talked about was being a credit and doing my family proud."

"I don't know. I guess I never talked about this kind of thing with anyone before. To be honest, I don't really feel like an American sometimes."

"What?"

"I don't know. I've always felt like I belong to some imaginary country, someplace my family made up."

"I've felt that way too."

"I feel like talking to you makes me a smarter person. Thanks."

"No problem." She grins and goes back to reading.

I suddenly wonder what this young woman is doing hanging out with me and how much longer it can possibly last.

Even though I don't have to, I ride over to the day care facility to be early on Thursday for the opening. I lock up my bike then clock in. Deedee, the owner, says I'm late and then tells me where to go. Everywhere there are kids with runny noses who are clawing at everything.

It's one thing to wipe the nose of a kid you are related to, someone you're obligated to keep clean, but it's another thing to go up to some snotty two-year-old you've never met and get in their face with some tissues. Before I know it, I'm over-

whelmed by the yelling, the crying, blinded by the acrid odor
of urine. I ask Deedee if I can wear my headphones and she
says as long as I can follow her directions, I can do whatever
I want. So I put my headphones on, find a spot where some
kids are drawing at a desk, and sing while drawing beside
them.

Over and over, I change diapers. A little kid cries and I
sing along with my headphones to block out the noise. The
kid stops crying as I make exaggerated faces. I finish changing him and put him on the ground and he asks to listen, so
I put the earphones over his ears and let him hear N.W.A's
"Express Yourself." Deedee looks over at me and shakes her
head. I change more diapers, put a bandage on a bloody knee.
I wipe fecal matter off the toilet seat. I try to keep toddlers
from biting each other and sometimes fail. I put the snack
out. I lead them in a game of tag. One of the kids won't let go
of my leg. Another looks at me and says, "Your face is too big.
I don't like you."

A kid named Oliver is three and has enormous glasses. He
is one of those children who already looks like an older version
of himself. As I am washing his face after snacks, he puts both
his hands over my ears. He stares at me like he is telling me
something, but I don't know what it is. And so I close my eyes
and at first all I hear is the chatter and noise of the kids around
us, and then I hear the muffled sound of his palms, and a
heartbeat, and I don't know whose it is, and I hear something
I have forgotten, quiet, which is at the center of everything.
In the last couple months, I have forgotten what it means to
be silent, to be in the moment and not have to worry, and like
that, the boy takes his hands away and for once I feel like I'm
not running.

* * *

One night we take Alex's father's car to Taco Bell. We go to the drive-through and order a ton of food and then eat it in the parking lot.

With my mouth full of burrito, I say, "I want you to know I have some strong feelings for you."

"What?"

"I said I have some strong feelings for you."

"I thought that's what you said. Well, that's good."

"No, I mean it," I say. I try to give her an earnest look. "These feelings I have for you. They're like really strong."

"If I understand you correctly," she says, "you have feelings which are strong."

"Exactly. For you."

"Great."

"It *is* great. It's pretty freaking great," I say.

"Good," she says laughing.

"Am I making you uncomfortable?"

"No." Then she looks down, clearly uncomfortable.

"You seem a little uncomfortable," I say.

"No way. I am totally comfortable talking about your feelings while I eat a burrito with you in a car."

"Cool. Because I don't want anything to be weird between us. I want us to be, you know, on the same page."

She smiles at me, then goes back to eating, brushing her bangs out of her eyes.

"Do you . . . you know . . . do you want to say anything to me?" I ask. It gets quiet for a moment as she is contemplating what to say.

"I like you. You're really funny. And I like that we can go to Taco Bell together."

"Cool." I wait a moment. "Is there anything else you want to say? About us? Or your feelings or anything?"

"I'm sorry. I thought we were eating."

"I just want you to know I'm serious about you. About us."

"Okay."

"I mean, what I'm trying to say is maybe we should think about taking this to the next level?"

"What does that even mean?" she asks and rolls her eyes.

"I really don't know."

"I like you," she says, shrugging. "I just don't know how much yet."

I nod.

Alex sighs and sets down her burrito. "And an uncomfortable silence enters the vehicle," she says with a frown.

"I'm sorry if I just messed this up. I just haven't been into someone like this in a long time."

She smiles and quietly goes back to eating.

It gets seriously awkward inside the cabin of the rusted-out Mercedes. It feels like I have probably said too much. We eat our sad burritos, sip our sad drinks. She drives me back to the train station and when I pull my bike out of the backseat it is like we are strangers, like we don't know each other at all.

In the last week of October, on a Wednesday, there is an orange sticker placed over the glass door of the day care. I pull up on my bike and see it has been closed for licensing violations. I'm supposed to be the assistant manager but I had no idea this was coming.

All around the way, nobody's hiring. When the mortgage bill arrives two days later, I get desperate and call my father, but he doesn't answer. I leave a message, knowing it's like waiting for the apocalypse—you wait for it and wait for it, and when it comes, it's like, *Why did I spend so much time waiting on this?*

A few days later, I go by the convenience store for a bottle of Yoo-hoo. I lock my bike up and see two people making out in the front seat of a car, faces shrouded by hooded sweatshirts. I ignore them, go inside, grab the drink, pay for it, and am on the way out when I notice it is Benny in a small blue hatchback laughing with the young man with blond hair.

Good for him, I think. *Let someone in this family finally find something resembling happiness.*

Before bed that night, Jazzy has a stomachache. I ask her what she ate for dinner and she says mac and cheese, which is all she ever eats. She asks for her mom but Isobel is nowhere to be found. Again. I try to get her calm and switch off the light, then go downstairs. After a few minutes, she gets up and rushes into the bathroom, and I can hear her beginning to get sick. She starts crying and I clean her up, try to get her back to bed. Another ten minutes goes by and she's back out of the bed, in the bathroom, with her head hanging over the toilet, crying again. I ask her what's wrong and she says it's her stomach. I rub her back and let her catch her breath.

I come down and find Daniel at the kitchen table and see he is pretending to be studying. I ask: "Where's Isobel?"

"I don't know. What's wrong?"

"Jazzy is making herself sick. Something is really bothering her."

"What is it?"

"I think it's school."

"Do you want me to try and go up there?"

I nod. "I think I'm going to go find Isobel. I'll be back in a while. Keep an eye on her."

I go out into the garage and grab my bike and start pedaling without having any sense of where I am going.

This is 99th. This is 103rd Street. This is 111th Street. This is Kedzie. This is Pulaski. It's cold because it is the end of October but I'm so angry I don't feel any of it. The streetlights flash over me like falling satellites. I ride, my thoughts going in circles as I blur through the neighborhood.

Fa. Fa. Fa. Fa. Fa. Fa. Fa. Fa.

I hear everyone saying as I ride by.

Fa. Fa. Fa. Fa. Fa. Fa. Fa. Fa.

I can hear them saying as I slow down.

This is the sign for bird.

This is the sign for sister.

This is the sign for hurt.

I pull my bicycle up to the first bar on Western Avenue. I pause and throw my bike against a fence and walk past a line of other twenty-year-olds waiting to get inside. I explain to the bouncer and he lets me in. I go around the bar once, then again, don't find her, and then force my way back outside.

I pedal to the next bar, then the next, all the way up and down Western—O'Flannagan's, O'Toole's, O'Leary's, with their fake Irish names and fake Irish decorations, fake Irish photographs, fake Irish history. I rush past the ruddy faces smelling of beer and sweat and perfume purchased at convenience stores, the classless droves of my neighborhood, the fake laughter, the commiseration of epic loneliness, all acknowledging that their generation will be the first in decades to make less than their parents. I go in and out of bars for the next hour and a half, and by the time I find her, I am so tired I can't even yell. I hear her laughter first, hear the shape of it hanging in the air, even with my hearing, even in the midst of this noisy crowd, as it is the one single sound I have come to rely on my whole life, the one thing I could always count on, and it just about breaks my heart. I find some of her coworkers, or who I assume are her coworkers, other people in cheap business attire, I recognize them from my mother's house, but Isobel is not among them and then I look around and see her jean jacket on the back of a chair, and I turn and go toward the restrooms and some terrible nineties music is playing and I go into the men's room which is empty and then I knock on the women's room door and no one answers and I go inside and find Isobel with one of her coworkers enjoying herself like she does not have a child at home, doing a line of what I assume is cocaine. I just stare at her until she looks up and stares back, as if she expected to find me here in the women's room of some idiotic bar on Western Avenue this whole time. I go over and don't say anything and lead her out and grab her coat and shove it at her and she shoves me back as she struggles to get it on and then we are outside, both of us breathing heavy, the cold coming down on us like a curtain, and I push her toward my bike and then she starts laughing, laughing with all the cruelty and anger she possesses, has carried around for the past four years.

"Be quiet. Get on the bike and go home. Your kid is waiting for you."

She sneers at me and refuses to take the ten-speed. "Why don't you mind your own fucking business for once?"

"I would love to. But someone keeps pushing all their problems on me. Which is actually what you *always* do. You make a mess and other people always have to clean it up."

She gives another brutal laugh and says, "I have cancer. I don't have to listen to this right now."

"Fuck you and fuck your cancer. Look at you. You need to stop feeling sorry for yourself and be a mom."

She slaps me hard across the face, which is something she has never done before. Ever. Both of us are so stunned, we just stand there, breathing in the cold night air. I put a hand to my face and laugh a little out of shock.

Finally we walk over to her car and I shove my bicycle in the back. She holds her hands on the steering wheel but doesn't start it up. We sit in the cabin of her car and watch the shapes our exhalations make. I reach into my back pocket and pull out my wallet. I have a folded-up check inside which has not been cashed for two hundred and twenty-five dollars, all my pay from before the day care folded. I flatten out the check and hand it to her.

"What's this?"

"If I give this to you, will you go away?"

"What?"

"Will you just go away and leave us alone for a while?"

"___"

"Will you please just leave? Until you get yourself together. Just for a while. Move in with Billy. Or somewhere else. Until you are better or ready to become a different person."

I can see the anger turn in her eyes. She crushes the check in her hand and tosses it at me. It bounces off my cheek and lands awkwardly between my feet. She grips the steering wheel even harder.

I say: "I don't know what else to do. What can I do? Tell me. What do you want me to do?"

We sit in her car for a long time, until finally she turns to me and murmurs, "I don't know what you want me to say. I'm not sorry. I'm just trying to get through this."

"I know."

"I know I messed things up. I know I need to make some changes. I just don't know how," and she begins crying. After a while she adds: "It's been a really bad year."

I put an arm out and hug her and am surprised to find her so close. We sit there for some endless length of time, waiting, watching as our breath, as the whole world, becomes visible and then invisible.

CHAPTER FOURTEEN

ONE MORNING AT THE BEGINNING OF NOVEMBER, I AWAKE before my brother and try to imagine another AMAZING COMPOSITION, putting together a single symphony for each passing hour, with instrumentalists playing different kinds of clocks—watches, cuckoo clocks, grandfather clocks— ending with all their alarms clanging at the same time. I lie there and listen to my ears ring, and when my brother's calculator wristwatch rings out, I know it's time to get up.

A half hour later, as I'm making breakfast, Daniel comes down and hands me a folded-up piece of green construction paper.

"What's this?" I ask, and he only shrugs. I open it and see he has drawn a picture of a submarine with a date and time.

"I'm launching my submarine this Saturday," he says. "I'd like it if you could be there."

"Oh, I don't know if this is a good idea, Daniel. I mean, do you have any clue what you're doing?"

"I've double-checked everything twice and it's perfect."

"Okay, I'll be there," I tell him. "But if it sinks, you're on your own."

He shrugs, grabs his backpack, and heads through the back door, hopefully for school.

Isobel comes down a few moments later. She sips a cup of coffee by the sink and says, "I think you should know, I haven't done anything illegal in over two weeks. I haven't even had a drink."

"Really?"

"Really."

"What about those people you hang out with from the bank?"

"I'm becoming incredibly boring. Exactly like you." Then she says something I've never heard her say before: "Thanks for looking out for me."

I am so shocked I don't know what to say. When I look up again, she is gone from the room.

I pick up Jazzy from school that day, and with her on the handlebars, we ride around looking for anywhere that is hiring. We also search for things to recycle: bottles, cans, old newspapers. We bust a lock with a rock and pick through the garbage behind the 7-Eleven and come up with treasure—two unopened bottles of Yoo-hoo. One of them is cracked but the other is in perfect condition. We share it and giggle accordingly, signing exclamations to each other, chocolate soda streaming down our faces.

Later we find a dozen balloons outside a used-car dealership on Western. Jazzy is the lookout while I carefully untie them. We ride off before we have any idea where we might sell them. We try a day care, a laundromat, and finally a funeral parlor, but no one's interested, so we let them go over Circle Park. As they lift into the air, my niece smiles, seeming to forget her troubles at school. I realize then that I have not seen her smile like that since she started kindergarten more than two months ago.

In the evening, I take the train down to UIC, pretending to be just another undergraduate student, stroll the campus, wait for Alex to finish class. We hang out in her dorm room for a while, go to a cheap restaurant, then I watch her study. Essentially, we are still kids, even though we are twenty. Alex spent all of her life overachieving, then started partying late in high school, and then barely finished. Apparently she got a reputation for being easy, then stopped going out anywhere at all. She explains this is why she cannot get distracted, why she cannot mess up again. I listen and nod and wait for her to finish her assignments and then the two of us fall asleep together. Everything from that point on gets even more serious.

Soon I begin to sleep over at her dorm room every other night. We make our way through her extensive DVD collection of classic French movies. One evening she cuts my hair, spreading out newspaper on the floor of her dorm, snipping my ear and making a general mess of things on one side. Her bed is so small I usually end up falling on the floor. But I don't mind. In the morning, I wake up before her and read one of her books. We pretend not to be falling for each other even though both of us already have.

My father finally calls me back. I tell him the situation about being out of work and the mortgage being six months late and he says he can use my help. He instructs me to meet him on the corner of Pulaski and 103rd, and when I climb in his van, he has two cups of Dunkin' Donuts coffee and some donuts. It's eight p.m. and already it's pitch black outside like light itself will never return to the world.

"Where are we going?" I ask as I buckle up.

"What do you know about architecture?"

"Not much. The Sears Tower, that's about it."

"You're going to learn a lot by the end of the night," he tells me.

The first place we stop is a foundry or steel plant of some kind, way over on the eastside of Chicago. The hulking skeletal structure has a pitched metal roof and an enormous fence that seems to run for miles in both directions.

"This is where both of your grandfathers used to work. I worked here a little while in the eighties before it closed. Lot of Bosnians, lot of Poles."

"What are we doing here?"

"I've got a friend who works security. He told me about some pieces that were being moved or thrown away."

"But what are we doing?"

"Picking up."

"Picking up what?"

Outside it is brutally cold, the kind where your toes begin to lose feeling within moments. My father stops the van, climbs out, unlocks one of the gates, drives the van through, and then locks the gate again. He pulls up to one of several outbuildings. There are dozens of piles of rusted-looking tools, forklifts, gears, engines. One by one, he inspects them, and asks me to help carry various pieces back to the van. Once we're inside his vehicle again, he turns up the heat and blows on his hands. He blows the steam from the cup of coffee and takes a sip.

"When your grandfather came over here, he said this is the only place that would hire him. In my twenties, I worked here awhile too. I guess there was a time, back in 1981 or '82, when there were four or five different time cards with the name Fa on them. Your grandfather and me, plus a few cousins we didn't even know, all working here. The city practically began and ended here for a lot of Bosnians and Poles. They worked here, then would go back to their own neighborhoods, churches, where other Bosnians and Croats and Poles all lived. It was like they came here, found work, then tried to recreate their villages back home, in the middle of the southside. All of this, until they closed this place down in the nineties."

Someone flashes a light outside. My father turns to me and smiles and says, "Stay here."

He climbs out again, slipping on his gloves, and goes to shake hands with a man who is dressed in a hooded coat. It says *Security* on the back of his coat in yellow. His face is vaguely Balkan or Eastern European. My father slips the guard something for his trouble, then pats him on the shoulder and climbs back inside the van.

"Just so you know. There's places like this all over the city, sitting vacant, full of treasure. You only have to know where to look, how to listen. I can get a couple hundred bucks for all of this stuff. The Internet makes everything easy now."

The second stop is a Chicago Public Library branch that's been recently closed.

"You probably don't know all this, but when the Bosnians began coming over here right before World War I, a lot of them ended up in Chicago. On the southside. A lot ended up in construction or in manufacturing. So our ancestors helped build this entire city. All those buildings downtown, those were built by your people."

I don't know what I feel after he says this. I watch him take out a pair of bolt cutters and snap the chain on the fence. He pulls the van past the fence and there, near the back of the single-story building, are some ornate cornice pieces of limestone in the shape of owls. He motions for me to come out. I follow and have no idea why we're standing in the dark. He quietly pulls a ladder off the roof of his truck and sets it up alongside the building.

Over the course of the next three hours, we steal three beautiful cornice pieces. We also very carefully pull down elaborate limestone work with baroque, hand-chiseled details—a face, a globe, a book—and one by one we strip the rear entrance of the library bare, wrapping each piece in a heavy towel before setting it in the back of the van.

From eight p.m. to three in the morning, we pull up to abandoned building after abandoned building, removing any trace of grandeur, any sense of history, from their facades.

I do it every night for the next week because I need the money and it's also the only way I get to see my father. I pay off some of the mortgage and then put some money aside for the overdue water and electricity bills.

After going by the bank, I am so overjoyed that I don't know what to do, so I ride by the water-reclamation plant, which, even in the cold, still has a lovely pink haze to it. I stare over the chemically treated water. I see some geese crossing in the sky, see the formation they make like an arrow piercing the chest of some unnamed, foreign saint.

It seems like something Alex would enjoy, like a painting in one of the books on modern art she is always reading.

* * *

I go pick up Jazzy from school later that day and my niece has tears in her eyes. When we get home Isobel happens to be there and so she is able to kneel down and give Jazzy a hug. She emails the teacher and makes an appointment to talk with her after school. Then she asks me if I'd be willing to come with.

"As long as I don't have to say anything," I tell her.

The next afternoon we wait in front of the classroom like we are in trouble and I can see how nervous Isobel is by the way she is tapping her foot.

Finally, the teacher calls us in and it is exactly like we are both in grade school, even though this teacher is only a few years older than us. Ms. Pascal is how she introduces herself, which I find slightly odd, as all of us are adults. Already there is an air of condescension between us. Isobel keeps adjusting her skirt.

"It sounds like you have some concerns about Jazz."

I watch my sister try on her best fake smile. "We know she's been having a tough time and we're only a few months in. We want to know what we can do to support her."

I nod, glad to hear Isobel talking like a professional.

"We love Jasmine," the teacher says, referring to herself in the fourth person. "We think she is an amazing kid."

"Okay, good, we do too. You're aware she has a hearing disability. And she could use some support. Last year the school was able to get a grant and have an aide help her out."

"We told your brother," and here Ms. Pascal shines a frustrated little smile my way, "that those accommodations are up to the family to try to implement."

Isobel looks over at me and I can see the anger beginning

to rise. "Okay, but we could use your help in navigating some of those questions. So how can we do that?"

"You need to request accommodations through the administration. I believe you need a doctor to recommend whatever accommodations they think are necessary."

Isobel's eyebrows become violently sharp. Before she can utter something inappropriate, I say, "Last year, Ms. Green requested support. So we're just trying to figure out what we need to do."

"Unfortunately, I am not Ms. Green. We have twenty-four other children in this classroom. We definitely recommend you try to make arrangements for accommodations on your own."

It ends with a tense silence then. I can hear the electricity vibrating in the fluorescent lights overhead before my sister and I get to our feet.

Back in the car, my sister looks at me and puts together some exceptional curses. She turns the radio on, then immediately switches it off. "She doesn't want to deal with Jazzy's hearing problem. She wants to act like it's not her responsibility."

"She's young so maybe she's got her hands full with the other kids."

"Well, that's too bad. Being a teacher means being a teacher of *all* the kids, not just the ones who get it. Jazzy is as smart as those other kids. She just needs help."

Isobel backs the car out of the lot. I look over at her and feel proud, even if, at the moment, she's glowing with rage.

On Saturday, Benny and I go to the launch of Daniel's submarine. It is the second week of November and the wind is freezing, seems to hang over our winter clothes like icy sheets. Benny and I wait in his van until my brother appears on his bicycle. He has hooked the three-foot submarine up to the back of his bike and somehow pedals it over to the desolate-looking pond near the community college. The sub is black with a round bubble of plastic on top and wheels on the back. Daniel unhooks the submarine and begins to drag it toward the pond. No one is around. I keep waiting for a security guard or police officer to stop us but none do.

Together we help Daniel slide the sub to the shore of the pond where it miraculously floats and then he climbs inside. Somehow, even more miraculously, the motor starts, and we hear the propeller upsetting the surface of the water. Daniel gives me an uncertain look and asks, "Where's Isobel?" and I shrug and say, "Maybe it's too cold for her."

He hands me a stopwatch. "I'd like to see how long I'm able to go under for."

"Sure."

He nods toward me in a serious way. "Ready."

"Ready." I nod back and he motions toward the plastic bubble, which has to be locked in place from the outside apparently. Of course, this seems like a gigantic safety concern, but I don't say anything. Benny and I wrestle the clamp into place and give the black and silver submarine a push. Off it goes, descending into the water.

I don't know if I can accurately describe what happens next. What happens is, for a few seconds the submarine behaves wonderfully, it does everything you imagine a submarine is supposed to do. It drifts away from the shore, toward the center of the pond, and starts to describe a small circle as it sinks deeper and deeper. Finally you can only see the very top of the plastic bubble and then, eventually, that sinks too. Several large bubbles rise to the surface. Benny and I look at each other, amazed and terrified.

"Should we . . . ?" he asks and begins removing his winter jacket.

Eight seconds later, the submarine unexpectedly rises and then turns perilously on its side. I see Daniel pounding on the inside of the plastic bubble with the palms of both hands.

Benny and I look at each other and begin pulling off our coats and shoes and wade ankle-deep into the freezing water. By then, the sub has propelled itself near the shore on its right side but Daniel is still trapped, trying to loosen the plastic bubble himself. We make our way over to him and unclasp the clamp and he starts coughing and pulls himself out as black smoke pours from the overheated motor. In the end, all three of us sit on the shore, shivering and out of breath.

"It failed," Daniel says, his teeth chattering. "Everything I do is a failure."

"No, it completely worked," I tell him. "Look. I mean, technically it was submerged for eight seconds."

"At least eight seconds," Benny adds.

"Eight seconds is a lot longer than I actually thought it would be," my brother says, quietly proud, raising his chin. We help him drag the submarine out of the icy water and then he hooks it up to the back of his bicycle. All of us ride home together, the van following Daniel's bicycle and submarine, like a very short, unpopular parade.

Later that same night, I become invisible, following my father into another empty building. Once we have pulled all the architectural pieces from the historical facades all over the southwest side, we go through a number of apartment complexes which have all been foreclosed. Inside one boarded-up apartment, I find a box in the corner of a closet filled with baby clothes. I look through a photo album on top of the box and find pictures of a woman who was pregnant, but there are no photographs of the baby being born. I realize that maybe the box has been left there on purpose.

I look over at my father pulling copper pipes out of the ceiling of a basement apartment. "Can I ask you something?"

He nods.

"How did you end up marrying Mom? I mean, how did the two of you end up together?"

There is plaster dust in the stubble of his short hair. Even though it is close to December, the basement is warm. My father looks up and smiles softly and pauses his work. "I saw her dancing and I liked her legs. And her laugh. We went out a few times. But even then I knew it probably wouldn't work out in the end."

"But why did you get married, if you didn't think it was going to work?"

He hands me another piece of cut pipe as quietly as he can. He wipes his forehead with the back of his coat and shrugs. "Why do people do anything?"

I put the hammer down for a second and stare at him even though he does not seem to notice. A coldness creeps in. I realize I am only pretending, that I don't actually know this person at all.

Later that same night we are pulling more copper from a retirement home that recently went out of business and I look over and say it, holding the pipe in place: "I don't know what I'm supposed to be doing here."

"You're supposed to be pulling copper. Go ahead and cut it here."

"No, I mean like why are we doing this? We're taking pipes from a retirement home."

"So?"

"So why?"

"We're doing what we need to survive."

"But it's not like we're robbing mansions. We're not up in the Gold Coast. This is some old folks' home." I hold my breath for a moment and then let it all go. "I don't know if I want to do this anymore."

"Do what?"

"I'm not like you. You make up reasons. You do the wrong thing and make up reasons for it."

"We're talking about making a living, kid. We're talking about survival. We're talking about who gets to live. You have to put yourself first. You just haven't figured it out yet."

I look away and sit stupidly in the dark. I put the hammer down and wait.

He doesn't pay me at the end of the night and I don't call him the next day. I wait by the corner the following evening but he never shows. I wait and I wait and it is like I am thirteen waiting for him to come by all over again. The wind gets stuck humming inside my ears. Finally I climb aboard my bike and ride home, cold and alone.

A few evenings later, there's a knock at the door in the middle of the night. I come down in my pajamas and Benny is in his winter coat holding a large CVS box in his arms. He gestures toward the van and I yawn and walk over and find several CVS boxes full of Halloween costumes.

"What's all this?"

"Discounted Halloween costumes. The store was going to toss them out."

"I thought you gave up this sort of thing."

"If they were going to throw it out, it doesn't count as stealing. And it was too good to pass up. We can sell these next year before Halloween and make some money. Besides, I thought Jazzy would like them. Who doesn't like Darth Vader or the fancy ballerina?"

On top of the box, there's an off-brand *Star Wars* uniform, a ballerina costume, a withered-looking Dracula cape, and several silvery-white ghost costumes with opaque black eyes. One by one, we stack them inside the garage and then I crawl back to my bed which is no longer warm.

In the morning I come down to breakfast and Daniel is sitting at the table, wearing one of the ghost outfits.

I shout and jump in shock but Daniel doesn't move. He just lifts the spoon of cereal to where his mouth should be and pretends to be eating.

One afternoon I call Alex and ask how she's doing. She says midterms are coming up and that she has to study. I feel like she's blowing me off. But then an hour later she calls back and asks if I want to come over.

"Just for a few hours," she says.

I take the train up and right away we get in a fight about I don't know what, something about how I expect too much and may have arrested development, and I know she won't be asking me to come by again. I sleep in her bed beside her but it's exactly like sleeping alone.

As I am riding back from the train the next morning, I no-

tice building by building, house by house, parts of our neighborhood have begun to vanish.

Here's how a neighborhood, an entire part of the city,
looks as it falls apart. First the White Hen convenience store
becomes a 7-Eleven. A few months after that it closes. The
video store that has managed to hang on for decades finally
goes under. Nothing goes in its place, its front windows staying permanently black. The Baskin-Robbins vanishes. All that
is left is the Chinese takeout where they won't accept credit
cards after being ripped off too many times. One by one other
businesses go under, until everything, even the air, feels empty.

Over the following week, Daniel, too, begins to disappear.
One second he is sitting at the kitchen table or reading comics
in his room, and the next he's gone. It's like watching someone slowly fade right in front of your eyes. I get suspicious.
Is he using drugs? Vandalizing other peoples' homes? Going
back to stealing strangers' belongings from the airport? Other
existential dangers are always present. There is delinquency,
pregnancy, drug abuse, somnambulance, overstimulation, cigarette burns, infected tattoos. One has to wonder, as a young
man at this particular moment, in this particular time, in this
particular place, at all the different opportunities a person like
him has to fail.

Before he goes to school on Wednesday, I watch him put the
ghost costume on over his winter coat then drag his bicycle
out of the garage. I shake my head, embarrassed on his behalf.
Moments later I follow on my own bicycle from half a block
behind, see his black and green backpack bobbing along. He
turns down a street near the park and then hops off his bike
and walks it up the driveway of a ranch house that's for sale.

He enters through the side walkway, lays his bicycle down in the grass, and lifts himself awkwardly over the wood fence. Then he is gone.

I put my bike down and walk slowly over to the back fence and see his leg disappear up into a gigantic oak tree. There are still some leaves in the branches, which obscure where he is sitting high up on a wide limb, still wearing the ghost costume. I watch him open his backpack and pull out a large library book and then he starts reading at the top of the tree. I wait for a while before I realize that he's actually studying.

Before he climbs down, I pedal off on my bike and wonder what is going to happen to him or any of us.

The next day I get a part-time job mopping floors at a rehabilitation center for people who have just had surgery. It's across from an abandoned shopping mall, which makes it somewhat surreal. It's like the patients can see real life happening outside but most of them will never return to it. There is a small forest nearby. Sometimes you can see deer going in and out of the mall's long, rectangular parking lot, picking their way through the overturned shopping carts. When that happens, all of the patients crowd around the windows, wheelchairs and crutches all knocking against each other, a beautiful catastrophe.

On the second floor, inside the recreation room, there is a large glass cage with two orange lovebirds inside. I spend as much time as I can watching them prune each other's feathers and speculate about how they know each other: are they siblings, mates, only friends, fellow prisoners? It's hard to tell by how much they both seem to irritate and need each other.

* * *

Daniel comes home from school that afternoon with good news. He's smiling so much I almost don't recognize him.

"What is it?" I ask but he just sits there smirking. Finally he tells me that, after months of studying, he has qualified for the Academic Bowl team and that his first competition is in December.

"I can see how much work you put into this. You should be really proud of yourself," I tell him.

He only shrugs and then goes back to staring out the window and grinning by himself.

A few days after that, Alex calls and says we need to talk. I ride to the train on my bicycle, take the train up to UIC— the whole way wondering what's on her mind, what might be wrong. I knock on her dorm room door and see she's been crying. The mascara on her cheeks looks like it's been there awhile, overnight possibly. She doesn't say anything, just goes and sits on the bed.

I take a seat beside her and ask, "Wait, what happened? What's going on?"

"I think I'm pregnant," she says. I try to look at her then but she refuses to look back at me.

"Really? Are you sure? I mean, I don't . . . I mean, I don't know what to say."

"I don't either. Nothing like this has ever happened to me before. I was so stupid. I don't know why I did this."

"Both of us were stupid."

"No. I should have known better. I should have been more focused on school and then none of this would have ever happened."

"Do you know what you want to do?"

"I know I'm twenty-one. And I'm definitely not having a baby right now."

"Okay. I can get some money together, and you know, we can take care of it."

She sighs and gives the slightest nod. I stand up and think about kissing her but I don't.

I get back home, go through my things—but because it's near the end of the month, I've got no money. I stand in the bedroom, look at my brother's bed, and begin to search underneath it.

I find his blue shoebox and lift off the lid. Inside is a tiny notebook with a list of all the rare comic books he's working on acquiring through online auctions. The notepad is opened to a page that says, *Fantastic Four 48, first appearance of Galactus and Silver Surfer VG 4.0,* in his tight, neat writing. Beneath the notebook is an envelope with two hundred forty dollars inside. I don't know how much the procedure will cost exactly but I have to hope that this will be close. I take out the money and then place the shoebox back beneath the bed.

After that there are no words. Nothing to describe the institutional setting of the women's clinic, the distant politeness of the nurse, the young women crying next to their mothers, the disconsolate look on Alex's face, the silence, the awful endless silence, so I won't even try. You just need to know it's a place I don't want to go back to ever again. I am appalled by how quiet everything is as I drive Alex back to the dorm in her father's car. No one makes a sound. All the lights on her street are off, like everything's over for good.

I put the car keys on her dresser, ask if she needs anything. She tells me no and I stand there for a long time before closing the door behind me.

Somehow I get lost riding back to the train station and end up on Lower Wacker Drive, with its dank tunnels that roam circuitously beneath downtown like something out of a low-budget postapocalyptic movie. There is no sidewalk to ride on, nowhere to get away from the traffic, and the blare of headlights and honking horns nearly sends me flying from my bike. Finally I find the exit and return to street level to find faint stars dotting the sky above the tallest skyscrapers. But I don't feel like I deserve any of it.

The train ride home is the kind where all of your thoughts are manifested in the burned-out facades of the city flying past. Each rattle of the train over the tracks feels like being shaken out of a dream. Then the grim silence of all the tired workers returning home in the late afternoon. Even the quiet, the moments in between other noises, is filled with regret.

Back at home, I walk my bicycle into the garage. Before I get up the front steps, Daniel is already out of the house yelling, grabbing my coat.

"What the heck, Daniel? What is your problem?"

"You took my money! You took it and didn't even say anything! You . . ." he murmurs and then repeats, "You ruin everything," and then it gets bad. He yells some kind of inhuman, primal yell and tries to tackle me and then I have to grab him by the shoulders and wrestle him to the ground. We roll around like imbeciles on the frozen grass in the near dark. My brother is howling and crying and spitting and I'm afraid if I let him go, he will claw my eyes out.

"Calm down!" I say.

He catches me under the eye with one of his fists and screams, "You calm down! You calm down!"

I shove him off and shout, "Why do you have to be like this? Why do you have to make a nuisance of yourself?"

"Because!" he shouts. "Because!"

It is then that my mother comes out on the front porch. Barefoot, in her blue nightgown, she quietly walks over to the coiled-up garden hose on the side of the house and sprays it in both our faces. My brother and I are immediately soaked. I get up and stand on the sidewalk, holding my cheek where my brother has hit me.

"You people are all crazy," is all I can say.

I grab my bike and ride around for the next couple of hours. When it is sufficiently late and sufficiently dark, sometime past eleven o'clock, I pull back up the driveway. The garden hose is still running along the side of the house. I go over and shut it off and look up at our bedroom window. Then I go inside and find all the lights are on. As quietly as I can, I go through the house, shutting each light off. It is like a prayer of some kind. Finally I go upstairs and see our bedroom door halfway open. I see the shape of my brother, his shadow sitting cross-legged on the floor, reading a children's book he used to love, which came with a 45rpm record to read along with. I listen to him reading with the record for a few moments before heading downstairs to sleep on the couch.

In the morning, I wake up to Jazzy pulling on my ear. She is saying something but I can't make it out. The shape of the sound feels like a hummingbird beating against the side of my cheek, light and sharp. I search the shape of the word she is making and realize she is signing the word *Mom*.

I follow her upstairs and peek at Isobel, sitting in her room, still in her pajamas, softly playing a variation by Beethoven on the cello, her eyes closed, the bow moving carefully back and forth, in a kind of trance. Moments later she opens her eyes and sees us standing there and the bow drops to her side.

Both Jazzy and I clap and Isobel politely bows.

Daniel comes out from the bedroom and asks what is going on. I give him a hug and he looks at the bruise under my eye and says, "Are you all right? I didn't mean to use my full power on you. I don't know my own strength."

"I'll be okay," I tell him, and we all go down to breakfast.

In the last week of November, my grandfather tells me he has been feeling poorly so I convince my sister to drive all of us to Blessed Alojzije Stepinac Croatian Church on the far northside to kiss the hand of Blessed Kata, whose mummified body is kept in the church basement, after first being killed by Chetnik soldiers in 1941. According to my grandfather, a group of Croatian priests are responsible for transporting the saint's body from Croatian church to Croatian church around the world. If you kiss her hand you will have a long life, wealth, and health, which makes about as much sense as any of his other stories.

My grandfather, Isobel, Jazzy, Daniel, and myself all squash into my sister's hatchback. When we pull up, there is a long line of stern-looking Croatians standing out front in the snow. We help my grandfather out of the car and get in line. I do not know what I am going to do when it is our turn. Maybe just stand beside my grandfather and then help him walk off. Forty-five minutes go by as we move inside the church, then closer to the altar, then down a flight of stone steps behind the sacristy.

Finally we are in a mildewed basement full of pipes and electrical supplies and when the aged priest in golden vestments motions us forward, my grandfather leans over and kisses the air over the Little Shepherdess's hands. The body looks like a doll of some kind and is buried beneath ornate silver and red robes. I look down and see a pair of incredibly tiny silver shoes and, forgetting myself for a second, I do what my grandfather has just done. Even though I am an unbeliever, I kiss the open air above one of her mummified hands, praying for all of us to be different, for everything to change.

I come outside and the snow is falling, and back inside the car, somehow, Daniel and Isobel are already arguing, both their voices sounding indestructible and brilliant.

CHAPTER FIFTEEN

ONE AFTERNOON IN DECEMBER I COME HOME FROM DROPping Jazzy off at kindergarten and listen to how the cold has changed every sound: how differently the air resonates, becoming crystalline and brittle, how timorous the birds are, only alighting for a moment on a near-empty branch; even the sunlight sounds more distant, with its faint echo of heat. I wonder if it is just my hearing. I look up and see a white shape at the top of a barren tree near the end of the block, a ghost reading an old encyclopedia. I pause for a moment and stare at my brother and discover he has built an entire room up there. There is a canteen, a scarf, and a transistor radio that he has attached to one of the limbs by a strap. It takes me another moment to realize it is a Wednesday and he should be in school.

I call up to him and he waves, pretending not to hear. Eventually I give up and have to ride to work.

One morning that same week, I hear someone cursing from the bathroom, down the hallway. It is not just any cursing, it is glorious, expansive, filthy, and I quickly realize it's Isobel. The way she curses is like a disruption of language itself, combining sound, color, nouns, verbs, adverbs, a collision of meaning and emotion, into a completely improvised performance. I peek my head in the bathroom and see her hands shaking as she puts on eyeliner. She smudges it, swears, then tries again, dabbing on light-blue eye shadow. "I'm trying to look like an adult for once," she says. When she is done, she tilts her head forward to brush her blond hair, and then lifts her head back up, and all at once she is unrecognizable. All anybody can do is smile at such a transformation.

When Isobel comes downstairs for breakfast, she kisses Jazzy on the top of the head. They eat cereal side by side, mimicking each other. Daniel arrives a few minutes later wearing his ghost costume. I watch him gnaw his frozen waffles under the edge of the costume and ask if he knows Halloween has been over for a while and he says he does. "Then why are you wearing that?" I ask, and he only shrugs, still eating.

Isobel tells him he looks insane and asks him to take the costume off and then Jazzy sneaks up behind my brother and pulls on the sheet and there is a terrific wrestling match, and everyone is on the ground laughing, but when it is over we all notice Daniel has shaved off his eyebrows, and we ask why and he says because he thought they were too big and we tickle him some more and he says it was to impress a girl in his history class and that he accidentally cut too much off trying to trim his eyebrows, then had to do the other, and so he put on the ghost costume to draw attention away from his face, and we turn him loose and he calls us all manner of insults, but we see he is also smiling happily.

I put up my hood on my winter coat and ride to work and try to think of new AMAZING COMPOSITIONS. The sun peeks through the top of the barren-looking pines. Even though my hands inside my gloves and my feet inside my sneakers are freezing, the frost has made poetic etchings on all the car windows. I stop at a stoplight and think: *What is one symphony, one melody that captures all of this, the totality of human experience, the birds, the sun, the weather, the feeling of cold in your hands, and everything, one day late in winter 2008?*

Later I stand before the orange birds at work and try to get them to say my name, even though I am not sure if they know how to talk. I finish feeding them and I look over at the calendar behind the nurses' station and I realize it is December 5 and that I have not talked to Alex in two weeks. The thought makes me feel both sad and embarrassed. I call her once on a break, then again after work, and get no answer.

The next day I take the train over to UIC and try to talk to her one more time. When she comes out for her twelve thirty class, I say hello, but she seems to ignore me. I keep trying to talk to her as we cross the campus, pushing my bicycle beside me, trying to keep up. Eventually she walks over to the bus stop and turns up her earphones.

"Alex. Can we please just have an intelligent conversation for a second?"

I stare at her and recognize again how she is way too smart, way too pretty for me. I notice her winter jacket is slightly torn on her shoulder and wonder how that happened. I almost reach out and touch it. I look down Halsted and see the bus approaching, know it will be there in less than a minute.

"Alex," I whisper, "don't you still like me? Don't you like how it was? I think you still do. Please just talk to me."

But she doesn't say anything.

"I mean, if you still like me, if you like how it was, then I don't think you should leave. Just stay and talk for a second."

I see the bus stopping a few blocks away. I've only got about thirty seconds left. I look up and see two old ladies at the bus stop, huddled together, scoping us out.

"Alex," I say.

"What?" But she doesn't even look at me.

"Don't go. Just stay. Just stay for sixty seconds."

I turn to her and think maybe this is the last time I will ever see her. And I think, *What is the one word, the one phrase that could save this?* but even as I'm thinking it I know there isn't any. She waits her turn in line and climbs up and the bus driver looks at me to see if I'm getting on, but somehow both the driver and I know I'm not, and he gives me a look of sad knowledge and the bus doors fold closed. Once she's seated, I do the only thing I can think of, which is to wave, and she gives me a small, sad frown and waves back, and right then the bus pulls away.

Through the unclear glass I can see the look on Alex's face, then the look on all of the passengers' faces, all of them staring, the grandmothers, a security guard, a minister, an eight-year-old girl with pink barrettes, they are only a blur that fades to a smudgy gray. I walk beside the bus and Alex seems to be saying something, she is looking at me and saying something, but I can't tell what it is and this is the last thing she will ever say to me and then the bus is gone.

For the next four or five minutes I stand there in the cold. The wind is all I can hear, carrying echoes from other parts of the city. Eventually I give up and ride back on my bicycle to the train.

The next day, Daniel comes home from school with his backpack over his shoulder, rushing past me into the kitchen. His eyes look small and dark and some of his hair is hanging in his eyes.

"Hold up. Where's your costume?"

"They took it."

"Who did?"

"At school. The assistant principal."

"You wore it to school?"

He shrugs, his back to me. "The other day. They took it."

"Daniel, what's going on?" I ask.

"Nothing."

"Come on, tell me." I motion to the table and he sighs and slowly sits down, refusing to look me in the eye. "What is it?"

"I just don't like going to school anymore."

"What about the Academic Bowl team? I thought you were excited about that."

"The assistant principal is the coach. He's awful. All he ever does is yell. He took away some of my comic books today."

"Why?"

"I was reading them during practice instead of participating and he took them and now he won't give them back."

"But that's on you. You know better than that. You need to apologize and ask for them back."

He nods and I think we're okay. But then later that night I go upstairs to ask him what he wants for dinner and find he is gone. I sit on his bed and wonder where he is and feel like nothing good can come from this.

On her last chemotherapy appointment in early December, Isobel throws up in her car four times, which sets a new record. After I clean it out, we commemorate this accomplishment, marking it as a particular kind of triumph. Back at home, I hand her one of Daniel's academic trophies and she laughs but also threatens to throw it at my head.

After what seems like two months of filling out paperwork

and making phone calls, Isobel gets an email that says Jazzy has finally been approved for an in-school aide. It's only a few hours a week, but it will still mean a lot to her.

I stand over my sister's shoulder and read the email once, then again, and can see in her face how proud she is. We give Jazzy the good news that night at the kitchen table. For dinner I cook pancakes, which are Jazz's favorite, and when Isobel tells her that she will be getting an aide, Jazzy asks: "Will they be a boy or girl? And will they have stickers?"

Isobel brings her to school and introduces her to a middle-aged African American woman named Miss Sheila. Apparently the first thing Miss Sheila does is put a sticker on the back of Jasmine's hand, which she refuses to remove for the next several days.

In the middle of December, Daniel has a hard time getting out of bed. I go wake him up once, then again. I go back downstairs and make him peanut butter and jelly toast. I go back upstairs and find him still asleep in his underwear. I pull off the blankets and drag him to the floor and finally he gets dressed.

Before I know it, he has finished eating and says he is ready to go. Out in front of our house, I watch him walk his bicycle from the garage before grabbing my own bike and telling him to have a good day. The sun is in his eyes. His hair looks momentarily golden. He puts his hand on my shoulder and says, "Thanks."

I say, "For what?'"

He says, "For being my brother," and then looks back at the house, and it was then I should have known something wasn't right.

But now it's easy. Only later did we see.

Daniel rode to school and waited in the parking lot and instead of going directly inside, he hid behind the squat brick building, sitting on a curb. Approximately twenty minutes later, Mr. Callahan, the assistant principal, pulled up in his blue Toyota, parked, switched the ignition off, grabbed his things, and climbed out of his car. Apparently Daniel had been just sitting there, wearing the ghost costume and carrying his bow and several arrows in his backpack. Once the assistant principal went inside, Daniel took out the bow and went over and shot the Toyota's tires full of arrows. Just as he was about to make his escape, Mr. Callahan returned, having forgotten his lunch, and saw Daniel in the ghost costume, hurrying off. It was the ghost costume that gave him away, the assistant principal later said. Before my brother could get to his bicycle, he tripped over the costume and then Mr. Callahan tackled him and a security guard came running to intervene. A commotion ensued and Daniel tried to get free, kicking Mr. Callahan in a sensitive place. Yelling was heard afterward, by several teachers and administrators, as Daniel tried to call for help.

Daniel later said he had attacked the assistant principal's car for taking his costume and comic books away and refusing to give them back. And also that the school, under the current administration, suffered from a complete and total lack of imagination and bordered on a fascist dictatorship.

But none of us had any idea what happened for several hours.

Only later, after I speak with Mr. Callahan, who leaves several angry voice messages, do I come to find out what has happened. Even now, I think of my brother determined to avenge himself, but doing such a bad job of it, and don't know how to feel. When I get home from work, I listen to the voice mails from the assistant principal and find out that the police have been called and that Daniel has been taken into custody.

In that moment, I realize that I have failed as an older brother, as a sibling, as even the lowliest sort of friend. I sit at the kitchen table with the phone in one hand, listening to one voice mail after another buzzing in my right ear like a condemnation, and sink into a despair so deep, so black, as to be heretofore unrecognizable.

It takes Isobel and me an hour to figure out where they have taken Daniel and even then they don't make it easy for us. At the police station on 111th, there is a hassle because no legal guardian is present and Daniel is underage. I give them my ID and say I'm in charge and that my mom is ill, but they don't let me see him at first.

One of the cops finally takes pity on me and lets me go talk to him in a small interrogation room. Daniel smiles when I come in and I see he has a blue-black eye, and something about his expression reminds me of how young he is. After he hugs me, he refuses to talk so we sit there in silence. I wonder, *What does it mean to hold on to every failure, every grudge, your family's history, the history of the entire past, what does it mean to always have it hanging over your head?*

I look over and see it all there in his eyes, in his expression, this inability to let anything go. Soon a different cop comes in and tells us that because Daniel is thirteen and struck an adult, he has to go to family court. He can either go to juvenile detention or be put in a facility for young people with mental illness for an evaluation. But it's entirely up to the judge.

The next morning, the family court judge, a woman with a kind face, decides Daniel should go to a mental health facility for an evaluation. Daniel lets out a low moan and begins to cry.

Benny drives me downtown the next day to visit my brother.

We get lost looking for the facility, which is a block from the lake, near Lawrence. When we finally find it, an administrator won't let us in. "He's in process," one of the orderlies says. He hands me a document and I read:

ALL VISITORS, EXCLUDING CHILDREN UNDER 17 YEARS OF AGE, GOVERNMENT OFFICIALS, AND LEGAL VISITORS, MUST BE ON THE INMATE'S APPROVED VISITING LIST IN ORDER TO VISIT. PROSPECTIVE VISITORS SHOULD CONTACT THE INMATE TO HAVE THEM PLACED ON THE VISITING LIST.

Visitation is encouraged to help offenders maintain ties with family, friends, and others in the community. Visiting times, rules, and policies vary depending on the facility and security level.

• Inpatients may only receive one visit on any given day.
  ° Three adult visitors (any person, generally over two years of age, who can sit unassisted is considered an adult visitor) constitutes one visit for offenders confined in general population or protective custody status.
  o For offenders who are classified as an extremely high-level escape risk, offenders on Visiting Restriction, and those in Disciplinary Segregation status, two persons shall constitute one visit.

*Upon entering the Visiting Room, the Visiting Room Officer will assign a table for seating during the visit. No moves will be permitted once seated unless approved by security staff. **Visits are subject to monitoring and recording** at any time by departmental staff, unless prior special arrangements have been made for confidential attorney visits or other privileged visits.*

I sit in the waiting room with Benny and realize everything I have ever done is wrong. There's just not enough words to point out my stupidity; the alphabet doesn't have enough letters.

Forty-eight hours later Daniel is released. We all hug him as he climbs into the backseat of Isobel's car.

All he says is, "My roommate was seventeen and kept talking about masturbation. But he did some really cool sketches of me as a skeleton."

"Good to know," I say, and we watch the city fly past us like some edgy foreign film.

Outside, as I ride to work the next morning, the cold is like a punch to the face or having all your bones broken at exactly the same time. My nose runs and my fingers lose their feeling. But then when I step into the warmth of the rehabilitation center with my bicycle at my side, it is a moment of low-cost transcendence and I am grateful for the escape. I call home several times to make sure Daniel is okay. Apparently all he does is eat cereal and watch cartoons all day.

On Monday morning before school, Daniel comes down with another ghost costume on.

"Jesus. How many of those do you have?" I ask, and he only shrugs.

I put some frozen waffles down in front of him and he raises the end of the costume just enough to feed himself, which I take as a partial victory.

Later I go up and look in his part of the closet and see it is filled with another five or six ghost costumes, possibly taken from the garage, all hanging on hangers, the way a normal person would have different shirts or suits.

* * *

As I am riding home from work that afternoon, I find my brother sitting on the back porch, staring up at the crisscrossing telephone wires.

"What is it?" I ask, and he tells me that, after shooting his coach's tire with a bow and arrow, he has been disqualified from the Academic Bowl team.

"No," I say, more than a little sarcastically, but he doesn't seem to get the joke.

"The worst part is I never got my comics back."

In our bedroom that night, I find a map of some unidentifiable country on his bed. I can't tell if it is supposed to be Poland or Jugoslavia or somewhere else because the cities and names have all been covered with liquid eraser. For a moment, I get a glimpse of the entire world as my brother imagines it. There is something eerily beautiful about how open it is. It has the look of someplace I'd like to visit. Over the map, he has written, *Invisible Kingdom,* in his perfect penmanship, and I begin to wonder if this is the place my brother has been building up in the trees.

I call Alex once or twice that week, not expecting her to answer. I get her voice mail but don't leave a message. I call back just to hear the way she says, *"I'll give you a call as soon as I can,"* like she really means it.

After I hang up, I take my mom to dialysis. On the way back, as she stares dreamily out the bus window, I ask, "What's happening with your play?"

"I ran out of ribbon."

"I can get you a new ribbon."

"I don't think I want to keep writing it. The thing I realized is that Tom Cruise is a human being. So is Katie Holmes. I looked at what I had written and it made me sad. I think I'm becoming one of those people who only finds meaning in other people's unhappiness. I guess I don't really have anything else to look forward to. It just sometimes feels like life is too long."

I give her a hug and we sit together on the bus, speaking in murmured tones. I tell her about Daniel, about my sister, I tell her about Jazzy as outside it becomes completely dark.

In the morning, my mother is not in her room. I go downstairs and find her outside, in front of the house, in a pair of oversized galoshes, wearing a winter coat over her pajamas. She has a large paintbrush in one hand and is painting the dead tree in front of our house a fluorescent shade of pink. It almost hurts to look at it, it's so bright.

After she is finished, she carries the brush and bucket half a block to another dead tree and begins painting that one. All I can do is watch and smile.

When I come home from work that night, Isobel is sitting in front of the television watching some crime show with her cell phone in hand. She holds the phone as if it is the only object of value left in the world.

"What is it?" I ask. "What's going on?"

"Billy called."

"So?"

"I want to call him back."

"Don't call him back. Calling him back is a terrible idea."

"I really miss him."

"If you call him back, you're a fool. You need to move

on. Things are going so good for you. Look at Jazzy. Look at yourself. Seriously. Don't do it."

"I know," she says but doesn't sound like she believes it herself.

I touch her bare foot and get up to leave. As I climb the stairs, I have no hope that what I have said has made any difference.

Alex calls the next day but I miss it while I am working. I call her back on a break but it just rings and rings. Still, when it goes to voice mail, even though I have heard this recording a dozen times, there is something about it that feels new, some sense of impossibility in the way she says, *"I'll give you a call as soon as I can,"* like she doesn't actually mean it.

I ride up the driveway after work and find Isobel sitting in the front seat of her hatchback, with her forehead against the steering wheel. I pause and watch her for a moment. The engine is off but the snow is still melting on the hood and so I have no idea how long she's been sitting there in the dark. It's almost eight p.m. I watch her for a long time, waiting for her to lift her head, but she never does. I put my bicycle in the garage and go quietly knock on her windshield. Finally she looks up and slowly rolls down the window.

"What is? What's wrong?" I ask.

"I'm so stupid."

"What happened?"

"I went by Billy's. To give him some of his things back. We started talking and then I fooled around with him. And afterward we got in a fight."

"Why did you do that, Isobel? I thought you were done with him."

"I am. I was. I don't know how I even ended up going over there."

"It's like you always want to punish yourself for being happy. Like the only thing you're committed to is failing."

"I know," she says. "I almost always choose disaster. The worst part is he said I was selfish and that I was a terrible person and that I don't even know how to care for my own child." I can see her eyes filling with tears. "I just sat there and listened to this terrible person say all these terrible things to me. I mean, he's a moron and I just sat there and didn't even say anything back. Part of me thinks maybe he's right, you know? I mean, look at me. Look at me." She rubs at her eyes with her palms.

After that, I don't say anything. I go into the garage and grab my bicycle and ride and ride and ride. Dark thoughts get the best of me. All I hear is my own heart beating hard in my ears. I pass the bankrupt bank, the bank that has run out of money, and see its large digital clock, which is the only part of the bank that is still functioning. It's almost nine at night. I pull up the hood on my coat. I ride and ride and find myself sitting in front of the water-reclamation plant but it is not pink, it is a dark purple, like death.

I ride off again. A couple hours go by. I don't really know how many. I don't know what I'm supposed to do. I only know I've got to do something. For a while I circle the neighborhood around and around without thinking and end up in front of Billy's mother's house. I see the blue roof is slanting over the sunken porch. I throw my bicycle down on the front lawn and walk along the side of the building. Someone is laughing at the back of the house. Some people around my age smoking dope, playing video games in the back room. I open the back screen door and ask if they have seen Billy and they shrug and shout something at the screen and then go back to playing.

I can tell some lo-fi hip-hop music is playing from somewhere upstairs by the sound of the bass but I don't even hear it. I wander around and see an oxygen tank, a green one, sitting in the kitchen beside a cabinet of antique china. I remember Billy lives with his mother, see the wheelchair folded by the bottom of the stairs, and pause. I have no idea what I am going to do. I give the first door on the left a gentle shove and find Billy in bed, shirtless, passed out with soft music playing from a stereo. Someone, some girl with a bare white shoulder, is lying beside him, also passed out. Incense fills the room. At the end of the bed is his prosthetic. I stare at it for a moment, see the Velcro strap and its smooth pink shape, then grab it and shove it under my coat. I go out the way I came. The two dudes in the back of the house playing video games wave at me and I nod and then I hurry through the back door, letting the screen slam quietly behind me.

I ignore all history and all facts and all reason and ride off as fast as I can. Where? I don't know. My hands are too cold to make a good decision. I find myself, moments later, standing in the no-name convenience store, before the freezers of soda pop and other drinks, staring at the bottles of Yoo-hoo. I put the prosthetic half leg on an empty shelf inside one of the freezers and then get a bottle of Yoo-hoo and take it up to the counter. I drink it outside and it is one of the single greatest drinks I have ever had in my life.

Before I make it back home, I see Billy's black Cutlass parked at the end of the block. I hit the brakes but it's already too late. Someone climbs out of the back of the car and grabs me by the shoulder. Looks like one of the guys who was playing video games. I see Billy climb unsteadily out of the passenger seat and when he comes at me, I know there's nothing I can do. I make myself small, ball up, try to cover my head with my hands. My right eye becomes a prized fruit, swollen and red. All I can feel is the dark and it hangs over me in ever-changing shadows, and some of these shadows keep punching me in the face. Both my ears begin to ring and I hear nothing as the blows rain down upon my back.

Later, after they're gone, after the car has pulled away, I open my eyes but there is nothing but the dark and a constant hum in my eardrums. Everything becomes silent then and I sit there, trying to imagine its shape.

For a long time, I sit on the curb in front of my mother's house listening to an otherworldly hum, staring at absolutely nothing. Then I pick up my bicycle, which they have dragged into the middle of the street, and ride over to the ER on 95th.

Hours later, I walk out with a bandaged-up eye and every part of my back and head hurting. I look like a boxer, like an Old Testament thief, both eyes swollen, arm in a sling. I get used to the surprise of feeling dizzy. I put my hood up on my coat so no one has to see my face. One time, as I cross Western, I nearly black out and have to pull over on my bike. Fainting feels like a relief.

I pause when I arrive at the house just as the sun is rising. A pleading, baleful sound hangs in the air, a single note followed by another, then another. The timbre is plaintive and bare. I know the melody right away: *Étude in C♯ Minor, Opus 25, No. 7* by Chopin, a composition the two of us used to play as children. I hold the handlebars and wait at the bottom of the concrete steps and listen to all that follows. Once she reaches the end of the short minor section, she starts again. I sit on the bottom of the steps, feeling the cut blooming under the bandage on my eye.

After some time, Daniel comes out wearing a winter coat. He sees me but doesn't say anything about my face, just takes a seat next to me. Eventually Jazzy comes out wearing her pajamas. The three of us sit on the steps beside each other as Isobel continues to play. The world seems to open, the sky becoming blank. When the notes shift to the quiet-sounding major part, I close my eyes and everything begins again.

MOVEMENT FOUR

SOMEWHERE

Allegro vivace e con brio.

CHAPTER SIXTEEN

CYMBALS CLASHING. OR A XYLOPHONE RINGING. OR A FAR-away trumpet producing mellifluous notes. I mop the entire rehabilitation building each night while the residents sleep, sometimes working two shifts in a row, coming up with a different AMAZING COMPOSITION for each room. On my break, I sit and watch the orange birds in their cage, sleeping with their beaks on each other's shoulders, and then punch out just past eleven o'clock. I put on my winter coat with the Polish flag on back and pedal off. Outside, my breath becomes smoke.

On my bicycle, I rush through the narrowing January evening, and try to imagine a single symphony that might include everything about the moment I am riding through: every question, every thought I have ever had, about myself, my family, all the minor compositions I have ever invented, all the exquisite silences I have discovered, something that feels epic, an orchestration of the ordinary and transcendent, of all of time and space that will forever be immortalized, that will leave a mark, that one day will somehow be heard and remembered.

But usually I only get as far as the first movement before I pass the line of video stores, restaurants, travel agencies, insurance agencies, bookstores, tanning salons that have all been permanently closed. I pass under a desolate billboard announcing, *100% Human Hair,* before I lose the melody and the air knocks the wind out of me.

I get home and am careful not to wake anyone, gently folding my uniform over the arm of the couch. I go to sleep on the sofa so that I don't disturb my brother. Feverish sounds emanate through the floorboards from the furnace below and I imagine their desperate melody as a variation on a funeral march. I go to sleep praying for the furnace and its continued existence. In the morning I feel Jazzy's hot breath against my cheek.

Hi, she signs. *Get up.*

I am up, I sign and pull the pillow over my head. She immediately pulls it away.

I know this game is probably going to be the best part of my day, so I like to draw it out.

My niece elbows me and signs, *You have to get up. Right now,* and finally I climb off the couch, hit the shower, and sit down next to Jazzy as she pours another bowl of cereal at the kitchen table. Daniel, still half asleep across from her, plows through another helping of frozen waffles, wearing the ghost costume over his shoulders like a shawl. I have told him multiple times not to wear it at breakfast but what can you do? All you can do is ask.

A few moments later Isobel comes down dressed for work in the same black blazer she wears every day, the one with the stitching coming undone at the collar, and says, "I'd like to make an announcement to everyone." Like a classic movie about some orphanage, all of us gaze up from our bowls of gruel as Isobel looks at each of us and says, "I'm going to audition for another orchestra. It's on the far northside. Apparently it's less fancy than the other one, so I think I've got a better chance. The audition's at the end of March. I know it's going to take a lot of practice, but I really want to do it."

Jazzy, Daniel, and I all look at each other and then offer a standing ovation. I can see how much it moves her, even if she refuses to admit it.

"All right, thanks." But we keep clapping. "Okay. That's enough," and then we play the game, seeing who will be the last one to clap.

Jazzy and I pull on our winter coats and ride off to school. Twice we skid in the snow. As soon as she climbs off the handlebars, she adjusts her backpack and signs: *Do you think my mom is good enough to play in the orchestra?*

I look at her and shrug. *I don't know*, I sign back. *But at least she's going to try.*

Jazzy seems to think about this for a moment. *I am going to try too*, and she makes her way into the depressing-looking building.

Later, on the way to work, I lose control of my bike and end up tumbling into a snowdrift. When I get up, my Walkman no longer works. I give it a shake, blow on it, do all the insensible things a person in a situation like that does, but nothing helps. My Brahms CD will no longer play. After more than four years, the CD player is dead. It's like a close friend and I think about burying it in the backyard but realize the ground is too frozen. Still, I find I am unable to put it in the trash and so I hide it in the drawer in the kitchen with the rest of the things my family is unwilling to get rid off: photos, keys, the sales slip for my old piano.

One evening at the end of January I call Alex, hoping enough time has passed. The phone just rings and rings and then a voice comes on saying her mailbox is full. I hang up and try again and get the same exact message over and over. Somehow the voice sounds different each time, more and more irritated.

I come back from work and pass five trees painted pink and one painted lime green. I find my mother's galoshes by the front door, splattered in paint. It is like a map she is making of infinite possibilities, entirely different worlds, color by color, tree by tree.

I get a call one afternoon in early February about an application for a part-time tennis coach that I left six months before at a Catholic school near 75th Street. Apparently their regular tennis coach is unable to work for some reason. Is this something I'd be willing to do?

"Absolutely, most definitely," I say. "When do I start?"

"We need you to come in for an interview first."

I immediately find a book on coaching at the library. I go to YouTube and watch every tennis video I can.

The interview is set for the following Monday. I cut my hair over the sink using clippers so the administration knows I am serious. I also decide to wear a warm-up suit to the interview so they will think I know more about tennis than I actually do.

I ride my bicycle to the interview, get a little lost. I realize my watch has stopped working and so I am ten minutes late. I lock my bike up and frown, surveying the crooked, upset pavement of the tennis courts—both of them missing their nets—and run into the school, ready to blow this interview up.

The school—St. Anthony's—looks like it's falling apart. The statue in front of the building has fallen over. The facade is caving in, the lawn is unmowed, trash bags are piled up in one corner of the building. The football field looks like a prison yard. Across the street, under the expressway, is a pile of used tires, some of which are on fire.

I check myself in the glass of the double doors. I see my face, see where the hair on the top and in the back has begun to thin a little, and think, *This is it. This is your chance.* I go inside and give my name to the receptionist and immediately begin to feel sweaty. I go to the bathroom to wash my face.

Everything is hung lower—the mirror, the sink, the urinal. I go to the bathroom but feel like an overgrown child. I check myself in the mirror again. I decide to put on a headband as an extra precaution; I think this will be my edge. I pull it out of the back of my pants and put it over my head. I look in the mirror and immediately take it off. I go back and wait by the principal's office for my name to be called, and when it is, I go inside and shake hands with three different administrators. It turns out they are mostly just looking for someone to babysit. They ask if I am Catholic; I say I am nonpracticing, then add I practice in my own way. I say lately I've been listening to a lot of Johann Sebastian Bach, whom I have always considered the greatest Catholic of all time.

"I believe Bach was Lutheran," one of the administrators tells me.

I nod aggressively. "Of course. Exactly. That's what I meant."

It turns out that the other tennis coach has come down

with gout. I laugh and then realize they are not joking. I apologize and say I always try to find humor in even the most
difficult of situations, that it's part of my coaching philosophy.
They nod. I tell them a wild one about how I was a semipro-
fessional tennis player in high school. They seem to buy it. I
tell them I don't teach tennis, I mold young people's spirits.
Also, I don't have a criminal record. Also, I am willing to help
the kids do personal inventories to maximize their emotional
growth.

"No," they say. "That won't be necessary. It's just an after-
school program. It's just supposed to be fun."

I say I will bring the state championship home and they
say that's okay. There is no state championship in intramural
tennis. They just want the kids to have a good experience as
most of them have never actually played tennis before. Also,
since the other coach came down with gout they are in a pinch
and they really just need someone to help monitor the kids.
This point cannot be emphasized enough.

When I come home, my mom is not in bed. She's actually in
the bathroom, taking a bath, which seems like it has not happened in several months. Isobel is in there with her, washing
her hair. I can hear the two of them talking. Isobel is cracking
jokes, and for a second I think I hear my mother laugh. I lie
on my bed with the record player turned low so I can listen to
them and also enjoy the glory of Puccini. When Cavaradossi
sings "Vittoria! Vittoria!" I feel the walls slip away and wonder: *When in life does that happen, when are you lifted out of
the moment? When does everything finally explode, break apart,
become something new and wondrous and different?*

Later that night the phone rings. Somehow, bewilderingly,

I have gotten the job. It is only part-time which is fine. I am not looking for full-time work anyway as I still have thirty-six hours at the rehab facility. But it feels like a victory, ridiculous or not.

The next morning, I notice Jazzy has her head down by her empty bowl of cereal. *What's up?* I sign, and she signs back something I don't recognize. Whatever it is, it is angry.

"I don't know what that means," I tell her.

She does the sign again and once more I shake my head. She gives an extravagant sigh then says, "There's a play at school. And I don't want to do it."

"How come?"

"I just don't want to."

"What's the play about?"

"Joan of Arc. Lotti Lorimer got the best part. She gets to be Joan of Arc and have a sword and shield and everything. She gets to witness the transfiguration."

"What does that mean?"

"It's when God appears."

"Right. Well, that sucks. Not being able to witness the transfiguration," I say. For a moment, I consider maybe that's all I ever wanted, to see beyond the present to something inexplicable, eternal. I turn back to my niece. "So what's your part?"

"The rest of us are trees and rocks. It's really embarrassing."

I try, "You should be the best tree or rock you can," but before it is out of my mouth, I can see I have already lost her.

That afternoon as I am riding home from work, I see a large black shape up in the tree in front of one of the houses for sale down the block. I slow up and see something white and green moving there and realize it is Daniel again. He is up there with his ghost costume on, reading a library book, covered in a sleeping bag. He is at least twenty feet up, near the top, and it looks like he could fall at any second.

"Daniel? What are you doing up there? Get down before you hurt yourself."

"I'm okay," he says.

"No way, you're too high up. You need to come down."

"I'm not coming down," he tells me. "I'm going to be like St. Francis. Or John the Baptist. I am going to find enlightenment in the wild."

"Enlightenment about what?"

He hold his hands out like a megaphone and says, "About how to try to live an extraordinary life," as if this is not something anyone in our family has ever thought of before.

I look at him and ask: "But what if nothing you do is extraordinary? What if a normal life is all there is?" and he frowns and goes back to reading St. Augustine.

In the middle of the night, there's a knock on the door. I leap off the sofa and make my way to the front of the house, suddenly afraid that someone's come to repossess our belongings, but it is only Benny. He has his hood up and is carrying a cardboard box full of clothes and old hip-hip records.

"Hello, kuzyn," he mutters sadly. After that, he doesn't need to say anything. I can see it all there in his face—his mother and father, who are staunch Catholics, have somehow discovered the truth about who Benny has been spending time with and have thrown him out. I look at him and he nods without us having to say a word.

All he says is that he has brought his own pillow. I give him a blanket and he goes to sleep in my bed while I crash on the couch again.

In the morning, all of us silently eat together. No one questions Benny being there. One by one, everyone drifts from the table. Isobel is the last to get up. She sits alone, drinking her black coffee with dark circles under her eyes. Everyone else is running back and forth trying to get themselves ready, grabbing book bags, pulling on boots. I take a seat beside my sister and ask, "Aren't you supposed to be going to work?"

"I'm late."

"It looks like you're not even moving. What's going on?"

"It's this new guy they hired last week, this assistant manager, Chad. He's completely insufferable."

"Why, what did he do?"

"He's one of those people that likes to look over your shoulder, like double-check everything. He thinks we're all his underlings or something. The thing is, I know for a fact he has an average IQ, at best," and then she repeats this a second time to herself, "at best."

"Well, why don't you ask to be transferred? Aren't there like a hundred other branches?"

"There are but . . . I don't want to give this imbecile the satisfaction."

"What else are you going to do? Quit?"

"I don't know. That's why I'm sitting here. There's an exam to get into the manager's training program coming up at the end of April. I don't know if I should do it or not. I feel like at some point I'm going to need to make a decision."

"I'm sorry," I say. "I've got to go to work. I'll see you later and we can talk about it." I leave her sitting at the table, her brows crossed like she is making her way through an uninteresting calculus problem or a piece of obtrusive music.

On our bicycles later that morning, I ride beside Daniel as he pedals to school, to make sure he's actually still going. As he locks up his bike, an angular shadow passes overhead. He turns to me and says, "Do you know what that was?"

"No."

"A hawk."

"Really? A hawk?"

"Did you know there are approximately thirty different hawks that live downtown?"

"No, I didn't know that," I say and look down at my watch.

"The city released three different kinds of hawks last winter to keep the pigeon population down. Cooper's hawks, red-tailed hawks, even a few falcons. Some of them even made it to the southside."

"Exciting," I say, checking my watch again.

"I'm going to make a map, based on what I find on the Internet, of all the different hawk sightings."

I look at him and then my watch again and say, "Sorry, Daniel, I've got to go. I'm going to be late for work. Have a good day at school."

I pedal off and glance back and see him smiling up at the sky.

I come home from work that afternoon and call out to what feels like an empty house. My mother's paint-spattered boots are by the front door with a brush and a can of bright-yellow paint. I call out again but no one calls back. Even with my hearing, I know at once something is wrong. I climb the carpeted stairs and go to my mom's room and find her lying on the floor, on her left side. There is drool down her cheek and I can tell she's having problems breathing by the ragged sounds she is making. I phone my sister at work but can't get ahold of her and have no choice but to call an ambulance.

The paramedics arrive and come upstairs, asking what's wrong, and all I can say is she's having some kind of breathing problem. In the back of the ambulance, they put the plastic oxygen mask over her nose and mouth and the sight of it's terrifying, like something out of a documentary or eighties horror movie.

Later, my brother, sister, and I wait in the emergency room in the blue plastic seats. Daniel and Isobel have fallen asleep, with Jazzy stretched across both their laps. Jazzy asks, "Is Grandma going to die?" and I smile and touch her hair and say probably not. At some point, Isobel takes Daniel and Jazzy home.

A nurse lets me into a semiprivate room where my mom is on a ventilator. She appears to be sleeping, with the oxygen tube in her nose, and then she wakes up smiling. I lean close and she begins to mutter something.

"Hey, Mom," I say. "You're okay. You're in the hospital. Are you all right?"

"I'm worried," she says, looking up at me. "I'm worried about George Clooney. I'm worried he'll never know what it means to truly love someone other than himself."

I murmur that it will all probably work out for George Clooney and squeeze her hand. A doctor, a young Indian American woman, comes in and debriefs me. "I just want you to know we have no idea why this is happening at the moment. She seems to be septic. We need to locate the source of the infection. We're doing everything we can."

"Okay. I appreciate your honesty."

"It most probably has something to do with her dialysis. Or some other immune response we've been unable to detect. We're going to keep running tests until we figure it out."

I walk home from the hospital on my own. It takes a lot longer than I expect and I enjoy the quiet.

All the lights are off when I get back. I go upstairs and find Daniel sitting outside on the roof. I take a seat beside him and try not to slip over the ice-covered edge. It is beyond cold out there. Icicles hang from the gutters like baroque chandeliers.

"How is she doing?" my brother asks.

"Okay," I say. "Alive and talking about George Clooney."

He smiles and we sit in silence for another half hour until finally I go back inside.

In the morning, my mom gets released but only because the doctors don't know what else to do, which is more than a little frightening. It's like she has turned to glass and, at any second, she may break, may stop breathing, may simply expire if one us says the wrong thing or talks too loudly. I try not to think about the hospital bill that will be coming as we push my mother in a wheelchair to the passenger seat of Isobel's car. My sister drives us all home, none of us knowing what to say. Finally my mom glances out the window of the passenger seat and says, "I'd really like some pancakes right about now. If it isn't a bother."

Isobel glances in the rearview mirror and asks a question with her eyes and I shrug and so we all take her to get pancakes. Watching her eat stack after stack with the blue hospital band on her thin arm, it's pretty hard not to smile.

I start tennis practice at the beginning of March. I get to the courts behind the school early but nobody is there yet. It's three o'clock and kids are mulling around the parking lot. I stand with my arms at my side in a very forceful pose, with a whistle in my mouth. I spit the whistle out because I think it might be a little too much.

Finally, around 3:17 p.m., some out-of-shape-looking kids show up, a group of seventh and eighth graders, boys with uncertain peach-fuzz mustaches, pimples, and unlaced tennis shoes. I ask, "Are any of you here for tennis?"

Some of them make obnoxious sounds with their armpits as a response.

"Great," I say. "I'm Coach Aleks. I'm here to make your tennis dreams come true. We're going to bring back State."

A very pasty kid raises his hand. "There's no finals for after-school tennis."

"Then the championship, wherever it is. I want to make you tennis maniacs. Does anybody here want to become a tennis maniac?"

All of them look at each other. "Yo," one of them says, "who is this person?"

"I am the future. Your future. And it's about to get real. Like John McEnroe real. Do you guys know who John McEnroe is?"

The boys all shake their heads no.

"Do you have the Internet in your house? If you do, you should go home and find out."

Some of them actually get up to leave.

"Not now, colleagues. Now is the time where we bond as a team. Hands out, everyone."

The boys look at each other.

"Don't be afraid. The first rule is to do the impossible; do what you think can't be done."

One of the kids laughs. "This guy is totally mental."

"I *am* mental. I am mental about tennis and your success. Because success on the tennis court translates to success in life. Now put out your hands!"

The boys shyly obey. I reach into my backpack and hand each of them an orange headband. One of them is pink. I hand the pink one to a large kid with gigantic bifocals. "Didn't have any more orange ones. Sorry. But this pink one, this is special. This makes you team captain."

The kid nods, dubious but still somewhat impressed.

"Put it on and assume the mantle of team leader."

The kid pulls it on lopsided over his large head.

"Outstanding," I say. "What's your name, team captain?"

"Perry," the kid mumbles.

"Again, but say it louder this time."

"Perry!" he shouts.

"Did you see that? Did you see Perry assume an air of victory? That's what I want from each of you guys, on and off the field."

Another pasty kid raises his hand. "It's actually a court."

"A court. Exactly. Okay, now's the time where we'll come up with our team names." I point at the very pale kid. He looks stricken. "You will be Blizzard of Oz."

"What?" the kid says, looking around.

"Blizzard for short. Go on and don the ornamental garb."

He gives a sullen face and puts the orange headband on. I turn to a squat boy with enormous braces on his teeth. "You. You will be Jaws. The Jaws of Death. You bring the hustle, am I right?"

The kid shrugs.

"Put on your headband and become one of us."

And on it goes. Fancy-pants. Shoo-fly-pie. Viking Hair. Nothing exactly inappropriate, but no nickname any kid would ever want.

"Now. If you want a better nickname, you need to perform on the court. If you don't show the right amount of hustle, I will have to downgrade you."

One of the kids—a boy with longer hair named Brendan Wooly who has been named Snakeskin—laughs.

"Snakeskin, you will now be known as Space Vomit. I'm not fooling around with this nickname business. I want you guys to refer to each other by these names on and off the field."

Blizzard of Oz raises his hand.

"Court," I say. "On and off the court. Ask your mom, your friends. Those of you who have relationships, ask your significant other to call you by these names. Any questions? No. Okay. Let's go do some laps."

The boys can handle maybe two laps, tops. I blow my whistle hard, so hard it pops my eardrums. They don't seem to notice. Some of them hang onto the chain-link fence that surrounds the courts. One of them lies down. One pretends to gag.

"Looking good," I say. "One more lap."

But none of them can make it past three. By the end, they are all on the ground, on their hands and knees, calling for water.

After that we work on our forehands, on our backhands, on our court positions. Twins—Donald and Ronald, who I christen McNugget and Other McNugget—are much quicker than I expected. They both return my volleys with graceful aplomb.

"Okay," I say, "I like what I see. You all are going to be winners."

Then we all sit down together when practice is over and share a gallon of ice water.

"Each of you guys has a spark of greatness," I say. "But right now it is covered in a layer of garbage. I am here to help you find that spark and do something with it. I am ready to fully commit to each of you as your new tennis coach. I am ready to help you grow into men. But first, I need to know: does anybody here feel like quitting right now?"

Almost all of them raise their hands.

"If you quit now, you'll be quitting the rest of your life. All of you have good hearts. We can work on the rest. Heart is what matters. Now let's put our hands in."

I am out of motivational speeches by this point. The kids all gather together and look at me, their faces streaked with sweat. It is amazing to feel so useful. Soon, I watch the boys all walk away with their schoolbags, exhausted and laughing.

I ride over to Taco Bell, lock my bike out front, and buy as much food as I can for seven dollars. I sit in the booth ruminating, and fill myself with seasoned meat by-product. I stare at the high school kids who are hanging out there, and think about telling them to get in their cars and drive as far away as they can before it is too late. *Become something else and get out of here while you can. Because once inertia sets in, there will be no escape.*

I go by my grandfather's apartment on Cicero the next day and he putters over to the door and unlocks each lock, one by one, and then looks me up and down, as if he is unimpressed. Finally he says, "I believe the last time you were here, you forgot something." He shuffles into the bedroom and returns with the enormous black suitcase, then heaves it beside me on the couch.

I sigh and unlatch one golden latch and then the other and slowly lift the lid.

I find it empty, or mostly empty, probably some Jugoslavian joke. The only thing inside is a package of several bound letters.

"Everything else was removed or stolen," my grandfather says. "The mail inspectors were famous for such things."

"But what is this?"

He nods, urging me to take a closer look. I slowly open the letters. I can see right away that they are not written in Jugoslavian or Croatian or even Cyrillic. They are letters from my grandfather's father, my great-grandfather, Nicolas, written entirely in music, notes and staffs filling page after page after page.

"He knew the bureaucrats would be unable to read it. So he wrote everything down in music. He knew this was the only way he could record it. So this is it. All your history. Everything you could ever want to know about your family, all right here, in this composition."

I look at the notes on the staffs and begin to hear the shape of the melody, scanning the measures with my first two fingers. It's a concerto for piano and cello and violin, written in my great-grandfather Nicolas's loose, unconcerned Jugoslavian penmanship. My grandfather pats me on the shoulder and says, "Family always finds a way."

I give him a hug and fold the bundled letters back up and then put them inside my coat, zipping them into the pocket.

Back on my bicycle, I feel the weight of history against my chest. Either it's my deafness or I can actually hear the lines my great-grandfather wrote coming to life behind me as I pedal off, a violet zigzag for the violin, a vibrant orange for the cello, an entire symphony following me down the unsuspecting street.

CHAPTER SEVENTEEN

I PICK UP JAZZY FROM KINDERGARTEN AND HER TEACHER TELLS me that my niece was lying down in class that day, pretending to be dead. I am flabbergasted. I say, "Oh, no, wait, what, really?" I glance over at where Jazz is standing and she gives me a dismissive look, inspecting the top of her gym shoes.

"It happened twice actually," the woman says. "I almost called home but decided to ignore it. Eventually she got up and went back to her seat."

I rub my neck and offer every lame excuse, every apology I can think of. "I don't really know, I just think she's nervous about the play. I'm so sorry. It won't happen again." I thank the teacher profusely and am angry that Jazzy has put me in the position to have to apologize to someone I did not previously like.

As she's climbing onto the handlebars, I ask, "What's going on with you, kid?"

"I don't want to go to school anymore."

"Why? Because of the play?"

She nods. "I don't want you to come see it."

"Why not?"

"Because," she says. "It's bad. It's terrible." Then she adds, "If you or my mom come, I'll cry."

I look at the side of her face and recognize she is not joking. I have seen that same expression with my sister a million times. Suddenly I am sorry that she has inherited so many of our challenges—our unconquerable stubbornness, our need to always be seen as perfect, our capacity to inflict self-harm. I stare at the back of her head as we ride, wishing she did not have to take things so seriously, knowing in our family what an impossibility that is.

On to my job at the rehab facility the next day, I mop the floor, feed the birds, and continue humming to myself. That afternoon, I am cleaning out a storage room on the second floor and find, under some boxes of misfiled reports and several gallons of paint, an upright piano missing seven of its keys. The varnish has been chipped off but, miraculously, it is still somewhat in tune. I drag it out on its sturdy wheels and clean it as best I can, then push it over to the lounge directly across from the lovebirds. I play a short sonata and then grab my mop. Only the orange birds seem to notice.

Later that day, I am taking out the trash at home and am walking back up the steps when I see Daniel sitting up in the tree three backyards away in his ghost costume, reading some book. I sigh and walk down the street.

"What are you doing?"

He makes his hands into a megaphone and says, "I'm studying for the Academic Bowl. There are tryouts again in a few weeks."

I wish him luck and ask him to please take off the costume. "It's time," I tell him. "You can do this without having to hide," and he promptly ignores me, lifting the book to cover his eyes.

On Saturday, Isobel asks me to go downtown with her to Cook County to get her latest test results. We take the train and then a bus over to Damen, and find our way into Cook County, or what used to be called Cook Country. Nobody calls it Stroger, because some places are bigger, more complicated than their names.

We sit in the waiting area in front of the oncology unit, which is full of men and women, though many of the people waiting seem to be older women. Every so often someone comes around selling something slightly strange—fruit, candy bars, soda pop, even electric hair trimmers.

Finally Isobel's name is called. She comes out forty-five minutes later and I can't tell what her face is doing.

I stand up. "Well?"

I see the faintest of smiles. "They couldn't find anything. He says I need to come back in six months but I don't have any sign of cancer. Apparently I'm back at stage zero."

I take her hand and give it a squeeze and we get out of the hospital as quick as we can.

On the train ride home we are silent. We take the bus back down to 95th and get off in the middle of what seems like a riot. Bodies, hundreds of them, are standing everywhere and there is nowhere to breathe. You can't tell who is a friend, an enemy, or a stranger, and I can't hear what my sister is shouting; people are yelling and are drunk and are falling against one another, there is a bevy of bright faces gone red, someone is vomiting now, someone is sitting on the curb crying, someone's clover antenna has been knocked from her head, someone has a black swollen eye and is yelling in delight, the world is a loud, cruel place, a nightmare of green faces, green scarves, green jackets, except for the bloody noses, and it is the southside parade for St. Patrick's Day and we push our way past the belligerent Irish American faces.

Isobel looks over at me as if this is just another part of what she has to endure and asks: "Why is this happening?"

"I don't know."

"I hate this neighborhood."

"I do too," I smile. "But apparently you can't just walk away from the place where you're from."

Both of us struggle through the crowd. Both of us are a mess, but finally it feels like we don't need to pretend anymore. We give in to the chaos, let the painted faces overtake us. Someone hits me in the back of the head with candy but what can you do? Once the parade has gone on, I walk with my arm in her arm, making our way toward home.

I get Jazzy from school on Monday afternoon and Ms. Pascal asks to talk to me again. I sign to Jazz to wait where she is and I follow the teacher inside the building and she tells me Jazzy has not been participating and lay down in the middle of gym class on three occasions.

"She was doing so well," she says. "Having an aide has been a huge help. But now she's acting out almost every day. Is everything okay at home?"

"I just think she's freaked out about this play. She's a perfectionist. I think she has performance anxiety or something. Everybody has some kind of emotional issue in our family. Everyone's too smart for their own good. I'm really sorry."

"I see it every day. All these kids, they have to deal with all the things adults do," and it's the first time I begin to see this person as a human.

After that, I ride over to the no-name pizza place with Jazzy on the handlebars and order us each a slice of pizza. I say, "I heard school was rough today," and she looks down at her pizza to avoid conversation.

Finally she says: "Some of the other kids were laughing."

"For lying down in the middle of class?"

She shrugs. "I don't want to be in the play."

"You have to stop trying to control everything. You have to be a little more flexible. This is not a big deal. It's just supposed to be fun."

She just keeps eating, unconvinced.

I study her face, see how intense she looks. She eats like someone might steal her food at any second, and I know it is because she has grown up in our strange family where everything is always up for grabs, everything is always uncertain.

After that, we play *Tetris*, which is the only arcade game the no-name pizza place has other than *Dance Dance Revolution*. As we're playing, I tell her that in our family we have a long history of poor decisions that usually only lead to disappointment. I tell her about my great-grandfather, and my grandfather, and even my father. I tell her I don't want to see the same things happen to her.

She nods though I don't think she understands. Mostly she just remains silent. When I turn back to face the screen, our game is already over.

On through the middle of March, Isobel keeps practicing the

cello but gets more and more frustrated the closer she gets to the audition date. She switches her audition piece twice, and ends up with something hideously difficult by Wagner. Out of the four of us—Daniel, Jazzy, Benny, and myself—only Daniel is able to pretend not to notice. At breakfast, my brother keeps his eyes down on the library book before him, ignoring the ignominy of an off-note splitting the air, harsh enough to curdle the milk in the fridge.

One evening Benny comes in through the back door, limping. His left eye is swollen. When I ask what happened, he waves me away and disappears into the bathroom upstairs. An hour later he comes down and sits beside me on the couch with several ice cubes wrapped in a hand towel. He holds the ice to his eye and groans. I know not to ask and just wait for him to speak. Eventually he clears his throat.

"Somebody saw us. In the parking lot. While I was on break. Kissing. They pounded on the windshield. When I got off work, someone jumped me as I was going to my van."

"Who jumped you?"

"I don't know. Someone who does not like the idea of two people kissing."

"It could be anyone."

"There were two or three of them. I'm not sure." He takes a breath. "I'm afraid to go back to work now," and then my cousin does something he has never done before. He begins to cry, but so quietly and without any actual tears. *This is how Polish people cry*, I think. I give him a hug and he says, "I haven't seen my mother in three weeks. It's the longest I've gone without seeing her. She won't talk to me. She said I've made my decision. I don't know what to do."

I see his invisible tears have made four or five perfect cir-

cles on the edge of my shirt. "I'm so sorry, Benny. You're welcome to stay here as long as you want. If you don't feel safe
going back to work, you should find somewhere else."

He wipes his eyes and says, "I will. I apologize for your
shirt."

I tell him, "It's fine," and both of us try to make ourselves
laugh.

Later that week, I go by St. John's on 55th, where I used to
work, to see my old boss, Maria. I sign in and one of the cor-
rectional officers rings me through. I find Maria sitting in her
office. Immediately she springs to her feet, gives me a hug, and
asks how I am. I start to tell her about my sister, my mother,
my brother, Benny.

"Oh, honey," she says, "you need to talk to someone. Like
somebody who does this for a living."

"I feel like I could really use some help."

For the next hour, I tell her everything, everything, even
about Alex and what happened between us. I guess sometimes
it just feels good to let it all out. I have never spoken so much,
all at once. When I'm done she hugs me again and I let my
head rest on her shoulder for some length of time I can't even
quantify.

As I ride home I keep telling myself I am going to make it.

The following day, I hear some kind of yelling and screaming
from upstairs and hurry up the carpeted steps to find Isobel
in the bathroom. There is brown hair everywhere and Jazzy is
standing there, looking at herself in the mirror. She has taken
a large pair of sewing scissors and cut off most of her hair.
What remains is short and brown and brittle. Isobel is holding

Jazzy by the shoulders and asking, "Why? Why would you do this? Are you mad at me?" but Jazzy doesn't bother to answer.

A few days after that, I go look for Daniel up in his tree but find Jazzy lying in the backyard in the snow instead. She is facedown in the wet-looking slush, with the hood of her winter coat pulled up. She looks like she has fallen from some unimaginable height. I go over and kneel beside her.

"Jazzy?"

"___"

"Jazzy?"

"___"

"What are you doing?"

"Practicing."

"Practicing what?"

"Being dead."

"For what?"

"For the play," she mumbles.

"For school?" I ask.

But she does not answer.

I frown and stand up. "Okay. If you get cold, come on in." I try not to let her see how alarmed I am as I go back inside.

I find Isobel holding a cup of tea, standing by the back window looking at her daughter, who is still lying inert in a mound of snow.

"What's she doing?" she asks.

"She said she was practicing being dead. I think it's for the play. Maybe. I'm not exactly sure."

Isobel winces. "I'm really worried about her. I'm worried I have messed her up beyond all recognition."

"It's possible. But she's not going to be any worse than the rest of us."

"That's not saying much."

"It's really not," I say.

Daniel comes home around nine thirty that night and I get in a rage and ask him where he's been and all he says is, "Working," and I say, "Working? Where?" and he says, "Places," and again I say, "Where?" and he looks at me and gives a soft smile and says, "At Fair Play," and I say, "Doing what?" and he says, "Chasing carts and bagging," and I say, "Since when?" and he says he went and got hired a week ago but no one noticed until now and then I find I am the one apologizing all of a sudden.

As we're riding home from school the next day, I ask Jazzy if rehearsals for the play are any better.

"Ms. Pascal gave me a line. I'm supposed to say, 'Only you can save France,' to Joan of Arc. And then I get to die."

I realize what Jazzy's teacher has done for her and feel overcome with gratitude. "That's tremendous news. It's sounds like an important part."

"Really?"

"Really. In some ways, it's even better than Joan of Arc."

At that moment she turns away and I can't tell if she believes me or not.

On the rest of the bicycle ride home, I keep having arguments with my niece in my mind. *Jazzy,* I want to say, *it doesn't take any kind of genius to see how difficult the world is and then to just lie down and give up. I know it seems like almost everyone else has given up. A lot of other people we know have given up, but that doesn't mean* you *have to give up.* In my head, I keep saying, *It doesn't take any kind of genius to give up. Or to quit. But you can't. You're four and it's too soon. Don't let this family, this world, get you down before you've even had a chance to figure out who you are or what you can do.* Even in my head, I know how small and phony it all sounds, and so I don't say any of it.

Before Jazzy goes to bed that night, I help brush her hair, which is a lot easier now that it's short. Still, I am terrible at it. As she sits on the floor before the sofa, I tell her stories about her mother while Isobel studies across the room for her managerial exam at the bank.

"Did you know your mother used to be a genius at math? She knew all the equations, all the formulas, before anyone ever taught her. It was amazing. No one knew how she did it. It was like a miracle or something."

"Like Joan of Arc?" she asks.

"Exactly. Like Joan of Arc. She just knew how to do everything on her own. It's like you. And your bike. Somehow you just figured it out."

She grins, happy to finally hear a story about herself. I go on and on, and every so often Isobel looks over at us and smiles in the exact same way.

One morning I go to feed the orange birds on the second floor at work, before any of the residents awake, and find an elderly woman with long gray hair sitting in front of the piano, playing a phenomenal Beethoven concerto. It is luxuriously slow, which allows each note to rise and fall on its own. I stand there with my eyes closed and listen. When she's done, I ask her name and she says it's Maribel and I tell her how amazing her playing is.

After she goes down to breakfast, I head to my locker and take out the bundle of letters from my coat, then have a seat in front of the piano and place my fingers on the keyboard.

Something about the color, the weight of the keys, feels intimidating. I fool around with a Dvořák piece, stop, change directions, then settle on good ol' Mahler. Eventually I stumble through the notes my great-grandfather composed, one by one, and hear them for the first time out loud, each a different moment, a different chapter of history.

There's something odd about the phrasing that seems both uncertain and overpowering, and the pauses in between each section feel way too long. Instead of two different melodies that eventually come together, his composition ends right in the middle, without any sort of resolution. I go through the piece once, then again, then place the bundle of letters back in my locker, believing both of us to be complete failures.

Isobel takes a seat beside me on the couch the next morning, waking me up. "I can't go to the school play. Jazzy said if I go she will throw up. Can you please go?"

"No. You need to go. She can't tell you not to go."

"I know she's trying to punish me. I don't want to make it worse for her. At this point, that's all I want: not to make things any worse."

"It'll be okay. We'll sit in the back."

Slowly she nods in agreement.

Two nights later, we hide in the back of the auditorium where no one can see us once the lights go down. Jazzy comes onstage and performs with a flawless intensity. You can see the concentration in her face. I don't hear her say her line but I see her lift her sword, mutter something, then get killed by an English soldier. The girl playing Joan of Arc kneels at her side and offers a silent gesture of comfort. Everyone is amazed at how realistic Jazzy's death is. They don't know she's been practicing for weeks, for months, maybe even years. A paper chalice—painted brilliantly gold—drops down from the stage lights. Someone shines a spotlight directly in the audience's eyes. Taped music plays from somewhere—a modern, glorious transfiguration.

After that everything goes horribly, indescribably wrong. The gigantic cardboard castle in the background collapses onto two kids. Joan gets distracted and forgets her lines. Some of the French soldiers decide to take that moment to walk offstage. The audience starts to laugh. But Jazzy never wavers. She lies there unbending, unwilling to quit. The play completely stops but she never gives up. Even as the curtain is pulled closed in uneven fits and the world comes apart, she remains lying on the stage, committed to the one part she has to play, and for the moment I feel like I can see her future. I wonder in those seconds if the things that make life so difficult for us are almost always the things that save us. I look over at Isobel and she is trying not to cry but having a hard time of it.

After the play, Isobel hurries home and I wait for Jazzy by the side of the gym. In the end, I think my niece is absolutely right. Why would anyone, in their right mind, ever try to do anything interesting? Why would someone put in the time, try to do something different, something difficult, to risk looking foolish, when all anybody wants is to see you fail? I think about our neighborhood and wonder why anyone would attempt to escape the inescapable. But somehow she has. She might be the most interesting one of us all, because she never gave up, not for one moment, even as the rest of the world was falling all around her.

Eventually she comes out and, like her mother, refuses to

smile. Other parents take pictures with their kids but Jazzy heads straight for the door. We step outside where the night is cold and full of echoes. I follow her down the block, understanding that she wants to be alone.

On the way back home, she is silent. I didn't know that I was supposed to bring her flowers. I can't tell if she is mad at that or the fact that I came. I glance over and try to see what she might be thinking but she's gotten too good at hiding her feelings over the last couple months. The neighborhood is different now with so many empty houses. There are long stretches in between the streetlights where the homes are dark and where both of us disappear. When we come out of the shadows, it feels good to see her face again. Each time it happens it's like a miracle, the immutable fact of her soft features.

We stop by the no-name pizza place and eat a slice of pizza. Then we will play *Dance Dance Revolution* until our bodies are sore. I will look over and still won't be able to read her expression, will still wonder what is going on in her head. I will put in coin after coin and we will play *Dance Dance Revolution* like there's no end to the quarters, all night, even as the Italian behind the counter gives us worried looks. We'll watch the numbers count down at the end of our turn and then begin again. We'll listen to the computerized music coming from the speakers. The beat of the music will become our beat as we become unstoppable.

CHAPTER EIGHTEEN

OH, WHERE IS THE GLORY OF IT ALL? BY THE MIDDLE of March, Isobel is practicing cello in the back room for forty-five minutes every day before work, which means all of us have to get up early too. No one is exactly happy about getting bombarded by all the symphonic masterpieces from Prague and Moscow at six thirty in the morning. But she ignores our collective sighs as she wanders from one Dvořák piece to another, and then makes her way back to the impossible Wagner number our old music teacher used to be in love with. Somehow she always ends up getting stuck near the end, and you can hear her frustration in the way she adjusts and readjusts the cello against the worn-out floor.

By the time breakfast is ready, there is a wave of fury and frustration accumulating on her face. I look over my runny eggs at her and murmur in hushed tones, "Why don't you just try another piece?"

"I've switched pieces three times already. I'm not going to quit again."

"It's not quitting."

"I'm not going to change pieces. The audition is in two weeks."

"You know this literally means you haven't learned anything from when you were ten years old? No one cares how hard that Wagner piece is. You don't have anything to prove. Just play something you love. Stop setting yourself up for failure."

"You stop."

"What?" I ask.

"I don't even know why I'm doing this anymore."

"You're doing this to prove anybody can start over if they want to. Now stop feeling sorry for yourself and be who you are."

She reaches out for the silver whistle around my neck. "You're taking this coaching thing pretty seriously, aren't you?"

"I guess."

"It's good to see you take something seriously for once," she says, and I roll my eyes and tell her: "See you later."

I come up the driveway that afternoon after tennis practice and Daniel asks if he can show me his new tree.

"What new tree?"

"I found a really good one."

I notice he is not wearing the ghost costume. We walk down half a block to another house that is for sale and then sneak around the back. An enormous tree, with branches that seem to cover the size of a small building, rises high into the air. Daniel has rigged up a rope-and-pulley system and easily makes his way up.

"Do you want to check out the fort I made?"

I shrug, knowing full well I might break my neck. He helps me up and we sit with our legs dangling over the lowest branches. To cover how afraid I am, I ask, "What kind of tree is this exactly?"

"I don't know for sure. I think it's an oak."

"It's impressive."

"I've named it. Do you want to know its name?"

"Not really. Is it going to make me uncomfortable? Like, am I going to worry about you, mentally or anything?"

"No. It's Quercus."

"Is that from some comic book?"

"No, that's the Latin name. I found out these kinds of trees originally came from Europe. Some of them have been here hundreds of years."

"Right. That's really cool." I look over at him and ask, "How's your job going, by the way?"

"It's good. I have a crush on a girl who works there," he says. "She's a cashier. Her name is Mallory. She's sixteen. I don't think I'm going to say anything to her about my feelings."

"I think that's a wise course of action for now. Just let your feelings, you know, develop for a while. You never know. They might change."

He nods. "I appreciate your advice on this matter."

"I'm going to climb down now," I say and almost fall out of the tree as I make my way back to the ground.

In late March, I finally hear back from Alex. She doesn't say much at first, just asks me how I have been. "Okay," I say. "Actually, not so good. I'm having some family issues. Which is pretty typical. What about you?"

"I've been the same. Just classes and everything. Do you have time to talk?"

That first day, we talk for about fifteen minutes. Later that week she calls me again and we talk for forty-five minutes. I never call her. I don't want to push or anything. I just wait to see if she'll reach out again. It might take a couple days or even a week but I am okay either way.

I get to work early one morning and sit in front of the piano. I like how the room sounds with the piano in it, vibrating in C♯. The heater in there causes everything to have a slightly sharper pitch so I try something in A minor. I put my hands on the keys and find the high G is missing but I don't fret. I try not to think of anything. I make up a short little tone poem, some obscure musical figure, and then a few lines and an entire melody, invent something to contain all my feelings. It feels good to be thinking about music again, even if it is only to keep my mind occupied. I imagine it as a way to clear out the ghosts from the second floor, from the rest of the facility.

Afterward, when I go to mop, the sunlight seems to hang in the unlikeliest corners of the building.

Alex and I keep talking every couple days. We fall back into the habit of reading poetry to each other or I will play one of my grandfather's records and tell her what I love about it. We listen to a few sonatas together over the phone that evening as a way to convince her that classical music has some lasting value.

"I like listening to you talk about this kind of music," she says. "Otherwise I'd have no interest in it. You should teach a class."

"Sad European Music for Beginners," I joke. "I could cover all the really amazing tragic compositions."

"Yeah, why are all these songs so tragic?"

"I don't know. Eastern Europeans really seem to enjoy feeling bad."

"It's like all this music for rich, sad white people played by poorer, sad white people. It's kind of off-putting when you think about it."

"I know, I understand what you're saying. But it's also more complicated than that. I think these composers were trying to figure out the shape of all these different moods, these different kinds of feelings, all these terrible things that happened in Europe—to find something useful or even beautiful in them. So that everybody could make sense of it. So, in a way, it belongs to everyone. I could be a kid from anywhere, from anyplace, and when I play this music it makes me feel important, like there's something timeless, like there's more to the world than just me and my problems. Listen to this," I say and play Mozart's famous unfinished *Requiem in D Minor*. After a few minutes, I put the phone back to my ear and tell her how ill Mozart was when he was composing it and how some of his students had to complete the piece after he died.

Alex says, "I don't like it but I understand why you do," and I thank her for even trying.

I go up to the bedroom later that night and find Benny reading *Esquire*. He frowns at me and says he is thinking about quitting his job. "My manager keeps making rude comments. He says he knows about me. My *persuasions*, he says. The other clerks, the workers, everyone keeps whispering. I don't know if there is anyplace for me in this neighborhood anymore."

I tell him I am sorry and go lie on the couch and listen to the Mozart requiem again, searching for answers, like

I'm waiting to find some missing puzzle piece, some musical phrase that will help everything come together. Studying that requiem over and over, I realize what has been missing from my great-grandfather's composition.

In the morning, I get to work early and sit before the piano with its missing keys. I follow the notes in my head and when they end, instead of going back and repeating, I think of every experimental composition I've ever imagined, every silence I've ever heard, all the figments and broken pieces I've been collecting, and map them all out, find a way for them to all fit together. I change the key up half a step, and follow a major scale in an entirely different direction, I look for pauses, for places in between the notes where the silence can build, where the silence, not the music, is being shaped, and I think that's what my great-grandfather was trying to do: compose something that was meant to be unfinished, that was meant to be added to, the story of a family told in fragments and intervals and pauses, the moments in between history where all the living happens, the moments that almost always get forgotten, where all the exceptional tragedies and invisible triumphs actually occur. One by one, I add our notes to the melody, and as I sound it out, the room seems to shift before me.

I come home from work that day and hear my sister laboring over the brutally difficult Wagner piece. I stop in the driveway and cover my ears. I think I see a bird fall dead from the sky at that exact same moment.

I go up to our bedroom and write out the rest of the composition in my notebook and come back down and show it to my sister. She reads through it, hums part of it out loud, shakes her head, and changes a good deal of the fourth part. Then she lifts the cello from the corner of the room and begins sketching out the notes in the air between us. It's brief, even for an étude, but it comes together beautifully, like a sculpture, a museum piece made entirely of glass, all angles and light and color, better than anything I could have ever done on my own.

A couple days later Isobel asks if I will go with her for her audition at a Chicago Park District field house. I think it is strange and lovely, playing classical music where an after-school program is just finishing up. Inside the field house I sit beside my sister in a metal folding chair and the whole room smells of wet paint. One wall is off-white where someone has covered up a long loop of graffiti. Isobel has worn her blue dress with the Peter Pan collar. She has brushed and styled her hair, but seems to be trying to hide behind her cello case while she is waiting for her number to be called. There are a few other people there to audition, almost all of them twenty, thirty years older. A number is called out and an elderly woman in a blue pillbox hat, who looks like a department store clerk from some other era, sits down at the piano and plays a very capable Brahms sonata. An elderly man in tan slacks plays the flute and seems to run out of breath halfway through a piece by Bach.

When it's Isobel's turn, she looks over at me and raises her eyebrows and then nods, which I guess is her way of asking me to leave. I go out into the hallway and put the back of my head against the wall, hoping I can hear something. After the first three or four notes, I cover both ears with my hands. Once she finishes with my great-grandfather's composition I imagine her going into the short Sibelius étude.

Moments later, I actually hear her footsteps on the dull wood floor. She comes out, lugging her case on its cart. She seems pleased and from the look in her eyes I know exactly how she has done.

On the car ride home, she doesn't say anything. I ask, "So how did it go?"

"About as well as the kidnapping of the Lindbergh baby."

"That good?"

"Either way, it's over. Thanks for your help with everything."

"I didn't do anything."

"No, you did. And I want you to know I appreciate it. You're special," she says, and both of us laugh like goofs.

Later that evening, when the orchestra director calls and asks to speak to Isobel to tell her the good news, none of us are surprised.

One evening in the first week of April, Alex asks if I want to come over and listen to some records. I tell her okay. I bet she can hear me smiling through the phone.

I am like *Wow* when I see her again, *Like how did the two of us ever meet? And why is she so beautiful?* I follow her around UIC as we talk and all I want to do is listen. We make our way over to the Chicago River which I must admit I have never seen before, not really, then we spend some time in her dorm, playing records. It's strange having a relationship with a very lovely person you used to sleep with. Before I leave later that afternoon, she asks if I want her old portable disc player, which she is getting rid off.

"Really?" I ask.

"I thought you said yours broke," she says, like it is no big thing. "Anyway, my dad got me a new iPod."

I give her a huge hug, and over the next few days listen to every CD, every symphony, every hip-hop record I own. I ride all over my neighborhood with Beethoven and RZA and Kid Cudi blaring from my headphones.

A couple of days after that, I go by my father's apartment. I see his van parked in the spot beneath his apartment and climb the concrete stairs to his door. I open my bag and pull out the notations for the composition my great-grandfather wrote, the piece that Isobel and I helped complete, and then leave it in an envelope beside the doorframe, knocking once and then hurrying back down.

Two days after that, Daniel gets in trouble at work. His manager leaves a message at home asking someone to come pick him up; I return from tennis practice and listen to the message then ride over to the supermarket and find my brother waiting in the manager's office. I make apologies and get him outside as quickly as possible. Both of us walk our bicycles beside each other as I ask, "Daniel, what the fuck happened?"

"I . . . I snuck into a coworker's car and sat there until she came out."

"Wait, what? You did what?"

"I climbed into someone's car. That girl I like. Mallory."

"Why would you do that?"

"I don't know. It was unlocked so I didn't break in. No actual crime was committed."

"No actual crime was committed? What the fuck's the matter with you?"

"I don't know. I . . . I just really like the way her hair looks. It's all jangly."

Both of us stop walking. Fumes from the nearby plastics

factory make the air feel sharp. "You like her hair? Are you serious?"

Daniel frowns, itching his arm. "I don't know. I think I'm becoming interested in dating."

"You're what?"

But he only shrugs.

"Well, you can't go sneaking into people's cars, man. They're going to lock you up again. You have to call your boss when we get home and apologize. Because nobody else in their right mind is going to hire you. You need to keep that job because we really need the money right now."

"Okay, I will."

"And no more being weird. If you need to pretend to be someone else right now, someone normal, then do it. Imagine you're in a comic book. Imagine you have a secret identity. I don't care. Stop hanging out in trees. Stop dressing in costumes. Stop saying odd things. Please. I need you to try and keep it together and be a more adult version of yourself."

"Okay," he says, "I'll try," and for once I am forced to believe him.

I come home and find a pink eviction notice stapled to the front door. I tear it off and go around back and find another one stapled there as well.

When I go inside, I see Jazzy sitting on the floor in front of the television, folding origami animals out of colored paper. She makes a pink giraffe and hands it to me before I realize it's an eviction notice from a few days before.

"Dang, Jazzy," I say, "looks like we're in trouble."

I go by Alex's the next night. I don't tell her about the eviction notices. I just sit in her bed and watch her do her schoolwork, writing an essay on hypersegregation in the city of Chicago. I keep playing with her feet, trying to distract her. At first she laughs, all flirty, but eventually she gets irritated.

"I really need to finish this," she says. "I told you when you called you could come over but I wasn't really going to be able to hang out."

"I thought that meant you wanted me to come over and bother you."

She smiles but does not seem amused. "I really have to get this done. My schoolwork is a priority."

"I know you've got priorities. I like that about you. You're going places."

She rolls her eyes. "I just take my work seriously. I have to."

It gets quiet all of a sudden. I look over at her and say, "I do too."

"No, I didn't mean that. I just meant . . . what we do is different. I want to be a teacher and change the way people think about themselves. Especially in this city. It means a lot to me."

"My job means a lot to me too."

"You mop floors part-time. And you're a substitute tennis coach."

I sit up angrily, shifting my weight away. "Hold up, hold up. What's that mean?"

She sighs a long sigh that pretty much signifies she is at the end of her patience with me. "My parents are paying for me to go here. I have people counting on me."

"I have people counting on me too," I say. "All the time. You know what? Just forget it. I don't think I want to talk about this right now."

"I just think we're in different places. I'm sorry. I don't know what else to say."

"You don't have to say anything. I think I'm going to go. I'll see you around." I sit up and put on my coat, then carry my bike outside.

Once I get home, I find Isobel in the back room with the lights off. It looks like she's been crying. There is a musical score by Beethoven on the floor beside her cello and her face is in her hands.

"What's up?"

"I don't think I can do this."

"What are you talking about?"

"I don't know if I want to do this anymore," she murmurs. "I don't know if I can perform in front of a bunch of strangers."

"Are you serious? What was the point of all this then? What have you been torturing yourself and the rest of us for?"

"I don't know. I'm afraid. And my playing sounds really terrible."

"I'm sorry to hear that. But I can't deal with this right now. I'm sorry. I've got to go," I say, and ride around the block on my bicycle until my legs are sore.

The next day is Friday. I pull up to the tennis courts on my bike. Tennis practice that afternoon is awful. I sit on the sidelines pretending to pay attention, thinking about the house, my sister, my brother, my mother, and then I hear a peal of laughter. Some of the boys are standing in a corner of the court; some are gawking, some are pointing. There's a large brown bird of some kind, a falcon or a hawk, feeding on what looks to be an eviscerated squirrel.

"Okay, guys," I say and stand up, "give it some space,"

but one of the kids who's been nicknamed Upchuck picks up a small triangular chip of concrete and throws it side-armed at the bird. There is a soft thump as the concrete collides with the bird's wing. The hawk tries to flee but quickly tumbles from the air, its wing broken. The boys all cry out. I can't tell if they're cheering or horrified.

I walk over and grab Upchuck by the shoulder. "You . . . you little fascist," I say and hurry toward the hawk. Some of the boys are taunting it with their rackets. I lean over and take off my coat and throw it over the bird. I carefully wrap it up, avoiding its sharp, rounded claws, and somehow get it under my arm. I turn and walk toward the parking lot.

"Wait, what about practice?" one of the boys asks, but I only frown and angrily climb on my bike and begin riding away. The bird is awkward under my arm as I am pedaling and makes weak though sharp sounds. I have to weave in and out of traffic and so it takes me a long time to make it through the neighborhood.

Back at home, I carry the animal upstairs and find my brother in the bedroom, reading a library book on Polish history. I place the bound-up hawk on the floor, and slowly unwrap my coat. Daniel's eyes go wide. It's like he doesn't even know what he's looking at.

"But how?" is all he gets out.

"I thought you could do something. Out of anybody, I know you could help."

He smiles and for a moment it is like he is five or six years old. The world is new and nothing bad has ever happened to us or anyone we know.

I call Alex the next day and ask if she is free and she says, "It depends," and I say, "I know school is important to you and I don't want to be a distraction but you are becoming one of my favorite people in the world, and so if your schoolwork is so important, maybe we can do some research together," and she says, "What kind of research?" and I say, "Human development," and she groans and laughs at once and says, "Where are we going to do this research?" and I say, "Let's take a field trip," and so we go to one of my favorite places in the world, the Field Museum.

We walk down the dark corridors, passing animals frozen in time, and, after an hour, hold hands in front of the pair of man-eating lions.

She turns to me and says, "I wanted to ask: What do you think your future looks like? Like, what do you imagine doing with the rest of your life?"

I feel my face go flush and I have no idea how to respond. "I don't really know. I can't even worry about that kind of question right now. I'm just trying to make it to the end of the week."

She nods and I know immediately what I have said is the wrong answer. It was some kind of test and I didn't even know it.

I try to recover by saying, "I just hope the two of us can keep hanging out," but I can tell she no longer thinks I am a serious person, which for her is one of the worst things in the world.

When we get off the bus, her heading down Roosevelt back to UIC, me taking the train back to the southside, I hug her and catch the scent of her hair and have a sinking feeling that we won't be seeing each other again.

* * *

I come home and bring a glass of water and some pills for my mother and she startles herself awake and then looks up at me, laughing. "I thought you were George Clooney for a second. I really did. I dreamed I was married to him and we lived in this enormous mansion." She swallows the pill with a mouthful of water and looks around. "I've got to be honest: after that, this is a little disappointing. I'm going to go back to sleep to see if I get back to that house again."

I say good luck, switch off the light, and creep downstairs.

Isobel asks, "What's wrong?" and for once I actually tell her, I actually say what's on my mind, tell her about the house and Alex and everything. We sit on the couch in the back room and play records for the rest of the night, each album a different story about our lives, trying to keep the sun from rising for just another hour or two.

CHAPTER NINETEEN

Everything terrible, everything tragic is what my fourteen-year-old brother spends his time studying: wars, plagues, assassinations, every other kind of human plight. These are the categories my brother memorizes as he falls asleep every night. In the middle of April, Daniel once again qualifies for the middle school Academic Bowl team. He comes home with the news, muttering it, and I hug him and then Benny and I try to lift him on our shoulders but we all just fall onto the worn-out yellow carpet and then we pick him up and carry him around by his arms and legs even after he asks us to put him down because we love him and are so proud of him and these kinds of moments seem to happen all too infrequently.

He keeps yelling and eventually we drop him on the floor and all three of us are out of breath and he is pushing us off and calling us crazy but also smiling because, for once, he knows no matter what, someone will always love him, even though this is not a thing people in our family, in our house, typically say out loud. So we chant, *Daniel, Daniel, we love you so*, and he runs from the room, covering his ears with a gigantic smile plastered across his face. After that, Daniel spends the next two weeks with his face buried in an ever-expanding stack of library books.

When he is not studying, he feeds the wounded hawk frozen mice from the pet store or raw hamburger meat. It learns to eat from my brother's hand and cries out in recognition whenever he enters the room. I am unsure how I feel about any of it.

On a Monday, something terrible and yet completely predictable happens: my mother nearly dies for the one-millionth time. I go in to check on her one morning and she is unable to move, unable to talk. An ambulance arrives but no one seems too worried. It's like nothing can faze us anymore. By this point, sitting in the ER's waiting room is like sitting in our own front parlor. We say hi to the nurses we've come to know. Benny brings donuts and hands them out to some of the doctors and interns.

"In Poland and in Chicago I have learned bribery goes a long way," he says. Later his boyfriend or ex-boyfriend or just friend shows up and introduces himself as William. It turns out William is a nursing student at Daley College and knows how to get answers from the medical staff. I immediately decide I love him like a family member. He comes back and sits down and says, "She has sepsis again but no one knows why."

I kiss him on both cheeks in the European style and Benny grins, looking slightly scandalized.

A few hours later, Daniel and I are the only ones left in the waiting room.

"Do you think she's going to die this time?" Daniel asks.

"I don't know. I don't understand why they can't figure out why she keeps getting sick."

"It's beginning to feel like she's just doing this to get attention," he says, and we both smile.

We wait, doctors and nurses come and go, and my mother is finally moved out of the ER and into a private room in the ICU.

Then we sit in another blank hospital room and look at how small she seems under all the blankets. I let the ringing in my ears take over, echoing along with the respirator and my own anxious thoughts.

"You should be at home," I tell my brother. "You have school tomorrow," I say. "How is school anyway? Are you still going?"

He looks at me and shrugs. Later he stands beside my mother and pokes her gently in the shoulder.

"Stop doing that," I say.

"I just wanted to make sure she was alive."

He leans beside her right ear and whispers, "Tom Cruise, Nicole Kidman. Tom Cruise, Nicole Kidman."

"What are you doing?"

"Giving her something to dream about."

"Don't you know? Tom Cruise is married to someone else now."

"Oh, right, I forgot," he says and then leans over and whispers, "Katie Holmes, Katie Holmes, Katie Holmes."

And so we wait some more. The moon comes up over the mostly empty parking lot. I stand by the window and try to imagine all the reasons people are walking away from the hospital, try to summon all their life stories as short pieces of music before they make it to their cars. My brother and I share a sandwich from the cafeteria. We watch a nature show about meerkats. Nothing much else happens.

But here is the amazing thing: once again, my mom does not die. Not that night anyway. I think it is because she doesn't want to go in the middle of so much upheaval, of so much excitement. Or maybe she doesn't want us to have to figure things out without her.

Around eight p.m., Daniel hands me a book about US foreign policy since 1945. "Quiz me," he says, and I do, for the next hour and a half.

Somehow he knows the answer to every question. Math, history, English, science. It's like he has done nothing but study for the last four months, and then I realize that's exactly what he has been doing. The Academic Bowl is shaping up to be his coup de grâce, though knowing my family, it will more likely be an unmistakably colorful disaster.

Alex calls that evening but I am too tired to talk, to try to explain everything, so I don't answer.

Back at the hospital on Wednesday afternoon, my mother wakes up for the first time in two days. Her eyes are open and somewhat opaque. They have given her several kinds of psychoactive drugs. I sit beside her and she looks over at me as if she hasn't seen me in months. She touches the back of my head and smiles.

"Did you cut your hair?"

I frown and say, "Daniel did it. But that was like two weeks ago."

"You look a lot like your grandfather. Both of them."

I touch her hand. "Are you feeling any better?"

"I'm doing great. I'm on so many different drugs right now, I think I could swim the English Channel."

In the middle of the conversation, she yawns and sud-

denly drifts off to sleep. Later, a doctor I have never seen before comes in and says her body has begun to shut down—her
lungs, her kidneys, her heart. "There's no way to know how
much time she has," he says. "Could be a month, could be a
year." One thing is clear: we're probably not going to be able
to take care of her on our own at home.

I talk to a social worker at the hospital, who suggests placing my mom in a long-term, state-run assisted-living facility. I
don't even know what most of those words mean, to be honest. I go home and talk it over with Isobel and all she can do
is sigh.

All the next day we wait to hear word from the hospital
about my mother. After work, Isobel comes home and throws
her cheap black shoes near the front door, then takes a seat
beside me on the floor as a Debussy record divides the air into
tiny pieces, like glorious fragments of stars.

"I'm done. I've just about had it," she says.

"Oh yeah. What is it?"

"Today. This guy Chad, he leans really close with his coffee breath and says, 'I hear you're training to replace me.' And
then he fake-laughed in my face like a movie villain."

"That's terrible. What are you going to do?"

"I don't know. He just got hired. It's not like they are going to fire him. I just have to pass this test and then asked to
be transferred."

"It sounds like a plan."

"I'm just having a hard time remembering all these customer protocols. They're all kind of pointless."

"Do you want to practice?"

"Really?"

For the next hour we lie on the floor and I pretend to be

an angry customer asking about my money market account, and before long Isobel is laughing, explaining the difference between two types of annuities and sounding like someone else entirely. Her voice gets lower and calmer and it's interesting to see this part of her I never get to see, where she is totally in her own element and asking if everything is clear and what other banking questions I have.

The day after that Benny tells me he and his friend—"friend" is what he calls his boyfriend—are breaking up because Benny is not willing to admit he is gay, even though most people who know him already assume this. I wonder why this is so hard for him. I find all of this out after Benny comes home from CVS and slams the back door, something he has never done before.

He mopes in front of the television, watching European football. I sit beside him and say, "I don't know if you know this, but here we call it soccer," and he laughs a little, rolling his eyes. "Sorry about your friend," I add.

He keeps his eyes on the screen and says, "No. No, he is right. He wants me to move to the northside. He says it's impossible for people like us to be happy in this neighborhood."

"What do you think?"

"I agree with him. But I'm not that kind of person. I don't feel ready for that."

We sit in silence and watch men in very tight shorts run after a spheroid for ninety minutes, never scoring a goal. The game ends in a zero–zero tie. All at once I understand why Eastern Europeans prefer this sport to all others. Maybe it is the tedium, the sense the players are merely trying to survive, that no one is supposed to be having any fun, and the best you can hope for is a draw.

I call the hospital in the morning and find out my mother is still unresponsive.

The Academic Bowl takes place on Saturday. For some reason it's called the Academic Decathlon, although there are nowhere near ten events. Daniel wears an orange headband and, with his longer hair, looks a little like Björn Borg. So be it.

Is it possible to feel any more hopeful or any more despondent at hearing thirteen- and fourteen-year-olds emotionlessly recite obscure facts and dates about history, science, literature, and math, knowing they are already smarter than you and also more likely to matriculate to private four-year colleges and universities, and that these same students will probably get their degrees before you do? I sit in the back of the gym, working out the distance between my life and theirs, as Daniel and his team dominate in category after category, question after question. At some point, I realize the competition is all part of an elaborate revenge scheme my brother has concocted, like an academically minded *Count of Monte Cristo*, as he attempts to avenge himself for what the assistant principal, Mr. Callahan, did to him by taking away his comic books, which led to him being sent to the mental health facility. I realize, all too late, that Daniel already told me this poor person is the coach of the Academic Bowl team. My brother keeps his eyes on Mr. Callahan the entire time, knocking down queries about Marie Curie, space exploration, even exponents. It would be a lot more psychologically thrilling, this battle of wills, if it wasn't all happening in a gym that smells like adolescent bodies and stale popcorn.

Of course the final question is about the sinking of the *Lusitania* and I see, even before the moderator finishes reading from his small blue index card, that Daniel has already hit the buzzer. Time slows to an existential crawl. The gym lights seem to fade to a single spotlight hanging over my brother. I look over at the coach and the coach looks over at Daniel. Some elaborate negotiation seems to be playing out but I am not certain what it means. Will my brother answer the question correctly and bring glory to his school, and thus find some kind of redemption? Or will he sink to his baser instincts and incorrectly answer the question on purpose, thus scuttling the coach's, and the school's, chance for victory? Everyone holds their breath except for me. I already know how this will play out. The middle-aged moderator calls on my brother and before he answers, he stares at the coach and grins once more. I close my eyes and hear my brother say, "The *Titanic*." The moderator apologizes, "No, that's not correct," and the other team is able to steal the win. Applause and cheers go up and the gym descends into a delirium of overexpectant parents and the cries of their overachieving children.

At the end of the day, Daniel's team captures second place. Considering he was arrested a few months back and put in an institution for three days, second places seems nothing short of amazing.

To celebrate his victory, I call Isobel and the five of us meet at Old Country Buffet. We do the trick where only one of us pays, even though five of us eat, and the hostess eyeballs us and we ignore her because we are impervious to evil looks at this point in our lives. We are immune to shame or guilt or embarrassment of any form. We have transcended ethics and morals and are doing what we have to in order to take care of ourselves and our family.

* * *

In the middle of all this, the intramural tennis team I am coaching has its second meet and the boys perform horribly, beyond horribly. I become irritated and angry and mostly just sit on the wooden bench, watching our players lose match after match. Because of my hearing, I lose track of how bad we are doing. The boys don't seem to know how to react. People with no concept of tennis would probably play better. I blame it on overconfidence. Perhaps I built these young people up too much? I'm not sure. There's also the possibility that I am actually a terrible coach, and I realize then that my future in coaching looks highly improbable.

The following week, fewer and fewer players show up for practice, until on Thursday, I am sitting by myself on the court alone. I ride home and find Daniel feeding the hawk what appears to be live mice. Here, asking no questions seems like the best plan.

One day a worker from the Department of Child and Family Services appears at our door, following up on Daniel's arrest and involuntary placement in a mental health facility. She comes into the house and does not seem impressed. She says the place should be condemned. But somehow I forget to panic, I forget to worry. For a week no one from the bank, no one from any collection agency, calls. Everyone is contributing toward the mortgage and groceries. Everyone is working as hard as they can. Isobel looks especially beat. She comes back from the bank and rubs her feet and lights a cigarette even though she knows there's no smoking in the house.

"I don't know if I can do this," she says. "As soon as I can, I'm going to try to get a place of my own. Something for Jazzy and me."

"You've got to get some money together first."

"I'm trying. I haven't been going out. I haven't been partying. I've been keeping to myself. I'm trying to make myself into a song."

I see how swollen her feet are, then go over and give her as much of a hug as she will let me.

Later I hear her practicing for her performance with the citywide symphony in May. I don't recognize the piece right away. Eventually I figure out it is an Erik Satie composition. I sit at the top of the stairs and listen, and at some point forget I am hearing someone I am related to.

In the morning, I wake up to some person poking my face very, very sharply.

I look over and see it is Jazzy. "I wanted to make you this but it was too hard," she says, and hands me a piece of colored paper. It is folded and creased and looks like an angular lump.

I squint the sleep out of my eyes and hold the paper before my face. "What is it?"

"A bat." Then she hands me a white piece of paper with instructions on it. "See? That's what it's supposed to look like."

"Why a bat?"

"You're like a bat."

"Really? How am I like a bat?"

"They hear things other animals don't."

I look at the piece of paper. "I will cherish these instructions for as long as I live. In some ways, it's better than the real thing."

Later that day I go and talk to Isobel's friend Jen at the bank about signing over my mother's assets to the state. Jen says she's been in a similar situation with her grandmother. She lays it all out for me: in order for my mom to go to a state-run assisted-living home, we have to sign over her remaining assets. This is a fairly easy process as my mother has almost nothing to begin with: a mortgage she owes on, a savings account with thirty-three dollars in it, some overdue credit cards, nothing but debt and more debt. I go through the paperwork with Jen, document after document.

As I am sitting there in the lobby, waiting for someone to come act as a witness, a car crashes into another car in front of the bank. Everyone stops to look out the glass windows. One of the cars actually catches fire. I get to my feet to watch. People are whispering and then I begin to think this might be my chance to make an escape. Maybe this is history telling me something, to run, to go, to look after myself and myself only.

I begin to panic. I look down at the papers and have the sudden urge to get as far away as possible. I sit and listen to the people moving around me but don't move.

Jen comes back. I don't run. I sign every paper with confidence although there is nothing actually legal about my signature. Jen helps me forge a document that gives me financial power of attorney, and she gets another one of Isobel's friends at the bank to notarize it after the fact.

Once the papers are all countersigned and accepted by the court, we will have thirty days to vacate the premises. Jen tells me this might take two or three months.

After that, I go home and Isobel picks me up with Daniel and Jazzy and Benny in the back and we all go to Old Country Buffet again but the hostess refuses to let us in. I think, *Our mother is in the hospital and all we want is mashed potatoes.* I whisper this to Jazzy and she begins to repeat it and then we are chanting it and marching back and forth and the manager comes and locks the door, and all of us begin to laugh so hard, our sides ache from the pain.

I begin to have this fantasy where my mom leaves the hospital fully recovered and I am somehow able to move into my own apartment with my old piano. I can see it in my mind, it is so clear, but when I open my eyes I find I am lying on the couch in the back room in the dark.

I go to the hospital after work the next day and my mom is still unresponsive. She laughs a little in her sleep and her fingers move like she is brushing away something imaginary, like dandelion fluff. She can't keep her eyes open and doesn't respond to anyone's voice. I sit in the chair beside the hospital bed and try to imagine what she is seeing, hearing. A forest, some trees. *Eine kleine Nachtmusik,* music from some unknown place. I close my eyes and let the ringing take over. Eventually a doctor comes in and discusses options. I call Isobel and she comes in with Benny and Daniel. Jazzy sits in the waiting area down the hall, filling out her coloring book. We don't want to make a decision so we wait, hassle the nurses for more information, argue about what game show to watch.

On the following Wednesday, one of the doctors, a young man, says, "You need to get you and your family ready," and I nod as if I have known this all along.

One day later and my mom is still completely unresponsive and an older doctor suggests signing a DNR and taking her off the ventilator. Before any of that happens, we all stand beside her, holding her hand, getting as close as we can. My mom's expression is oddly ethereal as if she is only playing a part. I look over and see Isobel gently brushing my mother's hair. Benny is silent. Only Daniel isn't there. It's too much for him. He goes outside and climbs the fire escape to the top of the parking garage where he can peer directly into the room. I look at the window and there he is, sitting with his legs over the top. He waves once and I wave back.

After that, time moves in incomprehensible waves. Everyone takes a turn alone in the room with her and says what they have to say. Even Daniel comes back inside. Then we sign the DNR. Isobel and I agree to stay with my mother. Two nurses work quietly together to take out the plastic tube and then we wait for another two hours, both of us falling asleep. Later we go outside where it is cold like winter again. I find Benny has taken Daniel and Jazz home. Isobel and I go back inside and wait some more and then the doctor says he will call us if anything happens.

Oh, yes, but then here is the thing. Once again nothing goes the way it's supposed to. Actually, what happens is that my mom gets up out of bed on her own in the middle of the night and scares the hell out of one of the nurses. In her sleep, she is trying to clean her room. It takes three nurses to get her back into bed. When they call to tell me all of this, all I can do is apologize and say, "No, yes, that does sound like something she'd do."

On Saturday, Isobel goes downtown to take her manager-training test. When she comes back a few hours later, I ask her how it went and she sighs. "I have absolutely no idea, my mind is a complete blank. I don't even remember how I got home." So all we can do is see what happens.

On Monday, the new manager calls Isobel into his office and gives her the news. My sister missed qualifying for the manager's program by only two questions. Isobel tells us this as she sits on the couch later that day, fighting back some tears.

"What are you going to do now?" Daniel asks. He has the hawk in the laundry basket and is feeding it chicken.

"I don't know," she says. "Change jobs."

"I think you should just try again," Daniel says quietly.

Isobel gives Daniel a kiss on the back of his head, which he quickly brushes off, as is the way in our family.

I call Alex the next day, even go by her dorm, but the young woman in the room next door says she is studying somewhere. I ride over to the river and walk around awhile on my own, looking at all the people downtown. Everything is finally feeling like spring.

I go and knock on my grandfather's door and no one answers. I knock again, then a third time, but still there's no response. I put my ear against the door. There's absolutely no sound coming from inside. The air is composed and still. I slowly walk down the stairs and one of his neighbors from the first floor, an elderly woman in a silky blue robe, carefully opens her door and asks if I know Mr. Fa on the second floor. I tell her I do, that he is my grandfather, and she says her husband is the building's superintendent just before she gives me the news.

Apparently, two days before, my grandfather was coming down the stairs, carrying a box that he wanted to mail, and fell. The superintendent's wife, Magda, came to help and found he had a large gash on the back of his head. She called an ambulance, and as she's telling me all this, her eyes get misty. "I could see something was very wrong," she says. "The way he cried out when he fell. As we are waiting, he was unable to keep his eyes on me. They went every which way."

I ask if she knows which hospital the paramedics took him to and she shakes her head. "You should try Holy Family. It's the closest."

I call and call and finally find out he was at Holy Family but was then transferred to Rush hospital on the westside because he was elderly and had a head trauma.

I call the other hospital but they have no record of him. I call the original hospital back and they tell me they don't know where else he could be. Then the operator or nurse or administrator says this, jokingly: "It's not like he's lost. We just don't know where he is."

I look at the phone then as if it is some unknown instrument and the voice coming from it some new, abstract form of music.

In the morning, my mother is strong enough to be moved to an assisted-living facility eight blocks from our house. That same day a nurse calls and says my mother is doing okay and I can hear her talking nonstop in the background, asking for some paints and brushes. "Good luck," I tell the nurse.

One day I come home from another uninspiring tennis practice and it is quiet and I wonder if everyone has possibly murdered each other. But no. Everybody is watching a nature show on TV in the back room: a lion is chasing down an antelope. It sinks its teeth into the animal's lithe neck. Benny is doing sit-ups with his shirt off, eyes locked on the screen. Jazzy is braiding Daniel's hair. He winces a little as she pulls too hard and she tells him to stop being a baby. "Obviously I'm not a baby," he says as the lion snaps the antelope's neck. I realize this moment is probably as close to functional as this family is ever going to get.

Upstairs someone is playing "John, I'm Only Dancing" by David Bowie. I creep up the steps and see Isobel hunched over the bathroom sink. She is in a blue terry-cloth bathrobe and has a pink towel wrapped around her shoulders. She is rinsing her hair. Dark spots of color drip into the sink. It looks like it's been dyed back to its natural color.

I don't dare say anything. She is so young in that moment, like a photograph of a person I have not seen in years. It is the beginning of something. I have no idea what it is the beginning of but as she smiles at herself in the mirror—a true smile—I quietly creep back downstairs and hold that image in my mind for as long as I can.

The other hospital calls finally and says they have possibly located my grandfather. The woman on the line apologizes, says she is very sorry, there has been some, ah, miscommunication, ah, some kind of mix-up, and then she apologizes again, and then a third time, and I slowly begin to understand what has happened. I hold the phone away from my ear and take a seat on the couch as she tries to explain, interrupting herself with long pauses.

He is lost. For good. As in expired. After falling down the stairs and hitting his head, he was taken to the hospital to be stabilized and was then moved to another hospital but apparently died in transit. An essential part of him simply disappeared somewhere along the way. When he arrived at the other hospital, they sent him back to the first hospital, which then sent him on to the Cook County Medical Examiner's. No family members or next of kin were informed because none had been listed. They hadn't even known his full name other than what he was able to tell the paramedics in the back of the ambulance, because he had been picked up without identification.

I think about tracing the journey he took from his apartment to the first hospital then to the other, to try to locate the exact place my grandfather left this mortal coil, but the hospital says they have no record of which route the ambulance took.

I ask where his body is now and she says she doesn't actually know and tells me someone will have to call me back. Something about this is mysterious and tragic but also slightly hilarious, that his body might be missing and never recovered. I have to believe he'd enjoy that kind of ambiguity. In the end, it looks like he found a way to run from history for good.

I call my father to let him know what happened but never get an answer. The phone only rings and rings, no voice mail, nothing, which in the end seems pretty typical.

One morning a few days later, Daniel takes the hawk into the backyard and we watch it flap its once-broken wing. It makes it to the top of the fence and then falls back down. It looks like it will be ready to fly in another couple of days.

On the following Monday, Isobel drives us over to Dan Ryan Woods on 87th. Daniel carries the laundry basket with a blanket over it and the hawk inside. He places the bin in the center of a clearing and then lifts the blanket off and we all watch the bird awkwardly take to the sky. Jazzy holds out a finger, marking its trajectory. The wind catches us all by surprise and pushes the hawk off course. Finally the animal lifts itself over the trees as it lets out a symphonic screech. The shape it traces, the path it describes, is unsure at first, but the farther it flies, the more certain it seems, exactly like a piece of music. My brother and I smile as we watch it disappear, and for some reason I think of my grandfather.

When we get back home, everyone goes to bed but I can't sleep. I take a seat before the invisible piano, hold both hands out, find middle C, and pretend to press down with both hands. I imagine all the sounds, all the noise coming forward, filling the house with an array of movement and color. I go through all my old practice pieces, sound by sound, experimental composition by experimental composition, until I get sleepy. Eventually I recognize I am only sitting before a blank wall and go collapse on the couch.

I wake to Jazzy pulling on my ear and muttering that it is time to get up. We sign to each other for a while before I realize how quick she's gotten and how much about the world she already knows.

CHAPTER TWENTY

CUE **STRING QUARTET NO. 12 IN E♭ MAJOR**
BY BEETHOVEN

EXT. STREET—DAY
Consider the possibility of a young man riding a bike with a four-year-old girl on the handlebars. Music builds as a neighborhood in decline flashes by. Still their faces beam with laughter as they avoid people on the sidewalk and dodge an oncoming car on the street. Imagine this as a scene in a movie never to be filmed, the strings growing louder, their laughter rising in the midst of a city that has become a comic tragedy.

I LIKE TO IMAGINE HOW WE MUST LOOK AS WE RIDE, UNVAN-quished, indestructible. Every day Jazzy shows me a new word as soon as we pull up to school. *Hit. Friend. Fool. Heart. Family.* The teacher's aide, Miss Sheila, has taught her more signs than I can ever hope to know. As soon as my niece climbs from the handlebars, I feel an ache of loneliness seeing her go to face another day of kindergarten on her own.

Later I ride down Pulaski and find the European Music School is closed for good. There is a *FOR LEASE* sign out front. I place my face against the glass and see that the small studio where I used to take lessons appears to be abandoned. I knock on the glass and ancient Mr. Gennaro answers in his moth-eaten sweater.

"Mr. Gennaro," I say, "what happened? What's going on? Is the school closing?"

"Ach, Aleks, the world decided it does not need music," he says in his lonesome Italian accent. "Everyone has their headphones and devices. No one needs to learn to play anymore. You, I bet you no longer even remember how to hold your fingers properly."

"I've been playing every so often. But this place, it was like another world. I used to love coming here so much," I tell him. He smiles softly.

I grieve with him awhile before saying goodbye and riding off.

Back at home, Isobel says she's feeling overwhelmed. She says she thinks she maybe made a terrible mistake auditioning for the symphony and she does not know if she will be able to perform at the upcoming recital. She sets her bow down and puts her cello away and says she feels like she is going to lose her mind.

"I can't stop thinking about it," she says. "I can't stop imagining everything that could go wrong. I just can't concentrate."

"You worked for this and now you've got this amazing opportunity . . ." I murmur but I don't know what else to say.

"I am absolutely terrified."

"Be terrified. Be unhappy. Or don't. You have to decide.
But I can't listen to this anymore."

"What does that mean?"

"It means I'm done. This . . . this relationship . . . I have
my own problems to deal with. I think both of us would be
better off figuring things out without the other person always
getting involved. If you want to play or if you don't want to
play—you need to decide by yourself. I just can't do this anymore. I think it's time we started facing things on our own."

She looks up and slowly nods before I leave the room.

Sometime, late in the night, I think I can hear her practicing, but with my deafness it could just be the house and the
sound of everyone in it settling.

Isobel and I don't speak for another several days. Even then,
it's only to figure out what to do about my grandfather. At the
beginning of May we go to the Cook County Medical Examiner's, which is on Harrison and Damen, on the westside of
the city. We go inside and talk to a kind though tired-looking
clerk, face wrinkled, eyes wise and weary.

"Are you here to claim someone's remains?"

"I guess so. But we really don't know the process."

"How long ago did the decease-ed pass away?" I pause. I
really like how he says *decease-ed*.

"I don't know. I think maybe a week ago. I'm trying to
figure it all out. Can I ask how much does everything cost, to
claim a body?"

"You have to work that out with a funeral home so that
they can arrange for transportation."

I look over at Isobel and she shrugs. "Are there any other
options?"

"You can have him cremated here or you can donate the body to science. If you want the body cremated, you have to prove the person was indigent and cannot afford services. Then there's an investigation, which takes a minimum of thirty days. And then it's two hundred and fifty dollars to retrieve the cremated remains, unless you can file a petition saying you also have indigent status."

I look around and whisper, "What happens if no one claims the body?"

"The body gets donated to research through the Anatomical Gift Association."

"And how long do we have to think about it?"

"Thirty days."

"Okay."

"But the body's been here a week already so you have a little less than that."

We go out and sit in the car but neither of us says a word, even though I am sure we are thinking the exact same thing.

I call my father to tell him the news that night. Finally, he answers and I explain the situation. After a ridiculously long pause, possibly the longest pause I've ever heard, he says, with complete sincerity: "Do what you think is right. I trust you," and then he hangs up. I listen to the line go dead and decide I'm done trying to make sense of him.

I go by the assisted-living facility later the next day and find my mother sitting in a reclining chair, eating a fruit cup. I look in the corner of her room and see she is working on a painting, a blue background with an orange swirl in the center. She says, "It's part of a series I'm planning on doing. What different catastrophes look like a hundred years after they happen. This is the place where Grace Kelly died in a car crash.

See? This is the mountain. This is the sky. This is the sea."

A nurse comes in and stands beside me and both of us lean closer to the painting and stare in confused awe. After the nurse leaves, I tell my mom about losing the house, about having to sign everything over. I expect her to cry or yell or get upset but all she does is put her paintbrush down and look at me and say, "I really wanted to leave you all something. And now I don't have anything."

"But we have you," I say, and she nods, glancing away quick, because such direct sentiment is too much for her.

The next afternoon I lock up my bike in front of by my grandfather's apartment and see that a number of businesses in his neighborhood with their Polish, Bosnian, and Ukrainian signs are all closed for good. The Great Recession has entombed the Eastern European community—factories have shut down and home values have plummeted. Everyone on the street wears expressions of the dispossessed, expressions first worn by their ancestors. I knock on the superintendent's door on the first floor and the old lady in the blue robe gives me the keys to my grandfather's apartment. When I get to the green-carpeted landing on the second floor, I stand there for a minute before going inside.

Everything has been boxed up. For a moment I am surprised, a little shocked to see how empty the apartment looks. Then I wonder who exactly boxed up all of my grandfather's things. Did my grandfather do this before he fell? Was he planning on moving somewhere, going on a trip, or was he simply losing his mind? I look down and see the handwriting on the side of the box but don't recognize it. *2F*, it says, his apartment number. I look in one of the boxes and see his record player with a record still on the turntable. I inspect the label: *L'Orfeo* by Monteverdi, one of my all-time favorites. I pause, realizing this is probably the last record my grandfather ever listened to.

I call Isobel and she comes over to help me carry the boxes down the stairs. I decide to keep the old violin case of photos, some books, his slippers, and one of his boxes of records. The rest we drop off at Goodwill.

In the front seat of the car, Isobel and I look at each other and quietly agree to leave my grandfather at the Cook County Medical Examiner's Office, allowing his body to be donated to the Exciting World of Scientific Research. I assume that my grandfather, always a performer and storyteller, would enjoy this one final chance to be seen, to participate in the Great Pageant of History. Or so I tell Isobel. I call my father and tell him what we are planning but all I get is his voice mail.

One morning, a few days later, I go over to the blackboard in our kitchen, erase the quote that has been sitting there for the last eight years, and write out one of my favorite lines from *L'Orfeo*:

> *Ah, wicked, cruel Fate!*
> *Ah, baleful stars! Ah, avaricious heaven!*
> *Let not mortal man trust*
> *in fleeting and frail happiness,*
> *for soon it flies away.*

Everyone looks up as they're eating breakfast, puzzling over the words. After Daniel reads it, he gives a short nod.

The following week, we all gather at the foot of the pond near the community college, all five of us—Isobel, Jazzy, Benny, Daniel, and myself. Daniel has dragged his submarine out of the garage and filled it with some of our grandfather's remaining possessions—a few books, some photographs, and his pair of blue slippers. Jazzy places an origami owl on top of it all and Daniel seals the rounded plastic hatch and then, together, we all give it a shove into the murky water. Jazzy salutes and begins to recite the Pledge of Allegiance.

"Burial at sea," Daniel says.

"Classic," I say.

We watch the submarine drift deeper toward the center of the pond before rolling awkwardly onto its left side. It begins to sink, producing gigantic bubbles, and then it just stops. We stare at it, all of our telepathic energy willing it to go under, but it doesn't. It just lies there, half submerged, burbling in place.

"What should we do?" Benny asks, and Isobel says, "Nothing. It's better this way," and we all stare at the odd monument that has taken shape before us. The side of the submarine is perfectly legible from the shore, *INTREPID*. If it had been planned, it could not have turned out any better.

A couple of days after that I come home from work and find the front door has been barricaded with several red eviction notices. Apparently we are officially trespassing and are no longer supposed to be living there as the bank has finally foreclosed on the property. Someone has come and put a two-by-four across the front door with a padlock. The back door has also been boarded up. I sigh and walk along the side of the house and sneak in through a window. Inside Jazzy is lying on the floor listening to one of my grandfather's records on the record player and folding paper animals, all in a line.

"Looks like we're going to have to find somewhere else to live for a while. I thought we had another couples weeks or so," I say.

Daniel looks up at me. "Where are we going to go?"

Unfortunately, none of us know how to answer that question.

And so then we begin to panic. Isobel calls around, looking for an apartment we can all move into, immediately. Daniel suggests going to my grandfather's old place but none of us have the keys and besides it is probably rented anyway. "Should we call Dad?" Daniel asks, and Isobel looks over at me and says, "Absolutely not."

The next day, Isobel finds us an apartment over in Oak Lawn. It is a single-bedroom, six hundred dollars a month, but we can't move in for another two days as it's being repainted. It's not even remotely charming. There are burn marks on the carpet and the bedroom looks like it may have been the scene of a triple homicide. We all—Isobel, Jazzy, Daniel, Benny, and myself—stand in the "living room" and stare at the apartment's untidy conditions.

Jazz asks, "Where am I going to sleep?" and Isobel says, "We're going to have to figure that out," and Daniel looks at me and frowns in an exaggerated way, but he knows this is all any of us can afford, and then something soft and large and furry moves from under the bed to the bedroom closet and Isobel screams and Daniel kneels down to get a better look and Jazzy says, "Was that a bear?" and begins making kissy sounds.

Daniel stands up and says, "No, it's only a racoon."

We get back in the car after signing the lease and Daniel asks, "What now?"

No one says anything. We drive through our neighborhood like we are strangers, like there is no place we belong.

Later, Isobel pulls up before our old house—the only house my family and I have ever known—to collect our belongings. We all stare at it as if it is no longer there, has somehow disappeared. Daniel pulls down the two-by-fours on the back door without much of a struggle.

We all go inside and stand in the back room, in the dark, as the electricity has been shut off, and take in the sound of the house finally gone silent. We can hear each other's breath, and the sound of anger and laughter from all the years of accumulated living, and then nothing. I go upstairs and find my mother's room is completely empty. We have no idea where her things have gone, who has taken them. On the floor, in the hallway between the kitchen and back room, is the old blackboard. All I can make out is one part of the quote from *Orfeo* while the rest of the message is now completely obscure.

We grab as many of our things as we can and shove them into the hatchback. Isobel's cello takes up most of the room while clothes, records, stuffed animals, and comics fill the rest. Jazzy is forced to sit on Benny's lap.

But none of us can decide where to go. After paying the first month's rent on the new apartment, we don't have enough for a motel or hotel. Benny's parents are not talking to him. And there's no room to sleep in the car with all our belongings packed inside. From the backseat, Daniel says he knows a secret place and so that's where we go.

We ride over to the forest preserve on 87th Street. Daniel—on one of his escapades—has constructed a fort with a tent, way up in a tree about a half mile inside the forest. From the parking lot, it is entirely invisible. All you have to do is climb a rope ladder, which he has also kept hidden. "For my escape," he says as if this explains everything. About three hundred yards away from the base of the tree, there is a public restroom with clean drinking water. But unless you were looking for a group of people up in the trees, you would never find it. It is the perfect hiding spot, at least for a night or two.

Benny takes charge of the portable record player. All of us sit together up in the branches and quietly listen to music—classical, jazz—then, of course, David Bowie's *Honky Dory*. We could only pry five records from the cardboard box in the back of the car and so he plays these same ones over and over to keep us from arguing.

It rains that afternoon. Daniel cuts up some heavy-duty industrial bags and makes tarps to cover our belongings. We make peanut butter sandwiches for lunch and dinner, drink cold water from the public fountain. Everyone is hungry but laughing. Daniel disappears for several hours and no one has any idea where he has gone. When he comes back, he pulls out several cheap plastic raincoats from his backpack—ponchos with hoods, all in vibrant monochromatic colors.

"I got one for everybody," he says. "All different colors, so we know whose is whose."

I am stunned by his big-heartedness. Where does this sense of kindness come from? Certainly not from me or Isobel or our parents or the rest of our family. "Where did you get all these?" I ask.

"At the pharmacy. I hiked over there."

"Did you steal these?"

"No, I paid for them like an ordinary person."

I cannot help but smile at this. Daniel grins even though his face is wet from all the rain.

He also takes charge of security. He sits up in one of the trees and keeps watch, in between reading a book by Thoreau. He wears a green raincoat and looks like some kind of bird. He has a long stick for a spear and I don't want to imagine what he plans on doing with it.

All of us are here together and it reminds me of years before, of the family trips our parents forced us to take, the family they tried to make us become by going to art museums, concerts, driving by places of architectural interest. All of it failed except for the feeling that each of us would rather be somewhere else, and maybe that is the thing that keeps us together, our insistence on being individuals in a family of people who desperately need each other.

Everyone has a turn to invent their own game that night. *Exploding Elephants. Mouse Parade.* Isobel makes one up called *Shits and Giggles,* which everybody loves. A forest preserve employee drives by in a green truck and none of us move until the headlights are out of sight.

That night it stops raining and the sky opens up and Daniel tells everyone about the constellations, about Perseus and Cassiopeia. It feels like he is making some of it up but I don't correct him.

"How did you do all of this?" I ask as Daniel hangs a dull green tarp over the tent before we go to sleep.

"I just read about it," he says proudly. I can see his dogtooth poking out and his dimple shows—the same as my mom's and sister's.

I cannot believe he is now actually fourteen.

In the morning it rains again and we get up early, climb down from the tree, and vanish into the forest, leaving footprints in the wet dirt.

Into the woods, wearing raincoats.

Violet.

Orange.

Blue.

Green.

Pink.

I look back over my shoulder through the rain and smile. Everyone has their hood up, each a different color, all five of us, like notes in a pentatonic scale. Every time they move, slow down, speed up, cut in front of each other, the song changes, from a soft melody to a triumphant orchestral score.

When Daniel helps Jazzy over a branch or when Isobel pauses to look at some indescribable pink flowers and falls behind, it is an entirely different harmony, the movement becoming unpredictable, uncertain. The composition continues as all of us march through the forest. We go on a long hike to keep from fighting but we fight anyway, just more quietly, which is an admirable change. All of this lasts until the second night when a forest preserve employee spots the five of us taking turns using the bathroom.

He doesn't bother to ask us what we are doing but later two other forest preserve employees find us hiding in the trees in the middle of the night. An hour later the cops come to send us all home. They say no one is allowed to stay overnight in the park without a permit. I look at them through the open window of the squad car and don't try to argue. But we have travailed, we have triumphed, we have made it mostly through the night.

A few hours later, Isobel pulls up in front of the apartment building in Oak Lawn on 103rd and we drag all our bags up the narrow concrete stairs to the new place.

As we look for somewhere to stow our belongings, Benny takes a seat on the couch and says, "I think I am maybe going to go. I think I am maybe going to move in with William."

No one says anything at first and then one by one we give him a hug. He helps us get settled and even spends the first night sleeping on the mottled carpeted floor, pretending not to hear the racoon coming and going from the corner of the apartment. Jazzy lifts her head beside me and says, "I think this is the greatest apartment ever," and I tell her I appreciate her insight even if I don't share her enthusiasm.

In the morning I find the racoon sleeping in the sink in the bathroom and don't say anything, just close the door to give it some privacy.

I go to work and play piano for an hour before I remember there are floors to mop. When I look up, I see some residents standing in the hall and a few of them are clapping.

All I can do is laugh. I practice laughing as loud as possible as I am riding my bike, rushing across the southside like a mad person, trying out different kinds of guffaws and chortles in other voices. *Ha! Ha-ha-ha! He-he!* I am sure I look like an escapee but I no longer care. When I get back to Isobel's apartment that afternoon, there is a package, something wrapped in brightly colored paper, lying beside the door. *ALEKS*, it says. I open it, thinking it might be from Alex, but once I tear off the paper, I realize it is from my father.

I remove the rest of the paper and see it is an album, a CD, Mozart's eighth symphony, the one my dad always played for me when I was a child, the one I purposefully scratched so I wouldn't have to ever hear it again. I look at it and look at it and don't know what to think.

The day after that I ride my bike over to the train and go by Alex's at UIC one more time. The young woman who lives in the dorm room beside hers says Alex is doing her laundry. I go downstairs and unlock my bike and ride to every laundromat in the neighborhood. All I want is to talk to her and tell her how everything between us was not a mistake.

The first two laundromats are empty and the third has an old woman in it who has twelve different machines going. We stare at each other and smile.

The fourth one is where Alex is reading a big textbook on form and theory in poetry. She actually frowns when she sees me and then her face shifts into a curious smile. I have surprised her, which is remarkably hard to do.

I sit down next to her in a hard plastic seat. I do not know what to say so I decide to just tell her everything. Nobody is around to watch me go to pieces. I end up telling her everything that has been going on, everything that has ever happened, the truth, all of it, about my family, my sister, my brother, my niece, my cousin, my mother, my father, my grandfather, even my full name. She doesn't laugh when she hears it that first time. She just nods like it is this grave, serious thing, like even I don't know how important or meaningful it is. She puts a hand over mine and murmurs, "It sounds like you have a lot going on."

"I do. I really do."

"It seems like you could really use a friend right now."

"I could."

"You can have that," she says and leans forward, giving me a hug.

I tell her that all I want is to lie in her room with her and listen to records. She nods and, when her laundry is done, we go back to her dorm. She quietly walks over to the stereo and puts on a Debussy CD she asked to borrow a few weeks before. I sit on her bed beside her and watch her listening to the music unfold and it seems like something. Like looking at the sun going down through your hands. I know I don't have to pretend around her. I'm grateful. It's good enough for now; it's more than enough for anyone who comes from where I come from.

Later that week I take the train all the way up to the northside, off Belmont and Broadway, to see Benny and his boyfriend Will's apartment. Walking around, I am tense. Everybody on the streets looks like they have degrees in economics or art history. I keep waiting for someone to call me out, like there is a mark hanging over my head that tells everyone I am from the far southside and did not go to some fancy college. I look at my clothes and feel like they are from some other decade and then I realize maybe they are.

I go up to their place—it's a one-bedroom with a beautiful sunroom that has a futon. In the corner is a beige upright piano missing more than half of its keys. I walk over and gently touch middle C. It sounds like an animal that has been skinned alive.

"Where did this come from?"

"It was here when we moved in," Benny says with a grin.

William shakes his head. "No, it wasn't. He's been driving all over the city looking for one. He found it in the trash a few days ago and cleaned it up. The thing is, he doesn't even play piano."

I look over at Benny and he shrugs.

William hands me a cup of coffee and says, "After we moved in, they raised the rent. Benny and I talked and he mentioned you wanted to move to the northside. We wondered if you might want to live here awhile?"

I press the piano key again and the sound that comes out is like a note that is surprised to hear itself. It echoes off the walls and finally finds its place before diminishing into the street traffic below. I close my eyes and listen and begin to think that some of those sounds, the sounds of the city and his apartment, are something I could probably get used to.

Once I get back to Isobel's apartment that evening, I hear her practicing the cello in the tiny bathroom. Daniel is doing his homework at the kitchen table, Jazzy is coloring on the mottled, carpeted floor. I stand beside the bathroom door and listen to all the beautiful music escaping from between the cracks in the floor. It is the sonata from Franz Liszt's symphonic poem No. 4 and it sounds amazing.

When Isobel comes out, she looks at me and says, "I'm doing the concert. I've decided." I'm stunned and it must show. Then she says, "And you're right. I think I need to start figuring things out on my own. Maybe both of us do."

I don't tell her about Benny, about his apartment, about the piano sitting in the sunroom, not yet anyway. We stand in the narrow hallway, neither of us knowing what to say until she puts a hand to my ear and whispers, "Robert Kennedy assassinated by Sirhan Sirhan."

I look at her and pause and then say, "President-Elect Franklin Delano Roosevelt survives would-be attacker's plot."

She thinks on it awhile and then the two of smile and ironically shake hands.

A week later, in late May, we accompany Isobel to her performance with the citywide symphony on the far northside somewhere off Irving Park. I get dressed up in a suit from my high school graduation, ask Daniel to cut my hair again. We follow a small crowd of people in formal attire inside the Chicago Park District field house. There are no ushers, no velvet chairs, no fancy curtains. The floor squeaks as we take our seats in folding chairs at the back of the room. On the small platform, Isobel sits down and raises her bow. Finally the conductor, a dark-haired man in his late thirties, raises his baton and the orchestra goes still.

Everything falls away into silence after that. I feel like I am possibly having an out-of-body experience. At first all I can hear are my ears ringing, a single note reverberating over and over. I look around the room and see everyone listening. I see my brother Daniel in his clip-on tie and my cousin Benny sitting beside his boyfriend, afraid to hold his hand, and Jazzy is there on Benny's lap and her patent leather shoes are catching the light overhead. I get lost in the endless silence of that moment, in between all our anticipation and the beginning of the music. All I want is to live in that moment forever, before the shape of things is described too completely, before all of the inevitable conclusions. For a second, I see history, the entire world before us, all the selflessness and chaos and struggle, as the bombs begin to fall, my great-grandfather and grandfather and father each making his own decision when his moment comes.

I can see each of the instruments being played on its own,

and how they fit together, each note a different color, a single story connecting to some other larger story. I look at the program and see it is Beethoven's seventh symphony and I know it is about his deafness, about his fear and hope, and I realize something interesting, something finally becomes clear. Everything important is part of some larger tragedy, the beautiful failure of all human beings struggling against their own glorious mistakes. It's at the moment of weakness when people are most profoundly human, the one experience everyone has in common. There's just no running from it. All you can do is try to build something from the tragedies you've faced, to arrange them, to put the pieces together in some new, compelling way.

The echo in the room becomes a little too much, the way the music bounces off the wood floors. I don't hear a lot of the concert or any of my sister's solo during the third piece, but I can see the music and feel her playing. I watch Isobel lower her head and lean into her cello and I can tell from the way she holds her shoulders and lifts her chin at the end of the passage that she is content for the moment, which seems extraordinary, and I see the rest of the orchestra carrying her along and I know she won't give up for anything.

And when everyone stands to clap, I leap to my feet and whistle as loud as I can.

I get an application at a community college downtown a few days after that. Everybody in my neighborhood calls it a joke, but it's all I can afford. I look at the classes online and try to get excited about being around eighteen-year-olds who couldn't get into college anywhere else. What do you know? Maybe I can still learn something.

On the way to Isobel's apartment, I pass a piece of graffiti someone has thrown up across from the drive-in funeral
parlor:

EVEN IF YOU KNOW, YOU DON'T KNOW
UNLESS YOU LIVE HERE

There's a cartoon boom box with the words erupting from
its speakers in a speech bubble. I think it just about sums up
everything I have come to understand about the world.

On a Wednesday, the first in June, when I drop Jazzy off for
her last week of kindergarten, she puts both hands over my
ears. Everything goes quiet: the schoolyard, the neighborhood,
the sky overhead. Then she looks me in the eyes and makes the
sign for *hope,* one of the signs her aide taught her: both hands
up, palms facing each other, then the fingers fluttering toward
the palm. She takes my hand and slowly shows me how to do
it. I repeat it once awkwardly, do it again with a little more
confidence, and she nods.

Then she gives me a hug, fixes her backpack, and hurries
off. She joins another girl in line and the two of them start
talking excitedly. The school bell rings, and as the other kids
march inside, the girl takes Jazzy's hand. Something about this
gives me a greater sense of possibility than anything. I wave to
her teacher and pedal off.

I go over to the rehabilitation facility and punch in and
clean the entire second floor. I hear Michael Jackson playing
in the activity room and when I peek in, it's like everyone's
moving in slow motion. I hold the mop and watch the colors,
the shapes, the way the aides help the patients' hands and arms

dance through the air. It is like some kind of strange ballet but more real, more interesting, if you know what I mean, because of how slow, how carefully and painfully they move. All the glassy circles of light coming through the windows, the way the aides speak so softly, the residents' outstretched hands looking like birds unable to land—it is the most moving composition or performance I have seen in a long time. I linger there for a few moments. When the song is over, I smile and go back to mopping, humming the melody to myself.

I get off of work and head back to Isobel's apartment to find Daniel sitting at the small kitchen table doing his homework. I drop off a stack of *Fantastic Four* comics from the no-name convenience store and watch as he smiles in surprised wonder.

After that I go by the assisted-living facility on Kedzie. My mom is up on her own two feet, using a walker to get around, shuffling over to a canvas in the corner of her room. She sits down and begins painting, dabbing at the surface with some bright-orange paint. It is an abstract landscape, glowing with light.

"One hundred years after the firebombing of Dresden," she says.

Later I take the train downtown, get off at Roosevelt, and go over to the beach on 12th Street, the one no one knows about beside Meigs Field, just as the sun is setting. I sit down, search through my backpack, find the new Walkman, turn it on. I listen to *Graduation* by Kanye West and then put on Chopin.

Fa, you made it. Or, *Fa, it looks like you're going to make it.* That's all I'd like to hear anybody say.

I sit by the lake for an hour until it gets cold and I can no longer feel my face. I put on the recording my father left for me, Mozart's eighth. Even though I have heard it a million times, every note feels new. I listen to the opening movement, then the second, then the third. I realize it was the composition my grandfather had been playing on his cello a few months before when I was listening in the hallway. How had he known? Was it something he was trying to tell me, was it some message he had tried to pass on to my own father?

By the fourth movement I am overwhelmed. It's almost too much joy. When it's done, I go back and play it again. The voices of the instruments are all saying something about the shape and size of happiness, how impossible it is to ever contain, to see the beauty of the entire world—all you ever get is a glimpse before it quietly disappears, I think this is what my father wanted me to know, why he played that one record again and again: to be able to look for those moments in the moments that don't appear to be so beautiful at first.

Once the symphony is over, I put away my things and take the train back to the southside, unlock my bike from a *No Parking* sign. The buildings I pass on 95th are boarded up, full of broken windows, and covered in graffiti. Stop signs have been stickered over, cars have tickets in the windows, each of them looking like a fading flag.

As I ride down the street, I see the homes, the lawns, the trees, the sky itself, all looking empty. But it is no longer my neighborhood, it is someplace else, someplace foreign. I ride past our old house—someone has slapped a coat of paint on it, and there's a *For Sale* sign out front, and I wish whoever moves in the best of luck. I pause for a while by the curb and then put on my headphones again and press play. I think of all the different ways the composition might end, all the ways everything could have gone, and all the futures that lie ahead.

As I ride it's like the entire block is a symphony, the entire neighborhood, the southside, the city, all the instruments ringing out, everything—even the street signs—having something to say. Let the streetlights go dim. Let the traffic cop wear white gloves. Let the electric lines hum like an orchestra tuning. Let the curtains part. Let the sound, the music, begin. Let the dispossessed arise and sing. Every color is its own note. The graffiti, the parked cars, the people—each becomes a melody, every movement becomes a song, and I don't look back for anything.

Acknowledgments

As always, many thanks to my family, Koren, Lucia, and Nico. Also thank you to my siblings and parents, Alicia, Melissa, Alex, Joe Paul, and Joyce, as well as Maureen, for their many years of encouragement.

Thanks to friends and early readers, Jon Resh, James Vickery, and Dan Lerner, for their conversation and questions.

Much gratitude to my agent, Erin Hosier, for her unconditional support and guidance.

Thanks to my colleagues and fellow writers at Columbia College Chicago for building a community where writing feels relevant and necessary.

And to Johnny Temple, Johanna Ingalls, and Aaron Petrovich, for their insight, enthusiasm, and constancy. You have taken a publishing house and made it feel more like a family.